MAY CONTAIN NUTS

MAY CONTAIN NUTS

A Novel of Extreme Parenting

JOHN O'FARRELL

BLACK CAT
New York
a paperback original imprint of Grove/Atlantic, Inc.

First published in Great Britain in 2005 by Doubleday,
a division of Transworld Publishers, London

Printed in the United States of America
Published simultaneously in Canada

Library of Congress Cataloging-in-Publication Data

O'Farrell, John.
    May contain nuts : a novel of extreme parenting / John O'Farrell.
       p. cm.
    ISBN-10: 0-8021-7015-3
    ISBN-13: 978-0-8021-7015-6
    1. Parenting—Fiction. 2. Mother and child—Fiction. 3. Parental
overprotection—Fiction. 4. High schools—Entrance examination—Fiction.
    I. Title.
PR6065.F34M39 2005
823'914—dc22   2005046297

Black Cat
a paperback original imprint of Grove/Atlantic, Inc.
841 Broadway
New York, NY 10003

Distributed by Publishers Group West

www.groveatlantic.com

06 07 08 09 10   10 9 8 7 6 5 4 3 2

For Sally, Tom and Anna

MAY CONTAIN NUTS

— 1 —

I used to be such a cautious woman. David said I was the only person he knew who read the Microsoft License Agreement all the way through before clicking on 'I accept'. And yet there I was about to make a bold stand on behalf of mothers everywhere. For ten minutes I had been crouching behind a parked white van, waiting for the right moment to shove a little boy out into the path of a speeding car. It had to be done; you have to teach them a lesson. Obviously it wasn't a real child, I'm not some kind of nutcase. It was a model boy on the end of a long stick.

We lived on a long straight road in south London, and young men in throbbing cars regularly tore past at two hundred and fifty miles an hour. At least, I presumed they were young men. It was hard to tell through those tinted windows; maybe when I screamed 'Slow down!' that was an elderly nun who always stuck a single digit out of the car window.

I had fantasized about pulling a chain of tyre-piercing steel spikes across the road, or having David dress as a policeman to stop them, confiscate their car keys and ask them if they felt the need to drive that fast because they had a microscopic penis. I had written to the council demanding road humps and speed cameras and all sorts of other traffic-calming measures, but I couldn't wait any longer. I had come up with my own solution. I would construct a life-size model of a child and attach it to an old broom handle. When that BMW raced past I could thrust the pretend child out between the parked cars and he'd have to brake suddenly and then I would calmly step out and explain: 'See? See what might happen if you carry on driving like that?' and he'd be so relieved that it hadn't been a real child, so grateful, that he would humbly agree never to drive so fast down our road again.

'What are you doing?' David had asked as he came down into the kitchen to find me stuffing scrunched-up newspaper into a pair of Molly's old tights to make the legs.

'Oh, nothing. Just, um, making a pretend child.'

'Right. I'm not even going to ask.'

'It's like a scarecrow. Except this is a "scare-car". If speeding motorists spot a child about to cross the road, they'll automatically slow down.'

'What?'

'I'm going to position it peeking out between parked cars and then motorists will slow right down as they go past.'

I pulled an old pair of Jamie's school trousers over the tights and began attaching them to the stuffed torso. I could feel my husband's eyes boring into the back of my head, but I didn't look round.

'What, you're just going to leave him out on the streets on his own, are you?' He made it sound as if this would be wildly irresponsible parenting; as if the model child might be abducted by a model kidnapper.

'No – I'll be nearby . . .' I said, failing to include the

detail that I'd be holding the child on the end of a pole.

I inserted a bamboo spine to prevent him repeatedly flopping at the waist like a pre-school children's TV presenter and gave him one of Jamie's old school caps, a pair of gloves and some old Start-rite shoes that swung about on the end of his bendy boneless legs. The face was a problem. Among the masks at the joke shop there was a choice between Mickey Mouse, a witch, the devil, Frankenstein and Tony Blair. None of them looked particularly like a startled child.

So at ten o'clock I had taken up position beside a builder's van parked right outside our house. I crouched in front of the bonnet, waiting for an approaching maniac. A net curtain twitched over the road. Ten minutes on, I was starting to get dizzy from crouching so long between the cars. People were driving too sensibly; it was quite infuriating.

The model looked unnerving in Jamie's old clothes. It occurred to me that if I'd had this idea a few years earlier I could have taken a model child on a stick in place of little Jamie on his first day at nursery. At least then he wouldn't have nearly been knocked over in the playground like that. I'd wanted to say to those big scary four-year-old boys, 'Stop running around – can't you see you're frightening him?' In fact, I did say that to them, but they didn't take very much notice.

Finally the car approached, the black BMW with the tinted windows and an exhaust pipe so inconsiderate and deafening that you could barely hear the jumbo jets roaring overhead. I felt my adrenalin surge as this arrogant idiot tore down the road towards me. How dare he show such contempt, I thought to myself. How dare he risk the life of my children, I raged as the macho roar of his approaching engine reached a crescendo. As two tons of steel drew level with me, I dramatically thrust the model child out into his path to force him to slam on his brakes.

A lot of things seemed to happen simultaneously, although I perceived each of them separately like the distinctive notes that make up a musical chord. There was a dangerous-sounding screech of tyre-rubber on tarmac accompanied by a startlingly loud car horn and then almost immediately the loud thud of metal on metal, repeated twice very quickly and accompanied by the leitmotif percussion of breaking glass. Another vehicle's car alarm was set off, which incidentally kept exact time with the electrical bass drum that continued to throb from inside the BMW. Oh, and then I burst into tears. And all the blood had gone from my legs from crouching down for so long, so that I tried to shout at the driver while sort of half squatting at the side of the road.

David picked me up from the police station four hours later. I was charged with being reckless under section 1 of the Criminal Damage Act (1971), told I'd have to go to court and might even face a prison sentence. Our neighbour's car was an insurance write-off; another would cost over a thousand pounds in repairs to the bodywork. The offending driver didn't even get charged with speeding, so it shows you how much justice there is in the world. David later joked about how the driver's police statement made quite entertaining reading. He managed to get a copy of it, which is now framed in our downstairs loo.

Statement of Frank Penn, driver of black BMW reg. X418 NGN regarding incident in Oaken Avenue, London SW4.
At around ten a.m. on 27th March, I was driving down Oaken Avenue in a southerly direction at approximately thirty miles an hour. Suddenly right in front of me on the end of a long

pole appeared a four-foot-high model of Tony Blair dressed as a public schoolboy. I instinctively swerved, striking a parked car, though still hitting the figure with my nearside wing, which decapitated the dwarf Prime Minister model, sending his head up over the windscreen. I struck a second car before coming to a halt, which was when I saw Mrs Alice Chaplin holding the now headless torso on the end of a wooden pole. She was crying and crouching at the kerbside and began shouting at me, 'See? See what happens!' I realized that I had caused significant damage to two parked motor vehicles and I immediately called the police.

In the end I got off with a fine, and we had to pay for the damage to his BMW and the two vehicles in our road plus the cost of hire cars during repairs. David never told me the total amount, though he did float the idea that I might sell one of my kidneys on eBay. The young man, who had been very aggressive and rude to me immediately after the accident, swearing and shouting and calling me a 'mentalist', got himself another black car, a Lexus I think David said it was. But he never cut through our road again. And I bet he doesn't go quite so fast any more. Who knows – there might be a little child out there somewhere who is only alive today because my model four-foot-high Tony Blair laid down his life on his or her behalf. That's got to be worth it, hasn't it? One of the policemen had been convinced that I'd been making some sort of anarchist political statement and kept asking if I had ever been on any anti-capitalist demonstrations. I said no, I vote Liberal Democrat and my children go to Spencer House Preparatory School.

The court case seemed to make me something of a heroine

with all the other parents at school, for which I was very grateful because I'd always felt a little bit of an outsider. 'Weren't you scared?' asked my friend Sarah as the framed statement was passed around my living room one Saturday morning.

'To be honest, I never really thought about what might happen afterwards. Anyway, it's no big deal, any normal mother would have done the same . . .' I shrugged, putting down a tray of coffee and biscuits.

'No, any normal mother would *not* have done the same – I think that's the point,' said my husband.

'Well, I say bravo that woman!' declared Ffion. 'The roads have got so dangerous now that it's impossible to let the kids out of the front door. And then we're made to feel guilty for driving them everywhere.'

'What happened to the headless model boy?' asked Sarah.

'He went to Battersea Comprehensive,' said Philip. 'He's top of the class, apparently . . .'

Ffion's husband Philip was never able to fully participate in any social gathering as his desperate need for a cigarette generally banished him to the other side of the French doors. From there he would do his best to lean in and offer the occasional comment between puffs.

'Don't talk into the room, darling, you're letting smoke in,' said Ffion as the laughter died down.

I passed cups of coffee one way while the statement was passed the other and the assembled parents attempted polite conversation while remaining totally focused on the activities of their own children. Sarah warned her youngest to be careful with the wax crayons, while my little boy Alfie was quietly occupying himself with some Lego. Each of us watched our children play in the same way that a bit-part actor watches a film in which he features, seeing only one person in the scene.

David commented that Alfie's confidence with the plastic building bricks might suggest that he'd become an architect when he grew up.

'Or a brickie,' said William. Sarah's husband had a habit of standing and surveying my bookshelves, making me worry that he'd notice there were no cracks in the spines of the highbrow classics that nestled between all the chick-lit novels and self-help books. David was putting a CD in the stereo.

'Not *Peter and the Wolf* again, darling,' I groaned.

'It's not my choice, it's Alfie's.'

'What, our four-year-old requested Prokofiev, did he?'

'No, when you were making the coffee I suggested the wolf music and he said yes.'

'Anyway,' continued Ffion, 'at the moment we're just letting Gwilym do as much painting and drawing as he wants, but there'll come a point when we'll have to impose a limit on it otherwise we might find we'd pushed him towards art college rather than university.'

'He is only four, darling.'

'Shut the door, your smoke's blowing in.'

'Shh! Shh! Shh, everyone,' interjected David. 'This is the string section. What does the string section represent, Alfie?'

'Peter!' volunteered Alfie obediently, and there was an impressed murmur among the assembled parents before they resumed their conversation. Sarah agreed that it was difficult to know when to start structuring their play towards achieving specific goals when David interrupted again.

'Shhh, this is the flute – which character is the flute, Alfie?'

'The bird!'

'Oh, that's very good, Alfie,' said Ffion. 'Yes, you can't start them on music too early. When I was pregnant with Bronwyn,

I opened out a pair of headphones wide enough to fit over my bare bump and then whenever I was having a lie-down I played Shostakovich to her.'

'Aaah, that's lovely. And does she like Shostakovich now?'

'Um . . . well, about the same as any other classical music. I had been planning to play her all fifteen symphonies in order and then move on to the concertos but she was a month premature.'

'I'm not surprised – I bet she couldn't get out of there quick enough,' said William, and Ffion's laugh didn't even attempt to be convincing.

I had been struggling to keep up with Ffion and Sarah ever since I'd volunteered to go into my daughter's classroom to listen to the kids read. I remember feeling slightly indignant when they had given me someone else's child to sit with. And while this child was obligingly reading away to me, I was craning my neck round the corner trying to see how Molly was getting on with this other mum who'd also volunteered that morning. In fact, there were so many mothers who had come in to spy on the teachers that there wasn't very much room left for the children.

'G . . . good. D . . . dog. Said. Dad,' stammered Molly. 'Good. Dog. Said. M . . . M . . . M . . .'

'*Mum!* It's *Mum*, Molly darling,' I called across. 'You know that word, don't you?'

The other helper looked a little annoyed by the interruption but I could hardly stand by and do nothing. Molly *did* know 'Mum'. I mean, it was the first word she ever said; she just needed a bit of prompting, that's all. Unfortunately I discovered that being at school with Molly didn't stop me worrying about her. My daughter tortuously spelled out 'good' and 'dog' while the child I was sitting with seemed to whizz through her chosen book effortlessly: 'It is a truth universally acknowledged that a single man in possession of a large fortune must be in want of . . .' Well, it felt like it at the time.

'Yes, all right, Bronwyn,' I snapped, 'that's enough reading. Go and play in the home corner. Or the second-home corner in your case. Hello! I'm finished over here so would you like me to take over with Molly?'

Five years later those other mothers and their husbands had become our best friends, and, like mine, their eldest children would soon be taking their entrance exams for big school. While our daughters were having extra tuition on Saturday mornings, we would meet up like this in my kitchen and debate the major issues of the day. How many secondary schools are you applying to? Is it true that you can only get in to Chelsea College if you can speak fluent Latin? 'We looked at a lovely secondary school in Calais. The only downside is that Bronwyn would have to get up at 4.30 every morning to catch the Eurostar.' The regular Saturday morning gathering also gave us a bit of quality time with our younger children, ones who were stimulated and encouraged as they learnt the basic skills of life: writing, drawing and identifying all the characters in *Peter and the Wolf*.

'Listen, everyone. This is the oboe now. Whose theme is the oboe, Alfie?' continued David.

'The duck!' he shouted and our friends murmured their appreciation.

'My Cameron likes to clap along to nursery rhymes,' said Sarah bravely but nobody bothered to respond to that.

'Hang on, hang on, here it comes. This is the clarinet. Who does the clarinet represent, Alfie?'

'The cat!'

'Clever boy, Alfie! That's one of the wind instruments, isn't it? What other wind instruments are there?'

'The baboon!'

'Bassoon, that's right! And who does the bassoon represent?'

'The grandfather!'

'He's very musical, isn't he,' said Sarah, rather perceptively I thought.

'The grandfather is a baboon!' Alfie repeated delightedly.

'That's right, the grandfather is the bassoon,' said David firmly.

'He is a clever boy, isn't he? Have you had him professionally assessed?' asked Ffion. I thought I'd already told her about how Alfie had scored at the institute but she must have forgotten.

'Er, yes, we got the report back a couple of weeks ago; the institute said he was "approaching gifted",' said David.

'"*Approaching* gifted." That's wonderful news.' Ffion smiled faintly.

'Well, it's fine, yes, but I think they've underestimated him. Actually I think he's just straightforward "gifted". Ideally I'd like him to be aspiring to "exceptionally gifted".'

'He's only four years old, darling,' I said, noticing that William was looking slightly incredulous.

At that moment there was a panic as Sarah leapt across the room like a presidential bodyguard and snatched a biscuit from her child's hand. 'It's OK, everyone – I've got it. He didn't ingest any, he's OK . . .'

'Sorry – is he not allowed biscuits, then?'

Sarah read solemnly from the side of the packet. '"May contain nuts." Yes, I thought so.'

'I didn't know Cameron was allergic to nuts.'

'Well, we don't know whether he is or not, we've never exposed him to them. It's just not worth taking the risk, is it?'

'Er . . . no, well, it is a worry I suppose . . .'

'Oh dear. "May contain nuts." He can't have these either,' she said, reading the warning on another packet from the sideboard.

'Well, no, but then that is actually a packet of nuts.'

'Oh yes, so it is. I suppose they can't be too careful.'

With the intellectual credentials of our 'approaching gifted' son clearly established, Philip took his chance to counter-attack by demonstrating the nascent genius of his own four-year-old who was bashing a plastic tyrannosaurus rex against a stegosaurus that had dared stray onto the wrong part of the coffee table.

'That's very good, Gwilym,' said Philip, leaning in through the open French windows, holding his smouldering cigarette at arm's length outside. 'The tyrannosaurus rex is the carnivore, isn't he?'

Gwilym made an exploding noise as the two dinosaurs collided.

'And what is the stegosaurus?'

'A herbivore!' lisped little Gwilym proudly and there was a light ripple of applause from the assembled adults.

'And what is an oviraptor, Gwilym?' prompted Philip.

'An ommyvore!'

'That's right. An omnivore. Good boy.'

'He certainly has a very good vocabulary for a four-year-old,' said Sarah.

'Well, Gwilym's report from the institute singled out his particular aptitude for dinosaur-based play, so we are taking the opportunity to teach him about predators and the food chain.'

'Yes, well, why not?'

'Careful, darling. You blew some smoke in just then—'

'No, Gwilym, the herbivore can't eat the carnivore, can he?' interjected Philip. 'Play properly, darling!'

'No, exhale outside, and then talk into the room,' ordered Ffion.

Gwilym ignored his father, and, turning the food chain on its head, he granted the plant-eater the power to savage the normally unassailable tyrannosaurus rex. 'Grarrr! Grarrrr!' roared the veggy, who'd finally cracked after millions of years of never eating meat, not even at Christmas. Ffion tried to deflect attention away from the slightly strained atmosphere that had developed due to two differing male interpretations of prehistory.

'Yes, well, of course, we're very lucky our children are "exceptionally gifted". But you can't guarantee good news from the institute. The Johnsons had their five-year-old assessed and they were told that she was, er, "able".' She whispered this word in case the children overheard.

'I'm sorry, I didn't know,' said Sarah.

A shudder went round the assembled adults at the thought of such a heartbreaking misfortune befalling any parent. We all knew there was a statistical risk when we decided to have children; we all knew there was an outside chance of having a child that might only be 'able' rather than 'gifted' or 'approaching gifted', but you just pray it's never going to happen to you. David glanced at me, but I quickly looked away. For five years we had kept the secret of our eldest child's assessment result. It wasn't fair, Molly was actually very bright – she just didn't do well in exams.

'I'm just grateful that the institute said that Gwilym was "exceptionally gifted",' said Ffion, forging on and finding an opportunity to slip in the detail that her youngest had scored higher than ours. There was an embarrassed pause filled by an embarrassing husband.

'Oooh, here it comes, the French horn! Who does the French horn represent, Alfie?'

'The wolf!'

'I think that Alfie is probably "gifted" really,' said David. 'He had a cold on the morning of the assessment and so he only scored "approaching gifted". I'm thinking of going back and having him reassessed.'

'It's two hundred and fifty pounds, darling,' I pleaded.

'Yes, but I think it's worth it, just so that we know where he is in his development and what sort of school and tutors we should be thinking of.'

Sarah glanced anxiously at her husband, who failed to make any reassuring eye contact. 'So what is this institute exactly?'

'Have you not had Cameron assessed yet?' said Ffion, frowning.

'It's the Cambridge Institute for Child Development – I can give you the number,' I said.

'Is it in Cambridge?'

'No, that's just the name. It's in Balham. The lady who runs it specializes in testing brighter children,' I explained. 'She talks to the child, watches him play and looks at his drawings and then sends you a comprehensive report and grading.'

'It's just a posh woman in a house taking lots of money off gullible parents to tell them that their children are clever,' William sneered.

'Well, I think it's vital that parents know how their children are progressing,' said David. 'Even if she did get it a bit wrong first time.'

'She assessed you as "approaching gullible". If you go

back again, she re-grades you as "exceptionally gullible".'

'Shut up, William,' said his wife. She turned back to me. 'He's only joking. Don't let me go without getting the number off you.'

'And here's the timpani drum – who's the big drum, Alfie?' Alfie didn't respond.

'Alfie!' said David slightly too crossly.

'What?'

'Who does the timpani drum represent?'

'The hunter,' he said sulkily.

'Er, Philip?' called William, a little mischievously. 'I think the herbivores are forgetting their place in the food chain again' – and he gave a mock-concerned nod in the direction of the prehistoric landscape of our coffee table, where a Roman centurion came swooping in from the arm of the sofa and attacked with a sword.

'It doesn't matter, Philip, stay outside.' Ffion bristled.

'Of course, one shouldn't stifle their imagination too much,' shrugged Philip, stamping on his cigarette and returning indoors. 'He does, of course, know that the dinosaurs were extinct by the time of the Romans . . . What happened to the dinosaurs, Gwilym?'

'Their eggs stink!'

'You see?' said his father with a proud smile.

'Would anyone like to listen to *Peter and the Wolf* again?' offered David.

I had met David when we both worked in the City; I was a PA and he worked in banking. By the time we were married he had given up trying to explain exactly what he did. People who had never worked in international finance always struggled to understand how it was possible to 'buy and sell money'. Perhaps David didn't understand it either; maybe that's why he got the sack. After that he set himself up as a freelance financial consultant, which he said was the best thing that could ever have happened because working for himself would give him more time to be at home with the children. And he said this as if it was a good thing. Now my husband managed to pull off a scam in which he advised people what to do with their money while taking a large chunk of it off them. We remained sufficiently prosperous for me not to understand all the extra lines of numbers on the National Lottery draw.

I still worked full time as a PA, but now to three children called Molly, Jamie and Alfie. (No one had told us that the -ie/-y suffix wasn't actually compulsory.) I organized their diaries, made sure they had the correct soft toy for sleepovers, arranged their meals and transport; like any good personal assistant, I knew they would never be able to manage without me. Jamie had to be cheered from the touchline at tag rugby club, and Alfie had to be applauded for splashing his legs at Little Ducklings Water Confidence classes, and Molly still needed me to sit with her while she practised her violin or she would say she couldn't do it and it was too hard. 'No, it's not too hard, darling, you're doing really splendidly. I think that's the most beautiful bit of violin I've ever heard. I really do think you're doing marvellously.' Praise inflation had spiralled out of control in our home.

When I was pregnant with our first baby, David and I had bought this nice house near Clapham Common, where we could watch the sailing boats on the pond, drink coffee by the bandstand or have gay sex with strangers in the woods at night. It's funny how when you live somewhere you never use the facilities for which it's most famous. But as the children grew older it became a struggle to shield them from the dark underside of urban life. The expensive kids' school was separate, of course, and our friends came from a similarly protected minority. Our children played outside, but only in our back garden; they went to swimming lessons, but only at the private health club. Apparently you get a much better class of verruca. On the occasions when we did walk out of the house and down the high street, I wanted to shield their eyes from the drunks and beggars and smashed car windows and the big yellow police signs calling for witnesses to a recent stabbing.

'"Appeal for witnesses. Serious assault." Mummy, what does that mean?'

'It's just a sign, darling. Ooh, look at that funny pigeon in the road. What's he found there?' At which point I would realize that the pigeon was pecking at a dead fellow pigeon that had been squashed by a passing truck. 'Oh, and look over there, what pretty flowers in the shop window!'

'And look, Mummy, there's more pretty flowers over there, tied to that lamppost.'

'Oh yes, so there are.'

'Why are all those flowers tied to the lamppost? And there are cards – can we read the cards?'

'No, come on, darling, let's get to the bookshop before they run out of books. Look at that funny bicycle locked to the railings – it's got no wheels. I wonder why it's got no wheels?'

'Because someone stole them,' Molly would explain tersely.

Their school reading books hadn't prepared them for any of this. Not that it would necessarily be a good idea if they had.

Biff and Chip have found some dirty needles in the gutter. 'Let's have a sword fight!' says Chip. 'Stop!' says Dad. 'Stop!' says Mum. 'Those old needles have been left there by smackheads. They are probably infected with the AIDS virus,' says Dad. 'Which is also why your father and I never have unprotected sex with total strangers,' adds Mum. Everyone laughs.

I could cross the road three times to avoid them, but Alfie would still spot the spaced-out beggars slumped beside the cashpoint machines. 'Mummy, can we give that man some money?'

'No, Alfie dear, you're not supposed to.'

'But his sign says he's hungry. If we give him some money, he could buy some rice cakes and hummus.'

'You can put some money in the pretend dog outside the chemist's.'

'But he's got a real dog. Why's his dog got lots of big bosoms?'

'She must have had puppies recently, dear.'

'Where are the puppies? Can we get one of the puppies?'

'Oh yeah, right, if you want to fish them out from the bottom of the Thames.' Obviously I only thought this; I managed to prevent myself actually saying it.

In the end I found it preferable to avoid taking the children down the high street altogether and would drive them up to the King's Road for their shoes and books and Harry Potter stationery kits. Ideally I'd have liked to keep them inside a giant version of the rain cover that used to unfold over their pushchair: a big protective bubble that would shield them from breathing in the lorry fumes and stop them from witnessing the dirt and the sleaze of the inner city outside their front door. Instead I strapped them into the back of the 4x4 and whisked them off to their preparatory school on the other side of the common.

A four-wheel drive is vital in this sort of terrain. When you are transporting children across a remote mountain region such as Clapham and Battersea, the extra purchase you get with a four-wheel drive is absolutely essential. Ordinary vehicles would have to be abandoned at Base Camp at the bottom of Lavender Hill, while only hardy Sherpas with mules and four-wheel drives could cope with the sort of incline you face as you pull away from the KFC towards the Wandsworth one-way system. Of course, the traffic on the way to school is terrible, forcing us to leave so early in the morning that sometimes the children have to eat their breakfast while strapped in the back of the car.

'What's six times nine, Molly?' I would chirp on the day of her test as I swerved down a back street to try to beat the gridlock.

'Fifty-four,' she would splutter, spitting out bits of Marmite toast onto the upholstery as her brother shouted, 'Mummy, Molly talked with her mouth full!'

On one occasion a child stepped out on the road in front of us and I had to do an emergency stop. How could a mother just let her child walk to school on his own like that? Thank God it was me, I thought. Imagine if it had been one of those speeding drivers who tear down Oaken Avenue. Obviously I am aware that I'm contributing to the traffic by driving the children to school, but there's simply no choice; there are too many cars on the road to let my children out of the car. I do my bit for the environment in other ways. When I do my supermarket shop on the internet, I always try to click on the little green van symbol so that I have a delivery from a driver who's already in my area.

I suppose I liked my 4x4 because I felt safe in it. I could climb in, lock the doors and ferry my children through the dangerous traffic out there without feeling vulnerable to the big wide world. It helped me feel separate from everyone else. Except all the other mothers at Spencer House, of course. Ffion had a huge Japanese one: a 'Subaru Big Bastard' I think William said it was called. Even that mother with an only child drove a people carrier – or 'person carrier' in her case. Every morning at half past eight there was chaos outside the school as all the middle-class trucker-mums executed three-point turns to get round the mini-roundabout.

This world of school fees and purple blazers and children who shook their teacher's hand at the end of the day was not something I had started out with. Growing up in a leafy suburb in Middlesex, I had been among the last few children in the country to take the eleven-plus exam. This was a universal test once taken by every eleven-year-old in the country, which would determine whether you went to the nice traditional grammar school, whence you would progress to university, or the scruffy secondary modern, which you left at sixteen to get a job sweeping up in the hairdresser's. Basically it was a fairly crude test designed to establish whether you were middle class or working class. The questions themselves rather gave this away. Question one: What is a motor-car? Is it a) A smart vehicle for driving Daddy to his job at the bank, or b) That rusty thing stacked up on bricks in your front yard? Question two: What is a pony? Is it a) That lovely little horsey at the bottom of your garden, or b) Twenty-five nicker and a lot less than a monkey. You even got a head start for putting the right sort of name at the top of your sheet. 'Timothy' or 'Arabella' got full marks, but if you were called 'Wayne' or 'Rita' you were losing points already.

But occasionally the social sorting hat got it wrong, as I discovered on the afternoon that the results were announced to the class. It never took me as long to walk home as it did that day. In the end my parents cobbled together enough cash to send me to a third-division private school, which for generations had supplied the British Empire with its estate agents and PR girls. Soon after that they abolished the eleven-plus in Middlesex. In fact, they abolished the whole county as well, just to make sure. And all these years later, the only thing that my third-rate education had taught me was that my children were going to have better. They would know the capital of Canada and that a quaver wasn't just a type of crisp. They would naturally understand all those frightening dilemmas of modern etiquette, like is it rude not to reply to a humorous email that's been forwarded to every name on the sender's address book? That is why we were paying all that money to Spencer House and why Alfie had started at the best private nursery, where young teachers were already steering his limp four-year-old hand into making barely recognizable letter shapes, so my children wouldn't spend the rest of their life feeling that everyone else knew more than they did. By the way, it's Ottawa. I just looked it up.

Having failed the first big test of my life made me determined that I'd do everything possible to help Molly pass hers. When she was nine, we realized her friends' parents were already paying for extra coaching to get their children into Chelsea College two years later. And so the recommended private tutor was contacted and diaries were compared. Obviously when somebody is incredibly busy they can't always find the time to fit in another lesson. But Molly had an hour's window on Wednesdays between violin and ballet and so was able to squeeze her new tutor in there. Our children were like Olympic athletes: years and years seemed to be spent preparing for a single event, this one far-off academic high jump on which everything depended. If Molly was off-colour on the day, if her approach was wrong or her timing was out and she crashed through the bar, it would all have been for nothing.

Obviously we tried not to make a big deal of it in front of her, though I feared she was picking up our tension.

'Lots of kids bite their nails,' said David.

'Yes, but not on their toes as well.'

So I tried not to appear too worried about it. It was just that if she continued to let herself down in exams and failed the entrance test to Chelsea College, then she'd probably end up becoming a drug addict and selling her violin to pay for her next hit of crack cocaine. I'd always promised that I'd support my children in whatever they wanted to do, so if Molly ended up working as a prostitute under the derelict railway arches of King's Cross to pay for her drug addiction, then obviously I would try to back her decision.

'Mum, Dad – this is my pimp, Sergei.'

'Hello, Sergei, delighted to meet you at last.'

'Sergei's offered to handle all my finances for me and just pay me in low-grade heroin.'

'Whatever you think best, dear. I'm sure Sergei has only your interests at heart.'

It seemed a harsh punishment for failing a school's entrance exam back when she was eleven. And so we were determined to tutor her, test her, encourage her and bribe her. Oh, and there was one other thing we decided we had better do, just to give our precious eldest child the best possible chance. We would cheat.

The Herbal Homework Helper
How Ancient Herbal Therapies Can Unlock Your Child's
Academic Potential

By David Zinkin   Published by Sunrise Books £6.99

Did you know that the long-forgotten Manoai Indians
of the Amazon basin possessed a highly developed
understanding of the powers of natural and herbal
remedies, which they believed gave them immunity from
all diseases? Sadly many of these secrets were lost
when the Manoai were wiped out by chicken pox and
influenza following their first contact with European
explorers. But in among the data that survives is a
fascinating window into the various ways in which
wholly natural stimulants can also assist in specific
areas of brain activity.

We already know that the chemistry of the brain
depends upon complex proteins, vitamins and minerals to
help the synapses process all those billions of little
signals that are handled every day. So it's a small
step to realizing that nature's medicine cabinet can
help us improve our own mental agility and intellectual performance. Now using this book as your guide,
and with the help of the organic herbs which may be

ordered by using our credit card hotline, you can pre-
scribe the precise herbal restorative for whichever
academic discipline is confronting your child.

Echinacea is a natural facilitator for the part of the
brain which deals with logic and analysis. Ideal for
assisting in the study of mathematics, particularly
logarithms, equations and binary code. For algebra
take equal parts echinacea and belladonna.

Calendula assists the synapses that process language
and speech. Take two drops dissolved in filtered water
an hour before approaching novels, poetry or drama.
Three drops if your child is attempting to study
Beowulf.

St John's Wort For thousands of years recognized as
being a synergic aid to the study of geography. For
human and social geography, hypericum may be used as
an alternative.

Nettle assists the mental processes required for sustained periods of concentration, such as examinations.
NB Do not attempt to give your child nettle in its
natural form, as its ingestion may hinder rather than
enhance exam performance.

There is as yet no known herbal facilitator for
metalwork.

— 2 —

'I don't want it, it's disgusting!' protested Molly, confronted with a clear glass of water containing a mere couple of drops of nettle and echinacea.

'How can you say it's disgusting? It doesn't taste of anything, it's just water, your body hardly knows that the traces are in there!'

'So what's the point of taking them then?'

'It's a bit like homeopathy, darling. It's hard to explain but I've read a book about it and it'll help your synapses. It's all 100 per cent natural and organic echinacea and nettle.'

'Nettle? What, like stinging nettles?'

'Er, yes, but just tiny doses of plant extract – it won't hurt you.'

She lifted the glass. I'm not sure whether or not any actual liquid made contact with her lips, but the reaction was dramatic.

'Ow! It stings! You've stung me!'

'Don't be ridiculous,' I snapped. 'It's water, it can't sting you – now stop this nonsense and drink it up.'

Molly started crying just as David walked into the room.

'What's the matter, darling?'

'Mummy's trying to make me eat stinging nettles!'

'I told her there are tiny amounts of nettle extract in the water – it's a herbal therapy to speed up her synapses.'

'Well, don't make her drink it if she doesn't want it. We don't want her in tears just before she does the exam, do we? That's not going to help.'

The preparations for Molly's mock test were not going well. Then I made her go to bed early so that she wasn't tired. In protest she forced herself to stay awake and came down three times between eight o'clock and midnight before finally crashing out. And I noticed that Molly's nail-biting habit had now extended to the surrounding skin. There was a raw crescent of bloody skin around the base of each nail. She had talked about becoming a vegetarian but I told her she would have to stop eating her own fingers first.

Even though this was just a practice run, I couldn't help but feel that it was incredibly important, that tomorrow I would discover whether the rest of my daughter's life would be one of spiralling success and happiness or whether she would fall at the first fence in the high-pressure steeplechase of modern life. Did Molly sense my anxiety? Is it normal for parents to snap at their children like that just for asking to watch a second episode of *The Simpsons* and then burst into tears saying, 'Sorry, sorry, darling. God, I'm just so worried about your mock test – no, I didn't mean that, I'm not worried at all, just do your best and I'll buy you a really big present if you do well. Or even if you don't.' None of the parenting books had recommended this particular approach, but we all find our own methods for dealing with our children. Shouting at them, then crying, apologizing, then bribing: all within sixty seconds. I sometimes wondered if I simply wasn't cut out to be a mother. I tried to imagine myself as a single childless woman approaching forty, friends with lots of gay men and over-concerned about animal rights. Maybe I would have been just the same if I had lived on my own with a golden retriever. 'Oh my God, Shandy isn't retrieving as well as the other dogs in the park, maybe he's dyspraxic, maybe I pushed him too early, maybe I should get a private life-coach to help him with his stick-fetching.'

Molly's practice test would be modelled on the entrance exam for Chelsea College. Everyone knew that it was the only school to go to, because everyone else said so. Chelsea College had rapidly become one of the great London public schools after the government flogged off the Royal Hospital and shipped the few remaining Chelsea Pensioners off to a hospice somewhere on the south coast (pledging that they would jealously safeguard the dignity of the newly dubbed 'Bognor Pensioners'). The imposing pillars, vast courtyards and lush sports pitches all in a central riverside location had given this new school a grand air of tradition and magnificence and created a stampede in the panicking herd of middle-class parents desperately chasing places at 'the best school'.

My children simply had to go there. All the problems of the world would evaporate once my daughter had got herself a place, and every snippet of information was viewed through that lens. 'The main item on the news tonight: militant Islamic terrorists threaten bomb attack on Britain.'

Oh no, I'd think, what if Chelsea College got blown up? They wouldn't be able to admit any new pupils.

'. . . And how global warming could leave half of London under water . . .'

Yes, but which half? Molly's new school is right next to the river, are there enough classrooms upstairs?

Molly would not be taking the mock exam on her own. All her friends had gone to the same private tutor to give them an edge over their friends. And today the tutor's pupils were brought together in a rented hall where he did his best to recreate authentic exam conditions by sitting at the front sneezing and blowing his nose loudly for three hours. A practice run would allow them to approach the real thing with a little more confidence, we told one another, and, who knows, maybe the competitive element might spur them all on to try their very hardest. Not that we were making it into a competition, though Ffion did announce that there would be a giant tin of Quality Street for the child who got the highest score.

'Which I'm sure the winner will open so that everyone can pick a favourite,' I added.

'They're not having any green triangle ones,' said Ffion's charming daughter Bronwyn, clearly confident of being handed the chocolates to hold aloft on the open-top bus her mother had organized for the victory parade through the streets of Clapham. 'Don't worry, Molly,' she added, turning to my slightly podgy daughter, 'you can have the coconut ones. They're the least fattening.'

I thought it laudable that the government was bringing in legislation to prevent parents from slapping their children. But what about slapping other people's children? Surely they could add a clause saying: 'It is illegal to slap any child *except Bronwyn*.'

I dropped Molly off at the hall, got her settled and told her I was sure she'd do really well. I could see she had now passed the age where she believed everything her mother told her. The mock exam consisted of three separate papers, with two short breaks for the children to have a drink of juice and a biscuit. Sarah was just checking the ingredients on the side of the juice carton when I got there. I bumped into Philip and Ffion as well. They were off to the park so that Gwilym could have a few practice runs for the nursery school sports day. I'd forgotten we had that coming up on Tuesday, but it was no big deal, it was just a bit of fun.

'It's ridiculous,' said Ffion as she headed off to the running track at Battersea Park. 'I've looked all over – you just can't get running spikes for children under five.'

Molly was on my mind all morning. I did my best to send her positive vibes, to will her to do well, as if the strength of my desire would somehow transmit itself across the cosmos and fire her with enthusiasm and a new-found mental agility. But when Molly finally emerged at the end of her exam she looked pale and exhausted. Before either of us even had the chance to speak, her pasty pallor and defeated posture told me that she had not risen to the occasion.

'Hello, darling, well done. That was a marathon, wasn't it?'

Silence.

'You must be exhausted. Well done. What would you like for lunch?'

Silence.

'Do you want to have a run around in the park with Bronwyn and Kirsty first?'

Silence.

Before the test I'd told her that if she didn't know how to respond to a question she should ignore it and move on to the next one. She was clearly going to follow this advice for every query I put to her between now and her wedding day.

I hated myself for having forced my daughter to go in and face that test all on her own. She always got much higher marks for her homework when I sat right beside her, gently hinting that she might cross out that answer and put in this one. Every new step my children had taken in their lives had been with me beside them holding their hand. For days after Molly had first learned to ride a bike I had run wheezing and panting beside her, holding her firmly round the waist in case her handlebars showed the slightest wobble. I wanted to do everything for my children: clear every obstacle from their path, fight every battle and take every blow. Apparently the mother pelican plucks the meat from her own breast to feed her young, and when I heard that I recognized a little bit of myself. Though since my children turn their nose up at most things I serve them, persuading them to eat raw human flesh might be a bit of a long shot. Breaded human-flesh goujons in dinosaur shapes maybe.

Letting the children go off and do things without me felt wrong. As if part of me was suddenly missing. When each of my three children had been born, their father had ceremonially cut the umbilical cord, a moving and symbolic moment – but frankly it was far too early. I know it's the convention to go wireless as soon as possible, but I'm sure it would have been fine to keep the cord attached for another year or two. I suppose one or two of the less baby-friendly restaurants might have been a bit snooty about their diners having to look at the tangled flex of veins and skin connected to the toddler crawling around the floor of the pizza parlour.

'Alfie, keep still, darling. You've gone and got your umbilical cord tangled round the waiter's legs again.'

I think that's what those baby harnesses are all about really. A substitute umbilical cord. I'd had one for Alfie ever since he'd started walking. We all had them. And if we found ourselves within five hundred yards of open water or a moving car, the emergency procedure would be followed and the children would have their safety harnesses strapped across their chests and would then continue their day out tugging at their leashes like excited spaniels. Something had gone seriously wrong somewhere. The parks were full of big scary dogs that had been let off their leads, and the mums were all clutching restraints attached to their toddlers. Obviously after they're four years old you can't have them wearing those restricting safety harnesses. Then you can buy a Mothercare wristlink.

A few days later it was the nursery school sports day and we all gathered on Clapham Common. Sarah spotted a couple of large dogs in the middle distance and was so concerned she insisted that little Cameron took part in the running race wearing his reins and that she would run along behind him, clutching on.

'Oh, I'm sure they'll be fine,' said the young Australian nursery teacher, but Sarah was adamant that she couldn't possibly let her child off the reins when there were big dogs on the common. 'What if they're those Rottweiler dogs?' she said, looking around anxiously. 'A running toddler's like a rabbit to them, they're bred to grab their prey by the throat – did you see that piece in the *Mail*?'

Oh my God, I thought on hearing this. I'd seen that article. There'd been a huge colour photo of a poor little boy covered in bite marks and stitches after being attacked by some vicious 'devil dogs', as the paper called them, and there had been a big drawing of the beast savaging the child, and beside it an article by a TV animal expert explaining that dogs were actually descended from wolves. I was panicked by this terrible vision of an enormous killer hound bounding out of the woods, its ruthless hunting instinct reignited on seeing my little Alfie trying to run away, me hearing his screams as it leapt at his throat and shook him like some broken rag doll.

'I think I'll just put the harness on Alfie as well, just to be on the safe side,' I said.

'Yes, I think I better had as well then,' said Ffion. 'I wouldn't want Gwilym to think I was the only mum who wasn't there for him.'

'Well, you can't have some mothers allowed to run along behind and not others,' said another, slipping off her shoes in anticipation of the race. Before long all the other mums were lined up behind their children, clutching their reins like a row of novelty jockeys from some Japanese extreme sports channel.

'Um, ready, steady, go!' said the bemused nursery teacher, but several mothers had already shoved their kids off on hearing 'ready'.

Little Alfie tottered along at a reasonably determined pace and I did my best to run at exactly the same speed. But somehow his reins were a bit too short and I found myself having to run along at a sort of half-crouch. 'Go on, Alfie, faster, darling, faster!' I urged supportively as I scurried along behind him, but the other mothers were screaming so loudly that I found myself shouting as well.

Alfie and I were now lying about fourth with Ffion and Gwilym a yard or two in front of us. Suddenly Gwilym seemed to lose his footing, but fortunately Ffion was there to pull the leash violently upwards to prevent her son tumbling to the ground and hurting himself or, worse, coming second. In fact, she lifted him clean off the ground, where he remained swinging for a few seconds as she ran along, the pair of them suddenly seeming to make up a couple of yards on the front runners. On noticing this, some of the other more competitive mums also started to use the reins as a way of trying to force their children to run more quickly. No longer were they scurrying discreetly behind their kids, they were now dragging their children faster than their four-year-old legs could naturally run. The result was that the kids sort of bounced along the track, their mothers swinging them up into the air, occasionally touching their little leather sandals back onto the grass for appearance's sake. But because this pretence slowed them down slightly, soon any semblance of fair play had completely disappeared and the mothers were basically running the race themselves, dangling their confused children in front of them with their little legs still running six inches above the ground. I noticed an old lady watching us, shaking her head and mumbling to herself. She looked a little worried and confused about something. I remember thinking: That's old people for you.

'Well done, Gwilym!' said Ffion, who had been first to carry her suspended child way above the finishing line. 'You won, darling, you won!'

'That's not fair,' said another mother. 'Henry was winning! You carried Gwilym the last bit!'

'Alexander normally goes everywhere in his buggy. I still say I should have been allowed to push him in his buggy.'

'Why don't we say they all won?' chirped the Australian teacher hopefully, which was about the worst suggestion she could have possibly made. The mothers were united on this. The children did not *all* win; *their child* had won. I never saw that particular teacher after sports day. I think she wanted to keep a certain distance from us for a while. Like the distance between London and Australia.

As Gwilym accepted his prize for the hundred-metre

dangle, and Ffion cheered and clapped slightly louder than might have been considered appropriate, I sidled up to Sarah, who was warmly applauding the winner as if she'd already forgotten the manner of his victory.

'Have you had the result of Kirsty's mock test yet?' I asked her mother.

'Gosh no, but I'm not holding my breath, to be honest.'

'Oh God, I can't bear it, Sarah. This is just the mock, what am I going to be like when it's the real thing? Molly just has to get into Chelsea, Sarah, she just has to, there's no other choice.'

'Oh, you'll be all right. You're lucky – Molly's a clever little girl. Not like my Kirsty, thick as two short planks!' and Sarah let out a horsy laugh which gave the impression that it ran in the family.

'How can you be so relaxed about it? What are you going to do if Kirsty doesn't pass the entrance exam?'

'Oh golly, she'll never pass the test in a million years.' She chuckled.

'So how can you be so bloody happy, Sarah?'

She glanced left and right to check that no other mothers were in earshot.

'Can I let you into a little secret? I applied for an administration post at Chelsea College, and I just found out that I got the job!' And she held her arms out as if to say 'Ta-daa!' or 'Hug me!', but if it was the latter I didn't take up the offer.

'What?'

'Didn't you know? Children of school employees automatically get a place. Well, up to a point, obviously. I don't think they want the dinner ladies' kids going there, but for us it means Kirsty's already into Chelsea College, whatever happens! Isn't that fantastic?'

There was a cheer nearby as another group of children started a race. I was stunned. I actually felt a dizzy wave of sickness wash over me.

'I was very lucky to get it, really. They had over a hundred applications. All from mothers of ten- and eleven-year-olds, of course.'

'That's fantastic news, Sarah.' I smiled using all the wrong muscles. 'Congratulations.'

'Isn't it? Of course, she still has to take the entrance test for the streaming, so I thought it worth her having the practice. But however she does, she's in!'

'Well done, darling, you won, you won!' shouted a mother in the near distance.

I didn't ask Sarah why she had kept this job application secret from us, though I knew why. Because she knew Ffion and I would have applied for it as well. We all wanted the same thing, but while we pretended that this put us all on the same side, the exact opposite was true. When Ffion began having her eldest privately tutored for her secondary transfer tests, I had found out about it months later when Bronwyn was casually chatting to Molly. Though it had been hard to get the precise details with my ear pressed to the other side of Molly's bedroom door.

Of course, when I'd quizzed her, Ffion affected to be as helpful as possible, forwarding the contact details and offering to drive Molly there as well. And now when I asked her when she thought we might get the test results, she was as obliging as ever.

'You're right, we should have heard by now,' she said, clutching Gwilym's first prize certificate to her chest, face out. 'I'm dropping Bronwyn there this afternoon. I'll get all the results off him then and let you know.'

'Oh no, you don't have to get Molly's result for me, I just wondered when they might come through.'

'No, it's no trouble, he must have marked the papers by now, but the post could take days yet; I'll send you an email. I might as well get the rest of the gang's while I'm there as well.'

'No, really, I don't want to put you to any trouble.'

'It's no trouble – it'll be jolly interesting to see how they all got on.'

'Mummy, Mummy, I came first!'

'You *did*, you clever boy,' she said picking up her little champion. 'You're the *best* runner in the whole nursery!'

I always found it impossible to assert myself with Ffion. This might have been a simple problem of size. Physically speaking, the two of us could not have been less alike: I was very short and skinny, while she was tall and wide. She once claimed she was 'big boned' but if I was her I'd be a bit worried about the way those bones wobbled when she was winning races. I also had problems maintaining eye contact with her because I was permanently terrified that my eye would be magnetically drawn to the dark hairs on her upper lip. She might have worn the trousers in that relationship, but Philip still had sole use of the razor.

At six o'clock David wandered into his office to find me sitting there staring at a blank computer screen.

'What are you doing?'

'I was just seeing if Ffion's email had come through.'

'But you've been sitting here for nearly an hour. You don't have to be in for emails; they don't leave a postcard for you to collect the email from the e-post office the next day.'

'I just can't relax until I know how Molly got on . . .'

I clicked on 'send and receive' again, in the hope that the server might find there was one stray email lying around in the bottom of its bag that it had forgotten to forward, but the same bleak text blinked back at me. No new messages.

Finally at a quarter to ten at night there was a note on the screen. In fact, there were two emails, but I ignored the first one as I was confident I didn't want a bigger penis. Underneath, the second little yellow envelope glowed with the maddeningly enigmatic title: 'Test results – interesting!' 'Interesting' could mean anything, though the upbeat exclamation mark obviously meant that Bronwyn had done well. The first thing I noticed was that everyone's email address was on the one message, when I had presumed that Ffion would just send me Molly's result. After madly clicking I found that the results were not on the email itself, but in an attachment. I double-clicked, yes, yes, I don't care if some attachments may be unsafe blah blah blah, I don't care if my computer gets hepatitis B, just let me see the result. My eye went straight to Molly's name. It was as I had sensed from her demeanour after the exam. She had done really badly. Far worse than I had feared. I winced as I read along her scores: less than 50 per cent in every paper and a disastrous performance in the maths when she needed to be averaging 80 per cent and above to be sure of getting a place.

	Eng	NVR	Maths	Average
Bronwyn	87%	88%	87%	**87%** (excellent!!)
Eliza	82%	80%	74%	**78%** (very promising!)
Henrietta	70%	58%	82%	**70%** (very good!)
Druscilla	66%	58%	67%	**63%** (good!)
Fleur	77%	59%	50%	**62%** (not bad!)
Jemima	66%	60%	51%	**59%** (getting there!!)
Kirsty	54%	61%	39%	**51%** (improving!!)
Molly	44%	49%	23% (!)	**38%** (disappointing!)

I looked again at the scores and my disappointment turned to indignation and then anger. It was only then that I realized the children had actually been listed in order of merit. Ffion had taken the trouble to arrange them into her own little league table, with her child at the top and my child at the bottom. I felt myself shaking with fury. How dare she send this to everyone to show how clever her Bronwyn was and how badly my Molly had done! My God, Molly had even done worse than Kirsty 'Two plus two equals twenty-two' McDonald, I realized, looking at the chart once again. She's much smarter than Kirsty, I thought, and easily as clever as Bronwyn. Molly's actually very bright; she just doesn't do well in exams.

Ffion had even gone in for a little editorializing. Her daughter, she thought we might all like to know, was 'excellent', while my daughter – it was there for everyone to see – was 'disappointing'. And her disastrous maths result merited an exclamation mark. Yes, how fucking amusing, Ffion, she only got 23 per cent! Oh and there was a postscript to the message. 'Could everyone let me have the £1.07 towards the tin of Quality Street I bought for the winner.'

I checked Molly's totals with a calculator. It wasn't 38 per cent, it was 38.66 per cent, so it should be rounded up, not down. Molly had actually got 39 per cent, not 38 per cent. Not content with putting Molly bottom of the league table, Ffion had cheated her out of a percentage point as well. I angrily clicked the file closed but then realized David would want to see it and I called him into the office.

'Well?' I said angrily, as he stared at the computer screen.

'I didn't enquire about penis enlargement, it's just spam . . .'

'No, the one underneath. The test results.'

'Oh God, how did she get on?' He clicked calmly and there

followed a long silence. 'Oh shit. Oh dear. What was she doing? 23 per cent in numeracy!' he shrieked.

'You don't have to read it with Ffion's punctuation.' He saw the tears dripping on to his desk and put his arm around me to comfort me, deftly wiping the salty water from the immaculate polished teak.

'Look, it was only a mock test. Far better that she does this now than when it comes to the real thing.'

'Oh, come off it, David, she's never going to make up all that ground in a couple of months.'

In my fury I wanted to ring Ffion immediately and shout down the phone at her.

'You're angry because Molly has done so badly. Don't take it out on one of your best friends,' said David.

'She's not one of my best friends. She was just the first other mother I met. Do you think I should email everyone on the list and point out that Molly actually got 39 per cent?'

'No, it doesn't matter.'

'I mean, if Ffion is going to put an exclamation mark after Molly's maths score, then she ought to know that you round up from .66 recurring, not down. I mean, that's basic mathematics.'

'Forget about the half a per cent.'

'Well, it's a whole per cent the way she's done it. From 38 per cent to 39 per cent, that's a whole percentage point she's been robbed of there. Do you not think I should just do a quick email to everyone to point that out?'

'She'd still be bottom.'

'Well, I'm sorry, but I don't recognize her methodology. I'm sorry, but who's to say who is bottom here?'

'Molly is bottom,' said David firmly.

'In how she scored in one test, yes . . . but that doesn't take anything else into account. I mean, Molly's much better, well, she's much better . . . at the violin than Bronwyn.'

'Great!' he said sarcastically. 'She'll be the best violinist at Battersea Comprehensive.'

I thought of little Molly carrying her violin into that rough inner-city school. You could never walk in there with a violin, it would make you stand out too much. You'd have to hide your violin inside a machine-gun case.

That night I was sitting up in bed underlining passages in *The Self-Confident Parent* when David sprung his Plan B on me.

'We're going to have to go for St Jude's.'

'Boarding? No way.'

'She could get a music scholarship.'

'She's going to Chelsea College with all her friends.'

'Alice, she's never going to pass the entrance exam, you said so yourself. We're going to have to put her down for St Jude's and work on her music.'

'She'd never have got 23 per cent if she'd had that echinacea,' I said, and David looked at me as if I was insane. I was adamant that Molly was not going to boarding school. I couldn't bear the idea of her being taken away from me, but I didn't dare give this as the reason. I feared that David would say I was putting my own feelings ahead of what was best for our daughter.

'She's going to Chelsea College. That's what we always wanted for her. That's the best school. That's where her friends are going. That's where Molly is going.'

'And how is she going to get in?'

'I'll think of a way.'

'Good. Well, while you do that, I'm going to sleep. I'll phone St Jude's for a prospectus in the morning' – and suddenly everything was total darkness.

My hand fumbled across to my bedside table and I found something to occupy my hands while I worried.

'Are you popping bubble wrap again?'

'Sorry. I'll try and do it quietly.'

I slipped the old padded envelope underneath the duvet and tried to pop the polythene air pockets as gently as possible.

'For God's sake, how can I get to sleep with that racket? Pop! Rustle, rustle! Pop! Pop!'

Then silence. Then one more pop for defiance's sake and then I just sat there staring into the black nothingness of my daughter's future.

Anxiety had been my default setting ever since the children had been born. I remember when Molly and Jamie were little, there had been a feature on the radio about the risk of asteroids falling to Earth from outer space. The children couldn't understand why I was suddenly calling them in from the garden. In the end I had to force myself to stop being so irrational, though as they ran back out of the kitchen door I still heard myself shout, 'Be careful!' as I glanced nervously up at the heavens. When David came home he wanted to know why the children were splashing around in the paddling pool wearing their cycle helmets.

Be careful. That's all I ever seemed to say.

'Mum, can we go on the slide?'

'Um, all right, but *be careful.*'

'Mum, can we jump off the diving board?'

'Oh, er, OK, but *be careful.*'

Once when Jamie was swinging at the top of the climbing frame in the school playground he even heard his mother's voice booming, 'Jamie, be careful!' as I happened to drive past. The poor child looked skywards, wondering if he had just heard the voice of God. All right, I didn't *happen* to drive past their playground. I had taken a detour to check that he was all right. I couldn't help it – the worry was always there, a crippling sensation of permanent panic fluttering inside me, searching for something specific to land on.

The fear has many forms. When I was not worrying about something happening to my children, I worried that nothing would happen to my children. That they would end up as failures or embittered dropouts because we'd neglected to give them the best possible start in life. That by the time he was a teenager Jamie would end up bunking off school and spend his days lurking on the London Underground with other feral street urchins, riding up and down the escalators sticking chewing gum on the nipples of the girls in the bra adverts. And all because we'd mistimed the right moment to start clarinet lessons. So my children had to get the best education possible; they had to get into Chelsea College. The spectre of Big School loomed out of the sky like those approaching asteroids, beginning as a tiny far-off dot but growing ever closer, rapidly blocking out all light and warmth.

I went to nudge David but realized I didn't need to; he was wide awake as well.

'You know that nursery school running race I told you about the other day?'

'It doesn't matter that Alfie didn't win it. Gwilym's six months older . . .'

'No, it's not that. Anyway, Gwilym didn't win it, Ffion won it; she dangled him over the line.'

'I thought you all did?'

'Yeah, but Ffion started it, so she had a head start.'

'Forget about it. You're only five foot one, you were at a disadvantage.'

'Five foot two. No, my point is: little Gwilym won because *his mother ran the race for him.*'

'So?'

I paused for dramatic effect before telling him the idea that had been forming in my head.

'*I'll* take the exam.'

'What?'

'I'll pretend to be Molly and take the exam for her.'

David reached across and turned the light on. The way he screwed his face up in the sudden brightness made him look totally perplexed.

'You're not serious, are you?'

'Well, look at me – I'm short, flat-chested, and last year they charged me half price in the cinema. No one at Chelsea College knows what Molly looks like. If I worked on my appearance a bit I could sit there in the hall with all the other boys and girls, put Molly's name at the top of the page, make sure she gets 100 per cent and a guaranteed place at the best school in London.'

It was 4.30am and the first jumbo jet of the morning was shattering the still silence of the night.

'It would never work. You could pass for twenty-something, my darling, but eleven?'

'What about Henrietta in Molly's class? She's taller than me *and* she has bigger bosoms. The cow. She'll be in the exam hall, so will hundreds of other kids of all shapes and sizes. With a baseball cap pulled down over my face and wearing kids' clothes, who'd look twice at me?'

He paused for a moment as the plane turned sharply when the pilot realized he wasn't going directly over our bedroom.

'But what would we tell Molly?'

'She can sit a test paper at home – we'll tell her there wasn't enough room in the exam hall or something. That's the least of our problems . . .'

'It just feels like a pretty extreme thing to do . . .'

'It's no worse than going to church to get into a faith school, or lying about your address to get in on proximity.'

'Yes, it is.'

'All right, maybe a bit. But we have to do what we think is best for our children. I mean, it's not as if we'd be defrauding anyone, we're still going to be paying them thousands of pounds in school fees every year.'

The plane was right overhead now; it seemed to change gear or something as the roar shifted to a higher pitch.

'Well, that's true,' said David thoughtfully. 'And Molly would be an asset to any school.'

'A great asset. Lead violinist in the orchestra probably. And she *is* bright . . .' I insisted.

'. . . Very bright.'

'She just doesn't do well in exams . . .'

'Which is something Chelsea College might be able to help her with once she was actually in there . . .' said David.

The plane noise had begun to fade, but the sonic scream of the next jumbo was already building in the distance.

Make Fear Your Friend

By Barney Travers MGSc   *Sunrise Books £6.99*

Have you met your fears yet? No???? That's strange, you've been living with them for most of your life!!! Isn't it kinda rude to keep ignoring them like that? Maybe you should have gotten to know your fears a little better; find out who they are? 'Hello, Fear-of-Failure, my name's Barney, how do you do?' 'Hello, Fear-of-Embarrassment, how come you keep stopping me doing stuff?' Guess what? I nearly didn't write this book because I was kinda frightened it might come across as annoying phoney-baloney, but I MADE THAT FEAR MY FRIEND and now look: you're actually reading it!!!!

— 3 —

It is a Tuesday morning in February at the beginning of the 1980s. I am thirteen years old and I am sitting in the front row in the middle of the classroom. The ancient furniture dates from the era of slates and corporal punishment: a dark wooden bench and back rest connected to a gnarled desk with a worn flip-top lid upon which generations of girls have carved their initials or preserved for ever the names of boys they loved that week. There is still an inkwell but these days the ceramic pot inside is stuffed with old pencil shavings.

This is my worst, worst subject. Miss Torrance, squat and old, clothed in beige tweed, bulky rings on all fingers except the one that matters, has a smouldering temper capable of exploding at the unlikeliest of provocations. I stir the dusty inkwell with my pencil. I need a wee but there is only ten minutes till morning break and I daren't risk the wrath of Terrible Torrance.

'Tamara, what is nine in binary?'

'One, zero, zero, one.'

'Correct.'

'Susan, what is twelve in binary?'

'One, one, zero, zero.'

'Correct.'

Where is this place called Binary? I think. And why is everything there in ones and zeros?

'Jennifer, what is twenty-four expressed as a binary number?'

'One, one, zero, zero.'

'Sheep!'

On hearing the word 'sheep', Jennifer knows she must stand until she gets an answer right. If she gets her second answer wrong, she becomes a 'goat' and must stand on her seat; three wrong answers and the offending pupil becomes a 'billy goat' and must stand on her desk until coaxed down from the mountaintop by a correct answer. Miss Torrance thinks this makes it fun; she thinks this is her being 'a character'.

Five minutes later I am one of the half-dozen girls standing up for an answer that I knew was wrong, but which I judged as preferable to telling the truth, which was: 'I have not had the faintest bloody idea what you've been talking about all lesson.' I sway from side to side. My need to wee has increased since I was ordered to stand. It is beginning to crowd out everything else as Miss Torrance fires questions round the room at increasing speed, and there are giggles as girls sit or clamber onto classroom furniture.

'Jennifer, what is fourteen in binary?'

'Is it one, one, zero?'

'Goat!'

Jennifer unhesitatingly stands on her seat; she always makes it to goat, but never billy goat – soon a well-timed easy question will ensure that she is back to the floor.

'Alice, what is fourteen in binary?'

I am caught off guard. I had been hoping that if I didn't

make eye contact she might not notice me there, standing up right in the middle of the classroom.

'Er . . . one, zero, one, zero,' I say, making a random guess in this foreign language in which everyone else seems so fluent.

'Goat!'

I stand on my seat. I am seriously uncomfortable now. It comes in waves, it aches, and I try not to jiggle too obviously where I stand. Then an unprecedented breach of the un-written rules from Miss Torrance. She asks me a second question in a row. 'Billy goat!' shout a couple of her favourite pupils in unison with their teacher and now I am the only one in the room tottering on my desk, towering over my class-mates, who one by one answer correctly and return to the dignity of sitting down.

Think of deserts, I tell myself, dry, dry deserts, with no water for miles around, but a mirage appears with a cascading waterfall, which turns into a flushing lavatory, a hallowed private sanctuary, with a door and a lock and a place to sit and let go. Think of dust, think of sand, think of air, think of a big round toilet seat . . . no, no, put that out of your head.

'OK, Alice, today's billy goat,' says Miss Torrance finally. 'An easy one for you, I think . . .' but I don't even hear the question, it is as much as I can do to present a face of apparent total concentration, to appear to be working out the answer, when what I am really thinking is: I really, really need a wee now, lesson please end, school bell please ring . . . but the minute hand on the clock is still in the same place it was the last two times I looked. Silence. A room full of faces staring up at me.

'Please can I go to the toilet?'

'No, you're not getting out of it that easily, young lady!' she barks.

'Come on, Alice, you can do it!' whispers a friendly voice.

'Alice, have you listened to a single thing I have said this lesson?'

'Yes, miss.' It is hard to appear sincere when I am towering above her, worrying about spraying urine all over her classroom.

'So what is four expressed in binary code?'

'Go on, Alice, you know this . . .' whispers another voice.

All faces are staring up at me, all my classmates willing me to say the right answer. I think hard about the separate words that make up her question, repeating them slowly to myself, but this is a pointless exercise – it is like carefully pondering, 'What . . . is . . . blinky-blonky tum-te-tum?' and then hoping the answer may present itself.

'Well?' she says.

'Sorry, could you repeat the question?'

'It is basic binary. Set two, Alice, remember? What's four in binary?'

I have to say something. All this pressure on me, it is pressing on my bladder, it is squeezing and pushing – any answer, just say something . . . 'One, one, one, one.' It seems like an intelligent guess. Four ones are four, I am sure of that. I must be in with a chance.

'NO!' she booms incredulously. 'NO, NO, NO, NO! That's fifteen, isn't it?'

'Yes.'

'Do you understand why one, one, one, one is fifteen?'

'Er, yes.'

'So what is four?'

'Oh, what is four?' I repeat as if she hasn't made herself clear before now.

'Yes. What is four?'

Silence. Standing on this desk ten feet above the floor, I can see the top of her head, I can see out of the glass partition into the corridor where the salvation of the toilets is just a few yards away. My skinny bare legs are level with the faces of my classmates, white socks and black shoes shuffling nervously on the desktop. It feels like for ever but I suppose it can only be fifteen or twenty seconds that she lets me stand on that desk in silence with the whole class looking at me. The first thing I notice is how warm the liquid feels upon my leg, how quickly it flows down my inner thighs to my calves, then soaks into my socks, a little urine finding its way inside my shoes. The sheer amount of it, too, is surprising: it just keeps coming and coming, forming several fast-flowing streams that run to the edge of the desk, dripping down to bulging pools that spread across the dusty classroom floor, while a few splashes bounce off the desk and onto Miss Torrance's tweed jacket.

It was quite a few moments before she realized what was happening, before she understood why girls around me were shrieking 'Urgh!' and leaping away from the downpour. She was barking at them to be quiet and sit down, unaware that little flecks of dampness were appearing on her jacket. Miss Torrance never did tell me what four was in binary. She never wore that jacket again either. But at least we didn't do sheep, goat, billy goat again after that.

Most of the girls in my class wore badges on their lapel for outstanding achievements in their particular fields: choir or netball or library monitor. It turned out there was no enamel shield for having pissed on your maths teacher. Of course, I was completely traumatized and was off school for a while, but time passed and the worst thing that could have happened in the whole world was eventually forgotten. I went on to be appointed form captain, to win medals for the debating society and star in the school play. Life moved on. I peeked at my old school on *Friends Reunited*. Somebody had put: 'Whatever happened to old Alice Niagara-Knickers?'

'Oh, *Friends Reunited*,' said David, looking over my shoulder. 'Are you on there?'

'Er, no, can't be bothered with all that mid-life crisis nostalgia nonsense,' I said, hastily turning off the computer. Getting the children into bed that evening had been a greater battle than usual and I hauled myself up from the computer and collapsed on the sofa. It was only now that I realized how tired I was following the sleepless night we had spent debating our daughter's school entrance exam. I flicked through the TV channels until I found the programme about a young family leaving behind their hectic life in north London to become organic olive farmers in Tuscany. I wondered if olive farmers watch programmes about people who've decided to become anxious inner-city parents tooting their horns in traffic jams because they're already late for their daughter's Scottish country dancing lesson? I let out a long exhausted sigh, kicked off my shoes, wiggled my body slightly to get extra comfortable in the soft folds of my favourite sofa and raised a large glass of chilled white wine to my dry lips.

But the glass didn't stop there. The arc of its flight continued upwards as it was deftly removed from my hand and placed on the sideboard by David.

'No wine yet, I'm afraid, young lady. You've got work to do . . .'

'What? Don't be ridiculous. Give me my glass back!'

'You can't do a test paper after drinking alcohol. It will affect your score. You can have a drink when you've finished – that can be your reward.'

'Don't treat me like a child, David. I want my wine and I want it now!'

'After you've done a numeracy test. Come on! There's a paper waiting for you on my desk. And a glass of milk and some biscuits.'

Why was it that whenever I announced a project my husband had to be even more keen on it than I was? Why couldn't I be married to one of those wonderful husbands who are completely unsupportive and uninterested in their wives or children?

'I'll do it tomorrow,' I mumbled sulkily.

'No, tomorrow is non-verbal reasoning. I've worked out your revision timetable' – and he thrust his spreadsheet under my nose as if this was some higher authority that neither of us could argue with.

'Now, come on, if we're going to do this we've got to do it properly. All the kids going for this exam will have been tutored and tested for the past couple of years; you can't assume that you'll do better than them just because you're an adult. It's twenty years since you got your maths O level.'

This didn't seem the moment to mention to my husband that in fact I never got my maths O level. That I had failed it twice and then given up. Even now I regularly set the video for 18:30, thus failing to record the programme that started at half past eight.

'Well, I was just going to have ten minutes, but I can start now if you want,' I said getting to my feet. 'I am thirty-six. I would imagine that I'm going to be a bit smarter than any ten- or eleven-year-old . . .'

David's desk had been cleared of all clutter. Reflecting the harsh glare of the spotlight, a clean white test paper stared up at me from where it lay beside a freshly sharpened pencil. An alarm clock was placed on the desk where it ticked slightly too loudly.

'I've made it as much like the real thing as possible. Now remember to check your answers,' he said, 'and show any workings out.'

'Yes, yes, I know,' I said tersely.

'And if you get stuck on a question, just move on to the next one and come back to it if you have time at the end.'

'Right, that's it! I'm not doing it! If you are going to patronize me and exploit this exercise to try to make yourself appear all superior then I'll do the tests in my own time.'

'But that's what you say to Molly . . .'

'Molly is eleven.'

'And so are you, my darling. You have to walk like an eleven-year-old, talk like an eleven-year-old, write like an eleven-year-old and even fidget like an eleven-year-old. Now come on, do this paper and I'll buy you an Avril Lavigne CD.'

I read the first question and was surprised by how easy it was. Converting fractions to decimals . . . I remembered doing these with Molly. $\frac{1}{100}$ as a decimal is 0.01, so I quickly wrote the answer in the box and was aware of an approving grunt from behind me.

'Could you shut the door please, David?'

He pushed the door to and, without looking round, I added, 'No, from the other side.'

I occasionally wonder how husband-and-wife teams ever achieve anything. Did Hilary Clinton really think it would be possible to reform US healthcare policy when the president was her husband?

'Bill, have you read my draft report on Medicare reforms?'

'You don't have to say it in *that voice* . . .'

'I'm not saying it in any voice, I just want to know if you've bothered to read it?'

'Bothered? So you're saying I'm lazy now? Just because I forgot our anniversary when we were invading Somalia . . .'

I was determined not to give David a single incorrect answer at which he could tut and shake his head in disappointed pity. My husband considered himself something of an intellectual. When he watched *University Challenge* or *Mastermind*, he usually got the answers wrong, but still took pride in the fact that his wrong answers were the same as the wrong answers given by the super-brainy contestants. This evening he would have no reason to feel smug. He would mark my paper and force himself to say, 'Well done. A perfect score,' as he tried to remember why it was he felt a vague sense of disappointment. I finished the decimals and fractions and moved on to the next section.

'Which are the next *two* numbers in this sequence: 2, 3, 5, 7, 11, 13, 17 . . .?' OK, I thought, not immediately obvious, but these things are always very straightforward – it's just a question of working out a pattern. Now, let me see . . . the numbers increase by one unit once, then by two units twice, ah yes, I see the pattern, now it will be increasing by three units, three times, will it? No, it won't; damn. OK, there must be some other sequence . . . I reread the question just to make sure I wasn't missing something obvious.

Ah, I've got it. If you add 2 and 3 you get the next number, 5. So if I add 3 and 5 I should get the next number, which is . . . shit, it's 7. They must mean 8, it must be a misprint . . . Every time I tried to listen to my own quiet thoughts it was like there was a car alarm going off in another part of my head, and ten minutes later I was still staring at the numbers until eventually they blurred into dead meaningless shapes. Ugh, it is SO unfair, I sulked to myself, infuriated by being forced to endure extra maths homework like this. My head was resting on my hand and my arm was slumped resentfully across the desk. I let out a long grumpy sigh. I ran my fingers through my hair and noticed a few flecks of dandruff fall onto the test paper. Dandruff, urgh, how long had I had dandruff? There was none on my shoulders, but by vigorously scratching my scalp I was able to send a few more tiny specks of skin tumbling onto the exam paper. I adjusted the spotlight slightly to get a better look and tipped up the paper to pour the collection onto the desk. There were a couple of dark hairs in the mix and one that looked albino white. It wasn't enough that I was going grey, now the grey hairs were falling out as well. I was slowly turning into one of those old ladies with thin white hair and a shiny pink scalp clearly visible underneath. I might as well buy a tartan shopping trolley and fill it with half-price loaves of sliced white bread to empty out on the edge of the common for all the pigeons.

'You've had twenty minutes,' called David through the office door. 'You should be on section two by now!'

'Thank you, darling!' I shouted, sticking two fingers up at the closed door. I quickly brushed away the fascinating detritus of my scalp and returned to the paper. I was miles behind. I was not even halfway through section one. I left the stupid number sequence question with the obvious misprint and moved on to some straightforward percentages. 'If Simon has 7 apples, Peter has 6 apples and Jennifer has 11, what percentage of the total number of apples does Peter have?' Easy. There are 24 apples altogether, and Peter has 6, so to get the percentage you just multiply that by 24 and divide by 100, which gives . . . 1.44 per cent. Hmm, that doesn't sound right. OK, it must be the other way round. It is 24 divided by 6, times 100, which gives you the answer . . . 400. Peter has 400 per cent of the 24 apples. This was serious now. I was going to do badly. I wasn't anxious about the test I would be sitting for Molly just yet – strangely, that felt too far away to worry about right now. It was David's likely reaction to my failure this evening that I couldn't bear to contemplate. The prospect of him patiently explaining to me where I had gone wrong on each question between now and midnight, the tone of voice he would use when he said, 'You mean you don't even know how to work out a percentage?' . . . I had to do well, if only to ensure I wouldn't be convicted of murdering my husband, leaving my children to be taken into care while I spent the rest of my life in Holloway prison writing sexually explicit letters to Premiership footballers.

The next page of sums appeared to be completely in-comprehensible. I began to panic. Maybe I have 'dyscalculia', I thought to myself, maybe I'm 'number-phobic'. When I'd had lunch with Ffion and Sarah in Mange Tooting recently, the bill had been plonked down in front of me to be split into three. And I had stared at it for a while before announcing; 'By the way, this is my treat, let me get this . . . no, really, because you paid for the parking meter.' Not that Ffion had put up much of a fight.

My mind was just so cluttered and messy – it was worse than the loft. I used to know exactly where everything was up there but now there were so many useless bits of rubbish piled on top of one another that I could never lay my hands on any-thing. David's brain was like his office: methodical and ordered. Looking around his study it occurred to me that I had never dreamed in my wild student days that I'd end up being married to a man who put a polythene cover over his computer in the evening. He had a desk tidy on his tidy desk. He had CDs that were in their cases. He had a tear-off calendar actually showing today's date, a magnetic paper-clip sculpture in a perfect line between the Sellotape dispenser and the pocket calculator. A pocket calculator!

It stared at me, defying me to switch it on, just to check a couple of answers that I was pretty sure I had answered correctly already. Don't be ridiculous, I told myself. The point of this test is to see how much work I have to do between now and the examination at the end of next month. If I cheat now, I will be completely wasting my time. Anyway, knowing David's thoroughness, he would have already taken the batteries out as a precaution. I actually became indignant at this thought: that David should trust me so little, so I pressed the 'On' button to see if the screen came to life or not. A digital zero glowed at me, reminding me of the possibility that zero might well be my final mark. I double-checked my last answer and found that it was correct, so there was no harm done. But then the answer before that turned out to be wrong, so I wrote in the correct total, reasoning that there is no point in giving a response that you know to be incorrect. Then the calculator told me that the solution to the first question of section two was 147. I discovered that the average number of clothes pegs in question seven was 93. I worked out that 6 over 24 was in fact 25 per cent. The square root of 196 is 14. Lunch at Mange Tooting would have come to £13.72 each. I whizzed through all three sections making up for lost time. There were still a couple of questions too obtuse for me even to work out with a calculator, but most of them could be answered instantly, leaving me twenty minutes to realize that the numbers in the impossible sequence that I had struggled with had one thing in common. Of course, they were all prime numbers. Like Ffion and her money, they could not be divided. So the next two numbers in the sequence were 19 and 23. With my confidence brimming I managed the last remaining blank questions on my own. I had done it, I had completed the whole paper in time and even had a feeling that I might have done rather well. I went to turn the calculator off. It was the advanced model with all sorts of buttons that I didn't understand. There was a button that said 'sin', so I pressed it to see if it made the screen say 'repent'. 'Time up!' said David, bursting through the door. Giving out a little squeal of surprise, I quickly leant my arm over the calculator. The suddenness of my movement made it slide across the desk and it was now poised to fall off the edge unless I kept pressing it hard against the corner. 'Oh you made me jump!' I said. I couldn't move my arm or the calculator would clatter to the floor.

'Right, let's go see how we got on,' said David.

'Good idea,' I said, not moving a muscle, smiling up at him.

'Strange,' he said, looking at his perfectly ordered desk. 'That doesn't look right.'

There was a big gap between the magnetic paper-clip sculpture and the Sellotape dispenser. I couldn't keep pressing the missing calculator against the corner of the desk for much longer.

'My dispenser has run out of Sellotape. I wonder when that happened?'

He grabbed my exam paper from in front of me and headed through to the kitchen. I breathed a sigh of relief and replaced his calculator. And then I glanced down at where he had revealed the next sheet in the folder: 'For Parents Only: Answers to Paper One.'

'Congratulations! You did fantastically!' exclaimed David, coming into the lounge to find me draining the glass of wine that I had surrendered earlier in the evening. 'You got 91 per cent on your first go, and you'd said that maths was going to be your toughest paper . . .'

'Whatever,' I mumbled, brushing past him to refill my glass, not wanting to betray my guilt with any eye contact.

'Well, aren't you pleased?' he asked deflatedly.

'Yeah, great, where's that bottle of wine?'

'Alice, you just scored the sort of mark that is going to get Molly into Chelsea College and you seem disappointed.'

'No, I'm just tired.'

This was true enough, but deep down I felt angry. Those bastards had been right all along. I was only cheating myself. I was also irritated by his presumption that this was all going to be so easy for me. 'Anyway, I guessed a lot of the answers. I must have just got lucky . . .'

'What, you guessed that the square root of 196 is 14? Come on, you did brilliantly. You're going to walk it.'

'*I am not going to walk it, all right?*' I snapped. 'It is not as easy as you think! You don't understand what the pressure is like: having all this responsibility on my shoulders. It's bloody hard enough being a good mother without having to sit bloody maths exams to decide their future as well! As if there aren't enough tests already without having to hurriedly recheck that eight-twelfths expressed as a percentage is seventy-fucking-five, knowing that if I make one little mistake it might ruin my daughter's entire life!'

'Sixty-six.'

'What?'

'Eight-twelfths is two-thirds, which is 66.6 recurring. I'm sure you would have got it right if you'd checked it . . .' mumbled David, realizing that this probably wasn't the best time to correct me on my mental arithmetic.

'That's it! I quit! *You* take the bloody exam. You put on a pink gingham skirt and a blond wig and pretend to be an eleven-year-old girl, if you're so bloody great at maths.'

'But I'm six foot one.'

'So she's tall for her age . . .'

'And I have a moustache.'

'So what, so does Ffion, I don't care, I'm not doing it! I can't do it. It's not going to work.'

I claimed that I was going out to take Alfie's video back to Blockbuster, although it wasn't clear why this required me to slam the front door quite so hard. It wasn't until I was outside that I realized that I didn't have my car keys in my coat pocket. I couldn't go back inside and endure David's upbeat encouragement all over again, so I decided to walk. We only lived five minutes from the high street, or fifteen if you were in the car, but it suddenly struck me that I never made this journey on foot after dark. And as I took my first brisk steps between the towering 4x4s and the shadowy hedges, I realized that it was not just habitual laziness that prompted me to climb into the car every time I needed so much as a pint of milk. It was fear. I was nervous of walking down my own street after dark.

'Make Fear Your Friend,' I kept repeating to myself as I hurried past a couple of suspicious-looking wheelie-bins, which to my great relief did not have a couple of muggers waiting to pop out as I passed. 'Make Fear Your Friend.' Why did I have to have such noisy shoes? Their hasty clattering seemed to broadcast the message: 'Wealthy lone female taking mobile and bulging purse out for late-night walk. Probably wearing a Rolex. Help yourself.' A recent neighbourhood-watch leaflet had reported that the last local resident to have their briefcase stolen had managed to take a photo of the fleeing muggers with his new mobile phone. I'd thought this was rather inspired, until I read that the thieves had then turned round and nicked his phone as well. I clutched the prize booty marked 'Blockbuster video' tightly to my chest as I imagined members of the criminal underworld trying to unload a stolen copy of *Barney and Friends* for the price of a hit of crack cocaine. Fragments of broken car window glistened in the gutter; in the distance I could hear a police siren rushing to the scene of some other routine crime.

Then ahead of me from out of the shadows emerged two figures. A couple of teenage boys, both tall with their hoods up, had come out of a doorway and started to walk up the road towards me. This was it. Fear wasn't my friend at all – he always made me feel awful. My pace slowed while my heart was racing. For a second I carried on walking towards them, thinking that turning round now would be too obvious, that it would concede defeat too easily, surrendering myself as a willing target. I could see them more clearly as they passed under the orange sulphur glow of a flickering street light: they were both black, and looked lanky and sullen. They walked a couple of yards apart so that I would have to walk directly in between them. That would obviously be the moment when they'd strike. One of them was a giant, maybe six foot six; would he be the one who would hit me while the other demanded my purse? Would they want more than the usual? I'd read somewhere about a robber cutting off a woman's finger to take her wedding ring. Maybe they'd read the same article in the *Mail* and had decided to try this out? They were only twenty feet ahead of me when I suddenly turned and started to rush back towards the safety of my home. Without actually breaking into a run, I scurried back up the street, adrenalin pumping, my heart in overdrive. I heard them laughing close behind me and now I ended any pretence and just dashed to the electronic security gate that we'd had fitted at the end of the path. My hands were shaking as I entered my code on the keypad. Nine four nine six – Jamie's date of birth and the four-digit code number I used for everything. A tiny red light flashed at me and a defiant beep told me that this code had now expired. I had paid for the best system available, which meant having to change our security code every two months. I had had this gate fitted to protect me and my family from criminals and now it had trapped me outside with them: stranded and about to be mugged by two dead-eyed youths. I was frantically pressing the buzzer but it was too late. I glanced round and they were upon me.

Would they say anything first or would they just do it, I wondered as my eyes were squeezed shut and my shoulders hunched up. 'No!' I squealed. Then the split second became several seconds. I looked round and they had continued past me, walking at the same pace, still several feet apart, laughing and joking, and I saw in an instant that despite one of them being the height of a giant redwood, they were just a couple of kids walking down the street, not going anywhere in particular, but not the slightest bit interested in me.

I am scared of black teenage boys. There, I've said it. *I, Alice Chaplin, am scared of black teenage boys.* Is that a racist thing to say? I think it probably is. I never considered myself a racist. Racists are shaven-headed football supporters with tattoos and bulldogs and BNP posters in the window, and you don't get many of those in Oaken Avenue. Whereas I sign up to the generally accepted moral viewpoint that racism is *A Bad Thing*. Nelson Mandela and Martin Luther King? *Good people*, definitely. The Ku Klux Klan? *Bad people*, very bad; if ever I met someone with a pointy white hood burning a cross I would think worse of them, no question about it. But black teenage boys? Well, I'm sorry, but either I lie or I say 'scary people' –

that's just my honest reaction. Maybe when they were four-teen, Nelson Mandela and Martin Luther King hung about with their hoods up at the bottom of Oaken Avenue on bicycles that looked as if they didn't originally belong to them. Maybe Trevor McDonald began his interest in journalism by writing illegible graffiti on the side of railway bridges. Maybe those black teenage boys who don't ever seem to be in school and leave half-eaten Big Macs on underground trains will grow up to be respected newsreaders or great leaders giving moving speeches about freedom or whatever, but in the meantime I cannot be a hypocrite and pretend that I do not feel alienated from, threatened by and simply *scared of black teenage boys.*

My reaction is, of course, based upon the fear that a black teenage youth might try to rob me. That if I attempted to edge my way between the phalanx of pushbikes blocking the shadowy pavement, one of them might grab my handbag and cycle off to some concrete hideout where he'd feverishly empty out the contents, wildly estimating how much easy cash he might get for a pocket umbrella, a small bottle of Clarins Eau Dynamisante and a couple of battered old Lil-lets. And even if the police were to catch him, everyone knows you never get the tampons back. Could any insurance payment ever replace their full sentimental value? Would I ever find another pocket umbrella like that one with two broken spokes that cost £4.99 from Boots?

If it is not the material loss that would bother me, why am I so scared? I suppose it is the thought of so much naked hostility being directed towards me, the idea of another human being showing me that much hateful contempt that I find so terrifying. This fear is not based on any personal experience. I have never been assaulted, robbed or even bothered by a black teenager. I

72

have suffered more violence from old ladies elbowing me on buses, but I don't break out into a sweat when I see a pensioner coming along in a little electric buggy because I think they might be planning a drive-by shooting.

I suppose I'm actually scared of white teenage boys as well, at least the pasty hooded variety that ride bicycles on the pavement at night with no lights on and look like they eat only crisps for breakfast. Why can't criminal youths be like they were in the old days? All rosy-cheeked and tousle-haired and singing 'Consider Yourself' while dancing in formation behind Ron Moody? I can't imagine any teenage muggers these days cheekily helping themselves to an apple off the basket on the head of a tap-dancing Covent Garden porter. Mind you, my own kids wouldn't fancy the apple much either – they'd have to stop all the singing and dancing while I peeled and sliced it for them and mixed it up with some organic raisins.

Make Fear Your Friend said that the only way to overcome my greatest fears was to go out and experience them. Did this mean wandering up and down Brixton Road at midnight wearing a gold necklace and chatting on an expensive mobile phone? I wasn't sure I was ready for that yet. And this evening I had failed even to walk to the end of my road. Instead I slipped back inside the house, picked up the car keys and drove to Blockbuster, and rather than say anything to the pimply youth behind the counter, I dropped the tape in the 24-hour drop-box outside the shop and was soon back home, double-locking the door behind me. The ordeal had reminded me why I was so utterly determined to get Molly into Chelsea College. Because I wanted her kept separate from the gangs of teenage criminals that roamed the streets and the pond life that worked in Blockbuster who had piercings through their eyebrows, lips and probably through several internal organs as well. I wanted to protect her from all those people who scared me; I wanted her to meet only nice young people, teenagers who were concerned about the environment and thought knowing your twelve times table was cool and wrote thank-you letters after Christmas. Then she would grow up to be a lovely charming well-educated young lady and have a boyfriend who didn't have 'love' and 'hate' tattooed on his knuckles but who was maybe in the orchestra with her and said things like, 'Hello, Mrs Chaplin, I'll make sure we're back from the cinema by half past nine; it's jolly lucky they're showing *A Room with a View* because we're both study-ing that for A level, although of course it's no substitute for reading the actual book.'

I suppose if I was honest with myself, it all came down to social class. I didn't mix with people from the local council estates and I was frightened of allowing my children to. We had very few dinner parties where I found myself saying, 'Ffion, this is Shaz. Shaz works as the receptionist at Body Brown Instant Tan Centre and is hoping to win the National Lottery.' The indigenous population of this part of south London was a foreign tribe to me, and their forbidding grey tower blocks were another country. In fact, they were further away than that, because I was happy to fly off to Umbria or Provence, but nothing would ever tempt me to wander a few hundred yards away into the alien ghetto of the council estates. The drug dealers in there probably couldn't flog me any echinacea anyway.

Perhaps the schools should organize some sort of exchange programme. When I was a child we all went on French exchanges; I had two weeks staying with a 'typical French family' in Lille, though I couldn't believe it was typical to keep your spaniel tied up next to the washing machine in a cement-scented garage-basement or to force visiting English children to eat what I remain convinced was raw bacon. Maybe now we should be sending our children on 'class exchanges'; instead of sending them overseas they should just move down the road for a few weeks and stay with a bona fide working-class family: drinking Tango, wearing enormous puffer jackets with Yankees logos on the back and hanging around the streets after bedtime. Of course, we'd keep in touch. Jamie could send me a postcard telling me how he was adjusting to his new adoptive family amongst the urban working classes:

Dear Mum
Am doing my best to learn language, yer bitch. Was having a well wicked time till I is getting run over by a train I was tagging. Told Kev I need drugs to ease pain – he said he'd score some for me, innit? Is Strangeways the name of a hospital?
Love Jamie

David had obviously given some thought to how best to tackle my outburst because the following night as we both climbed into bed he casually mentioned that we ought to think about what sort of children's clothes I was going to wear for the exam. This was a bold tactic but one that had worked before. We both knew that the subtitles said: 'You didn't mean what you said last night, did you?' It was understood that my mock-casual response expressing an intention to visit Gap Kids translated as: 'All right, I take it all back, we're still going through with it.' Despite my abject failure when confronted with my first exam paper for twenty years, I could see no other way. I still wanted total control of this process; it was the only way I could envisage coping with it. My daughter was going to have the best life possible, if I just lived this one bit for her.

We lay beside one another in the dark. I was thinking that if I got David to tutor me and studied full time and kept practising, then surely I should be able to get full marks in an exam designed for eleven-year-olds, and that Molly would take a test at home and that way she'd think she got in on her own merit but we should also continue to tutor her anyway because she mustn't fall behind, oh, and we mustn't take our eyes off Jamie's education at the same time, and Alfie would be starting at the infants in September. Meanwhile, David was probably thinking: I wonder if there's any chance of us having sex.

I reached for the bedside cabinet, sensing David's irritation when the small sheet of polythene in my hand produced the first tiny pop.

'Do you have to do that?' he sighed.

Pop!

'It helps me get to sleep,' I countered, running the bubble wrap through my fingers in search of the few remaining air blisters.

Pop!

'Why can't you get some worry beads or maybe listen to the shipping forecast on the radio or something?'

'I tried that. But it keeps me awake. I lie there waiting to see if there is going to be a hurricane in Clapham.'

Pop!

Each little controlled explosion felt like another knot of anxiety had been kneaded away – each tiny release of trapped air was a problem solved. But there always seemed so many bubbles to get through; whenever one sheet was completed I'd have to find another one. Nearby a car alarm had gone off while a low-flying jet roared overhead.

'Do you think maybe we should move to Lundy?' I said into the darkness.

'Lundy?'

'It's a little island in the middle of the Bristol Channel.'

'I know where Lundy is. Why on earth would we want to go and live in bloody Lundy?'

'I read it has the lowest crime rate in Britain. And if we sold up here I bet we could get somewhere with a really big garden in Lundy.'

'Alice, I'm a financial consultant. Lundy's all cliffs and wildlife. What am I going to do – set up an investment portfolio for a load of seals? Advise them to buy shares in fish?'

'But think of the freedom the children would have. They could go to the local school with the children of the nature warden and the lighthouse keeper, and get lots of fresh air bird-watching.'

'And do you think you wouldn't find new things to worry about on Lundy? You wouldn't lie awake worrying about the children being dive-bombed by a killer puffin?'

David started to drift off to sleep, leaving me trying to shake off the image of my children being pecked to death by a vicious little seabird with a stripy beak. 'Can puffins fly then?' I said into the darkness five minutes later.

'Yes, puffins can fly . . .' mumbled his voice into the pillow. 'Go to sleep.'

'Oh, I thought they were a sort of penguin.'

'No.' He laughed patronizingly. 'You only get penguins in the southern hemisphere,' and he covered his head to block out the noise of the popping bubble wrap.

As if he sensed my anxiety, little Alfie suddenly came galloping into our room. He was frightened. It was the same fear as usual: he was afraid that there might be a bear in his toy cupboard.

'Darling, there are no bears in England,' David said,

spotting the opportunity for a lesson in natural history even though it was half past one in the morning. 'The last European bear in the British Isles was hunted to extinction in the thirteenth century, remember? And even a small bear, like the Himalayan black bear, needs a range of at least twenty square miles of woodland, so no bear could ever live in your toy cupboard, could it? So come on, let's go back to bed.'

'No . . .'

'Why not?'

'I'm scared of the bear in my toy cupboard.'

'*Look, don't be ridiculous!*' snapped David. 'I just explained to you that that's impossible. What's it going to live on? Lego?'

David always got upset about the wrong things. For example, he was furious about 9/11. '9/11 is an Americanism,' he would rage. 'In Britain it should be 11/9!' However, on this occasion I have to say I was with my husband. The chances of a colony of bears having continued to live in southern England undetected by naturalists for seven hundred years before finally settling just off London's South Circular seemed pretty remote. And then for one of these urban bears to successfully pick all the locks to our front door, type in the correct alarm code on the keypad with its great big claws and sneak up to hide in Alfie's toy cupboard, well, this was beyond a long shot.

I pulled back the duvet to allow him to climb in and I felt his arms lock round the back of my neck.

'You know you'll never get any sleep if you let him stay next to you . . .' groaned David.

'Hmm, you smell nice,' I told him, inhaling the scent of my son's scalp like an addicted ex-smoker hovering near a stranger's cigarette. I wanted this moment to last for ever, and I held him close, letting him drift off to sleep, pretending to myself that in six hours' time I wouldn't be snapping at him to hurry up and brush his teeth and put on his shoes: paying the debt of the previous night's intimacy with exhausted short-tempered tension.

Right now my children were as safe as they could possibly be. But tomorrow I would have to let them go back off to school, to face all sorts of perils and make all kinds of decisions that might be the wrong ones. I read somewhere that it was now possible to buy an electronic tag for your child so that if they were abducted they could be instantly located using a satellite tracking system. Imagine what it would be like when every kid had one: you'd have to have some sort of playground traffic control with stressed-out radar supervisors shouting desperate warnings that the slide was not clear for take-off yet, little Timothy was still sitting at the bottom. I wondered if soon it might be possible to fit a tiny camera to the top of your child's head, so that you could then sit at home watching what they were doing all day while they were away from you. You'd need one of those wireless talkback facilities that newsreaders have as well, in order that you could warn your child to hold on to the banister when they hurried down the stairs, or to guide them towards the grated carrot at school dinners.

Or maybe all the CCTV cameras in the country could be linked up to a central network so that we could tune in and watch our children wherever they were. Crossing the road in view of the traffic monitor by the pedestrian lights, then passing the security camera in the high street and now into range of the web-cam in the window of Dixons – wherever they happened to wander they would always be in their parents' sight, as long as Mum and Dad paid the £49.95 monthly rental on the personalized child-watch cable channel. Maybe

I could sell that thought to Philip as the next big computer idea he was searching for.

Molly had recently announced that she wanted to go un-accompanied to the newsagent's at the bottom of the road to buy a comic, and David said he thought it would be good for her, so I tried to appear as relaxed as possible in the face of this mad adventure. I talked through with her step by step exactly what she had to do, on her own, without her mother. And then she went out and did it. She walked out of our front gate, turned left along the pavement, walked a hundred yards down to the corner, went in and chose her comic, handed over the money (exact change already arranged) and then headed back towards home. And then she said, 'Mum, I can see you hiding behind that hedge.'

With Alfie's head tucked under my arm and the red digits on the alarm clock glowing a blurred 3:something, I began to drift off, when suddenly I was jolted awake by an unfamiliar noise. This wasn't a child on a landing, this was coming from outside. Someone had climbed the fence and was in our back garden. My heart was beating so fast it had sucked the energy from all my other muscles and I was completely frozen. They may well be trying to force open the back door at this very moment; they might have stun guns like those burglars on *Crimewatch* last week – it might be the same gang now on their way upstairs to rob us and then shoot me and the children so that we wouldn't be able to describe them to Nick Ross. I pictured the yellow police sign in our road. 'Appeal for Witnesses; Multiple Murder.' Some blurry photo of me and the kids being repeatedly shown on the news. Oh God, I hope David wouldn't give them that one of me looking hideous in a saggy bikini at Center Parcs.

Then I forced myself to fight such irrational thoughts, to be sensible about this. I'd heard noises before and David had always stomped back to bed to report that there was nothing out there. I'd been half asleep – maybe I'd dreamt it. Calmness, I thought to myself. Tranquillity. Composure. I am not afraid of anything in the back garden. I am in my own home, the doors are all locked, there are bars on the windows, there is no danger, there is nothing to fear.

And then I let out a small scream. The security spotlight had come on in the garden. Something was definitely out there. I'd only just had the light fitted for this very eventuality and already a burglar had set off the sensors.

'David! David, wake up! There's a burglar in the back garden.'

'What?'

'The light's come on . . . the security light – there's someone out there.'

He sat up. 'It's just a cat again.'

'Shall I phone the police? I'll phone the police,' I gabbled.

'No, let me just have a look,' he said as his pasty bottom disappeared out of the bedroom. Whenever David went to check that we were not being burgled, he never even bothered to put his dressing gown on. If I was a man going into battle with a gang of drug-crazed armed robbers, I wouldn't have thought that the most protective armour possible was a baggy old T-shirt with your willy swinging about underneath.

I held the phone in my hand all ready to ring the police, trying to remember whether it was still 999 or if they'd changed it to 118-something. But then he just waddled back upstairs and into the bedroom with a world-weary expression and threw me a sheet of polythene. 'It was the bear from the cupboard,' he sighed. 'I brought you up some more bubble wrap . . .'

The Zodiac Diet Book
Eat The Right Foods For Your Star Sign And Watch The Pounds Drop Off!
By David Zinkin   Sunrise Books £6.99

Are you a munching goat or a picky crab? Do you weigh out every calorie with your Libran scales or demand the lion's share of dinner like a typical Leo? Just as the position of the stars and planets affects our personalities, so our metabolisms and appetite vary enormously according to our star sign. Whether you are a Virgo who prefers pure, fresh food, or you are an Aquarian who often drinks water at meal times, by using the planetary charts in this book you will learn the astrological slimming secrets for your sign as practised by the Ancient Egyptians.

For example, I'm Gemini the twins and just one chocolate never felt like enough; my star sign had been urging me to eat them in pairs. But for Geminis like me, the solution to weight loss also demands what astrological dieticians call a 'Twin Approach': namely, 1) eating less and 2) exercising more. This has worked for every Gemini I know . . .

— 4 —

David was always completely contemptuous of anything to do with astrology and, rather annoyingly, that's not typical Aries. He never liked it when I knew more about something than he did. In any case, they got him exactly right: 'As one of the fire signs, you don't like your meals to be left to go cold. You also like your vegetables properly cooked and prefer not to eat cheap processed foods.' That was so true it was uncanny. The only bit of the book where I did wonder if they were stretching it a bit was when they suggested that you should try to select precise ingredients according to your astrological symbol. I'm Cancer the crab and I didn't really fancy snacking on a load of decaying seagull heads.

I lost quite a few pounds in the first weeks of my diet as I strove to make myself look more like an eleven-year-old. Former weight-loss regimes had failed when I'd thought it reasonable not to count rejected chicken goujons off the children's plates that I ate while standing up. But now I found that I had self-discipline. It's the new Alice Chaplin diet! All you need is your child's entire future to depend on it and you'd be amazed at your own willpower! That's why we can't lose weight after we have babies – because we are more focused on our children's lives than we are on our own. But now I'd found the secret: 'Lose half a stone or your children will get it.' If I put that in a book, I'd make a million, no question. Though David rather unhelpfully suggested that if I really wanted to look like a modern child, I should be stuffing my face with burgers till I was clinically obese.

In fact, even Molly had developed a bit of puppy fat in the last year or so. Well, quite a lot of puppy fat actually; we're talking about a St Bernard or Bull Mastiff puppy here. She didn't like sport because she hated losing, and anything that required sustained effort or vigorous movement, such as chopping up her sausages, I tended to do for her. Apart from music, the only pastime in which she really excelled was literacy: every day she'd seem to come back from school another fifty pages further on. 'We just did reading our books in English today.'

'Marvellous that you're reading so much, darling . . .' I would say, while I privately wondered why we were paying £3000 a term for someone to sit in the room with our children while they read a book. But it was good for Molly to be good at something, and doubly satisfying that it was an interest she'd inherited from me. It's very important for your children to see you reading proper books; I read that in *Your Child Is a Journey, You Are the Compass*.

So when one Saturday morning Ffion suggested our eleven-year-olds form their own junior book group to meet up and discuss whichever children's classic they had elected to read that month, I jumped at the idea. They were all reading the same books and we were all eager for our children to develop their literacy skills, so I thought it was a wonderful suggestion.

'That would be great fun, wouldn't it, Molly?' said Ffion, before I'd got the chance to talk to my daughter about it. 'You'd like that, wouldn't you, to have all your friends round and discuss books, you'd love that, wouldn't you, hmmm, hmm dear, you'd like your own book club, that'd be fun wouldn't it, dear, because you love reading and you'd love to discuss it with all your friends, wouldn't you, dear, wouldn't you, wouldn't you?'

Molly's mental cursor must have briefly scanned the choices that Ffion's enthusiastic onslaught had left her and quickly realized that 'yes' was the only available response.

'I thought we might choose *The Lion, the Witch and the Wardrobe* as their first book,' Ffion announced.

'Oh, that's a super idea. I loved that book when I was a little girl,' concurred Sarah.

'All right, so that's agreed. Why don't I pop into the bookshop and buy five copies of *The Lion, the Witch and the Wardrobe*, and we can arrange a date in a month's time for them all to meet up and discuss it?'

Clearly this book must have been on some sort of 'three for the price of two' offer and Ffion was planning to collect the money from each of us and get a free copy herself.

'Shouldn't we maybe give them the chance to choose which book they do?' I ventured.

Her cheery smile twitched slightly as she processed this suggestion, but instead of being thrown off balance, she rolled with my mutinous proposal, incorporating its weight to help force through her prearranged plan. She was a black belt in the art of aikido conversation.

'You're quite right, Alice, we ought to ask them, they're

the ones who are going to be reading it after all. Molly, you'd like to read *The Lion, the Witch and the Wardrobe*, wouldn't you, you'd like that, wouldn't you, it's all about a secret magical land and there're lions and there's a witch and there's a wardrobe and oh and children away from the grown-ups, that sounds fun, doesn't it, you'd like to read about that, wouldn't you, Molly, shall I buy you a copy of that, hmm? Because you love books like that, don't you, dear, you'd love to read *The Lion, the Witch and the Wardrobe*, wouldn't you?'

My poor Molly looked slightly terrified and I could just about hear her whisper, 'Yes, please, thank you,' as she looked at me for approval. If she hadn't agreed I think Ffion might have turned her into a statue.

The thinking behind a kids' book club had been that it might increase awareness of children's classics and on one level this plan was certainly successful. With two nights to go before the first meeting, both David and I were sitting up in bed reading separate copies of *The Lion, the Witch and the Wardrobe*. It was gone midnight, and David made another pencil note in the margin.

'What's that?'

'Edmund eating the Turkish delight. I must explain "allegory" to Molly in the morning.'

'But the whole book is an allegory, isn't it? Aslan is Christ, the children are disciples, Edmund is Judas . . . It says so in the notes I got off the internet.'

'Yes, but if Molly says all that it'll look obvious that we briefed her . . . But she might plausibly say that she thought the Turkish delight maybe represented all sorts of temptation, like drugs and things like that . . .'

'I think she should say that after the stuff on characterization . . .'

'Well, it depends – how much have you got so far?'

'I was concentrating on Lucy and Tumnus at the moment,' I said flicking through my notes, 'and then I was going to do the Snow Queen and Edmund.'

'Four characters is probably as much as we want to focus on if she's going to say anything about narrative style as well . . .'

'Yes, but we can't just tell Molly exactly what she's going to say, it has to come from her. This is just to help prompt her into discovering all these things for herself, isn't it?'

'Yes, of course it is. I'll sit down with her again tomorrow and ask her what the Turkish delight bit made her think about, you know, if she felt it had any wider meaning . . .'

'And if she still doesn't get the right answer?'

'Well, *then* I'll tell her what to say.'

My house had been volunteered for the first meeting of the junior book club, though not necessarily by anyone who lived there. I had realized earlier that day that I would have to provide appropriate refreshments and so there were bowls of organic kettle chips arranged around the room and a jug of iced elderflower cordial and five glasses placed on the table. The four other children arrived with their books under their arm, a parent or two excitedly ushering them in. My daughter, reader-in-residence of the South-west London Literary Society, welcomed her fellow academics with the usual enthusiasm.

'Say hello to Bronwyn, Molly,' I prompted.

'Hello.'

'Say hello to Molly, Bronwyn.'

'Hello.'

It was going very well so far. The children hovered in the hallway, a little unsure as to what they should do next, till they were manoeuvred into position under the persuasive guidance of Ffion. 'Well, this does all look lovely, doesn't it, hmmm, doesn't it? Why don't you all sit yourselves down, and look, Molly's mummy has even provided some crisps, that is kind, so get yourselves a drink and some crisps, not you, Bronwyn, you don't eat crisps, go on, that's it, everyone sit down, there you are, this is nice, and then when you're all sorted just sit yourselves down, that's it, you've all brought your books, haven't you, well, we won't interfere, and why don't you find your favourite bits or anything that you wanted to read out, hmmm? And we'll just be right here so you don't have to worry about anything.'

I had been just about to head through into the kitchen when I realized that every other parent was planning to stay in the room and watch. Well, everyone except Philip, who watched from outside the French doors where he stood puffing away in the light drizzle. William was there but wasn't there; he took a book of poetry from the shelves and attempted to escape from the book club with a book. The scholars sat on the chairs, their legs still not quite reaching the ground, while the remaining parents stood round the edge of the room in eager anticipation.

'Off you go then!' said David.

Silence.

Molly looked at me and I smiled and tried to give her an encouraging nod to say something to the group. Every child was looking at its mother or father, unsure what they were supposed to do. They looked as if they'd done something wrong.

'Well, somebody say something,' said Ffion.

'These crisps taste old,' said Kirsty.

'No, that's just posh crisps,' explained Molly. 'They're organic.'

'Somebody say something about the book. Bronwyn, why don't you start?' said her mother.

Bronwyn glared at her mother and furiously whispered, 'Mum! Don't!'

'Did you like the book? Why don't you start by saying whether you liked the book or not, darling?'

'I liked the book,' mumbled Bronwyn.

'Not to me, darling, don't look at me when you're saying it, say it to the rest of your book club.'

Bronwyn turned her head and, addressing the floor in front of her, announced, 'I liked the book.'

This inspirational literary insight failed to break the ice and another period of silence ensued, while various adult observers remained frozen round the edge of the room exchanging expressions of upbeat bravery. Someone coughed quietly. The children waited for the purgatory to be over.

'Maybe we should leave them to it,' I suggested.

'You had a thought about what it was all about, didn't you, Bronwyn?' her mother cut in. 'About why C.S. Lewis wrote it, didn't you, darling? What was it you thought about the book, an idea about what it all meant or something, why don't you say that now, Bronwyn, hmmm, darling, hmmm?' prompted Ffion, nodding expectantly at her daughter.

Bronwyn went a little red in the face and then said, 'I think the whole story is an allegory for the Christian story with Aslan representing Christ, the children as the disciples and Edmund as Judas.'

David shot me a furious look.

'Oh, Bronwyn is such a clever girl, Ffion,' whispered Sarah. 'She really is extremely bright for her age,' and Ffion felt forced to agree.

David smiled and half nodded agreement but clearly his

thoughts were elsewhere. 'What was it you wanted to say about the Turkish delight, Molly?' he interjected. Mortified at being put on the spot like this, our eldest mumbled 'Nothing' and glared furiously at her father.

'Come on, darling, didn't you think that it had some kind of wider meaning?'

Molly sighed and was forced resentfully to proclaim, 'I think that the Turkish delight that Edmund eats represents all sorts of temptation.'

'Oh I say, that's very sharp!' exclaimed Sarah. 'Well done!' And there was a murmur of impressed agreement round the room while David and I tried not to beam with pride too obviously. The evidence was there for all to see: our daughter was a highly literate, perceptive and intelligent eleven-year-old, even if she didn't do very well in exams.

'He told me to say that,' declared Molly, looking at her father. And all adult heads turned accusingly to the cheat in our midst.

'Well, I guided her towards it . . .' mumbled David.

'No, you wrote it down on a piece of paper for me to learn,' said Molly, grinning mischievously, though her smile fell away when she saw the thunderous expression on her father's red face.

'I think it's best if children can learn to discover the books for themselves,' commented Ffion sadly as her daughter discreetly turned her notepad face down. 'Shall we go through into the kitchen and leave them to it?' she said, leading the way.

'I liked the little drawings,' offered Kirsty as we headed out of the room, and her mother smiled at her but didn't comment on this insight, hoping that we hadn't heard.

I took orders for drinks – three teas, two coffees – and an ashtray for Philip.

'I guided her towards it and then we made notes,' David muttered to Sarah. He turned to William. 'I guided her towards it . . .'

Ffion glanced at Jamie's music sheet propped open on the piano. 'Ah, that brings back memories. Look, Philip, do you remember Gwilym doing this one?'

'Ah yes,' he said, craning his neck through the kitchen window, where his face had popped up so as not to be antisocial.

'Careful, darling, you're letting smoke in again . . .'

Inside I was still seething that Bronwyn had won the battle of the book club. I knew that I was perhaps a bit too competitive sometimes. But I was beginning to despair at the level of unrelenting competitiveness Ffion possessed. The level that always won, damn her. When Bronwyn had had to do a little song and dance presentation for the Spencer House talent night, Ffion asked a professional theatre director who lived in their road if he could just watch her practise it and give her any advice. She had him round there four times in the end, which is ridiculous. I mean, Molly could have won first prize if we'd got a professional theatre director. But he said no, he was already helping Bronwyn.

I went to fill the kettle but found that the water filter was empty, so we would have to wait for that first. 'I guided her towards it,' said David to William. As if my husband's humiliation was not already sufficient, his youngest son chose this moment to wander down from his playroom modelling a Disney fairy dress, his high heels clacking noisily and attracting attention. 'Oh, that's a pretty dress, Alfie – who are you?' asked Ffion.

'Tinkerbell!'

'Oh yes, the fairy . . .'

I told myself it was sweet that Alfie enjoyed dressing up so much, it was just David who struggled with the fact that his four-year-old son was a transvestite.

'Ooh, why don't you go and see what else you have got in your dressing-up box, Alfie?' said his father. 'There's that Bob the Builder outfit, isn't there? And your cowboy costume? Why don't you put one of those on?'

'My Esmerelda dress!' he announced excitedly.

'Er, I think *Molly's* old Esmerelda costume is getting a bit worn out now, isn't it? What about that soldier's helmet I bought you?'

'Sleeping Beauty!' he announced, and ran off to get changed.

'Sweet. So have you thought about what you are going to do if Molly doesn't get into Chelsea?' probed Ffion.

'Oh, I'm pretty confident that she'll pass the exam,' I said casually.

Ffion's silent smile seemed to suggest otherwise. 'Might be worth having one or two options up your sleeve though,' she continued. 'I mean, Chelsea College is a *very academic* school, it may not be the right place for a girl like Molly. That's not a criticism – she's a very cheerful, funny girl, and when it comes to music lessons I'm sure she'll really excel.'

David's glare implored me not to be provoked into saying too much.

'Actually, Ffion, Chelsea College is the only school we're going for. I've been doing quite a bit of work, I mean with Molly, obviously, and I'm pretty confident she'll get in . . .'

Out of the corner of my eye I noticed David placing a cookery book on a pile of Letts' secondary selection practice papers, which were filled with my handwriting.

'Goodness, well, that's very, umm . . . brave. I'm sure you're right, it was probably just a one-off that she came bottom in the league table.'

I went quiet for a moment and then steeled myself to say something. 'Yes, well, you can't make a league table from just one result. I mean, what about all the other things that should be taken into account? I mean, I could do a league table based on how good the children were at violin and Molly would come top, or what about playing Top Trumps or PlayStation Dancemat scores, or who was the first to finish *Harry Potter and the whatever the big fat fourth book was* – you can't do a league table on just one thing, it's not fair.'

'What about a league table on who can remember the most things that their parents told them about *The Lion, the Witch and the Wardrobe?*' suggested William unhelpfully.

'I *guided* her towards it . . .'

Sarah sensed that it might be time to change the subject. 'What about Bronwyn – have you got any back-ups in mind for her?'

'Well, we've got her down for a few other schools just in case. So she'll be sitting the exams for Alleyn's, JAG's, City of London, St Paul's, Streatham Hill and Clapham High, Godolphin and Latimer, Emanuel, Putney High, Francis Holland, oh and there's a boarding school in Massachusetts we're looking into . . .'

I was still seething inside, though part of me was wondering whether I should be writing all these names down to make sure I had twenty-seven reserve options for my own daughter.

'But her personal tutors are all pretty sure she'll get into Chelsea, aren't they, darling?'

Philip nodded through the window, but I don't think he could hear her. It was raining quite heavily now. Tutors in the plural. That was a slip. I thought Bronwyn was just having the one tutor that she shared with Molly.

That evening, David slumped on the sofa with a long cold glass of beer and I whisked it out of his hands and placed it in the fridge.

'What are you doing?'

'Come on, there's work to do. I am going to get Molly that place if it's the only thing I ever achieve in my life. I need you to explain multiplying fractions and long division again. Only the top 40 per cent of applicants get into Chelsea College, which out of nine hundred children is only . . . um . . . actually, could you go over percentages with me again as well?'

'Do we have to do this now?'

'This isn't for me, it's for our daughter,' I admonished. 'So she can get the best possible education, so that she has the best start in life we can give her. And so we can see the expression on Ffion's face when she learns that Molly beat Bronwyn in the entrance exam . . .'

The level of David's grasp of modern mathematics proved problematic. He knew everything. Having my husband tutor me in something in which he was so unarguably superior precipitated an unacceptable shift in the fragile balance of power that allowed our marriage to function. I was forced to admit I had no idea how to calculate the volume of a cube or what happened when you multiplied negative numbers, so later I'd feel compelled to introduce a conversation on something I knew more about, such as Jane Austen novels or putting the salt in the dishwasher. My literary knowledge was superior to David's; the only fiction he ever read involved scenarios in which Hitler developed the atom bomb after his invasion of Cornwall.

'What is minus nine times minus five?' David asked, as if this was the most obvious thing in the world.

I looked at him extra earnestly to show that I was listening. He had white hairs growing out of his nostrils.

'Sorry, can you repeat the question?'

'Minus nine multiplied by minus five?'

My husband really did have the hairiest nostrils I'd ever seen – which reminded me that I'd booked Jamie in for a haircut after school next day; I wondered if they could just give Alfie a quick trim as well. Except Alfie always made such a fuss, it might be better to do it myself when he was asleep, though last time I tried that I'd done it in the dark so as not to wake him up, which had the opposite effect when the scissors stabbed into his ear lobe.

'Are you just thinking or don't you know?'

'Don't know what?'

'The sum I just asked you.'

'No, I'm thinking. What was the sum again?'

I thought teachers were supposed to be positive and encouraging, not say things like, 'Please, please, in God's name listen to what I'm saying before my brain explodes from frustration.' The truth was that this project was making me feel even more stupid than I felt already.

I'd never had the intellectual self-confidence of David or our friends. We were sitting round in our favourite Italian restaurant and Ffion said, 'Of course, Granada is a wonderful mix of Islam and Old Spain,' and all I could think of was Granada services on the M4. But David could always summon up an appropriate response. 'Yes, well it is only five hundred years since the Ottoman Empire was driven out of the Iberian peninsula . . .' and I sat there wondering if my holiday in

Malaga was worth mentioning here. My husband seemed better educated than me, my friends all seemed better educated than me, and sometimes I just felt like a stupid little girl.

'So, er, why were you in Granada, Philip?' I called across to where Ffion's husband was sitting on his own in the smoking section of the restaurant.

'Computing conference. We're still trying to develop these recreational software ideas but it's got a bit bogged down.'

'What's recreational software?'

'Well, you have a home computer, right? You might shop on it, look up your star signs on it and write letters on it, but you'd never play any games on it, would you?' he said, craning to make eye contact over the plants.

'Maybe with the children. But that's because Jamie's not very good at computer games. The last time he played *Desert Storm*, the Americans actually lost.'

'Well, there's no end of programs that ordinary adults can use during their leisure time: Family Tree Maker, 3-D Garden Designer or whatever, but none of these has been a runaway bestseller. That's the idea I'm determined to find . . .'

Philip worked on the creative side of software development. He claimed that his most lucrative idea had been sending random email addresses the following message: 'Dear Pervert, your computer has been recorded accessing hardcore pornography sites. We have a complete record of all your email addresses; if you do not wish us to contact all your friends and work colleagues with details of the obscene websites you have visited, please send fifty pounds to the following bank account in the Cayman Islands . . .' He said he made nearly a million pounds from that one and I was never quite sure if he was joking or not.

'What about a computer game in which the object is to get your children to stop playing computer games?' suggested William. Philip couldn't hear him. 'Or, if everyone's doing internet shopping, then how about internet shoplifting? You order what you fancy on the website and they go round and nick it for you?'

'I've got an idea for a computer program!' announced David excitedly. 'A historical flow-chart challenge! Yes, yes, you start at, say, the Battle of Zama, right? And making various choices along the way you follow the course that history might have taken if the Carthaginians hadn't been defeated by Scipio in the Second Punic War so that Rome wasn't the dominant Mediterranean power! Now that would be massively popular!'

There was the sound of someone breaking a breadstick. 'I think it may need a speedy hedgehog in there somewhere . . .' said William.

Obviously David could not spend all day as my maths tutor because, as the only breadwinner, he had more important things to concentrate on, namely our son's school history project on World War Two. I tried to picture the reaction we would get at drinks parties when people said, 'And what do you do?' and he replied, 'I'm writing my nine-year-old son's school project on World War Two.'

'Oh right, does that pay well?'

'Not huge amounts, but we're hoping for a gold star at the end of term . . .'

David's professional focus seemed to have blurred some-what in the weeks since he'd volunteered to help Jamie with his project. There were still intricate diagrams and spread-sheets neatly pinned above his desk, but now instead of referring to revenue forecasts versus capital outlay, they tracked the encirclement of Von Paulus's German Sixth Army to the west of Stalingrad.

'Good day in the office, darling?'

'Excellent . . . found some wonderful archive material on the Volga offensive for Jamie.'

I tentatively suggested that he might possibly be going into a little too much detail for a nine-year-old's school project. He was quite defensive about such an idea. 'But the Battle of Rostov was vital to regaining the oilfields of the Caucasus; leave that out and all of Operation Uranus becomes illogical.'

'Look, I know we want Jamie to get a good mark for his project and everything, but don't you think it rather defeats the object if you do it all for him?'

'I'm just following his lead . . . and then sort of guiding him towards locating the stuff he's interested in . . .'

'What, so our nine-year-old son chose to chronicle the German annexation of, of . . . Estonia, did he?'

'The Germans didn't annex Estonia . . .' He laughed condescendingly. 'The Baltic states were seized by Russia as part of the Nazi–Soviet non-aggression treaty.'

'I knew that. 1941 . . .'

'1939.'

Secretly I rather resented the way this project seemed to have taken Jamie away from me. It felt as if I had lost two of the men in my home to the war. It seemed to drag on for ever: not knowing when my brave boys might be coming home on leave from the Imperial War Museum; keeping the home fires burning for the lads out there battling away on the school assignment front. David had declared martial law – this military commission became something exclusively for the boys; there were mines and barbed wire and signs all around it saying, '*Achtung! Frau Verboten!*' If I dared to stray over into David's territory, I immediately came under intensive fire. Just because I happened to comment on the nice colours Jamie had chosen for colouring in his map of Hiroshima. 'That's why there'll never be a female minister of defence,' laughed David. '"Which tank do you want to buy, minister?" "Well, I rather like the green one."'

I wished I had known lots of stuff about World War Two so that I could have spent a bit of time with my son talking about war and armies and history. I had helped him a little when his class had had to write a piece imagining they were evacuees. Though by the time his mother had checked out which was the best village to evacuate him to, the war would have been over. Maybe I should find out a bit more about it, I thought; maybe the Waffen SS could bring me and my son closer together.

'So this Nazi–Soviet non-aggression treaty? When did you say that was?' I asked David.

'August 1939. Just before the war broke out.'

'But Russia was on our side in the war?'

'Yes?' said David patiently.

'So what happened to stop them having a non-aggression treaty?'

David looked at me with almost pitiful disbelief. 'Well, I think Adolf Hitler *invading Russia* may have been a technical breach of one of the sub-clauses in the *non-aggression* treaty.'

'Oh, I see.'

'Yes, I think sending in hundreds of panzer divisions, occupying thousands of square miles of Soviet territory and killing twenty million Russians was deemed by some eagle-eyed legal pedant in the Kremlin to be in technical breach of sub-section three, paragraph two of a treaty based around the concept of *non-aggression* . . .'

'All right, all right . . .' David's blitzkrieg sarcasm had all the subtlety of his favourite warlords.

'I mean, maybe the Russians were being a bit oversensitive; maybe Stalin was a bit prickly that morning and just misread the signals. Maybe when Hitler set out to totally annihilate the Bolshevik *Untermenschen*, he didn't mean it in an *aggressive* way . . .'

'You know your trouble,' I said to him. 'You're too interested in the subject.'

'What?'

'You're unhealthily interested in the Nazis.'

'What are you talking about?'

'You! You're worse than the History Channel. I think there's something vaguely suspect about being that fascinated by the Third Reich . . . Next you'll be going to medal fairs and collecting Nazi insignia.'

'Look, just because there's something I can teach the children that you can't . . .'

'Well, that's the trouble, isn't it? You're just doing it all for him, not letting him find out for himself.'

'I can't believe I'm hearing this! From the woman who's going to disguise herself as an eleven-year-old girl so that she can take her daughter's exam for her!'

'Yeah, which leaves me stuck in the study trying to do non-verbal bloody reasoning while you have all the time with the kids! I thought men were supposed to balance work and home. But not you, oh no, it's just family, family, family the whole time! You never think once about coming home late because you were out drinking with some important clients, do you? Not one weekend where I'm abandoned with the children because you've taken off on some vital work crisis that came up at the last minute. I mean, other husbands leave it to their wives to sit down with the children and go through all the homework, but you're so selfish you have to do it all, don't you?'

David never took criticism well. One bit of negative feedback on eBay and he was in a bad mood all weekend. But I did come home a couple of days after our row to notice Jamie sitting at the kitchen table enthusiastically drawing a big exploding battleship rather than taking dictation from his father on geopolitical fall-out from the Japanese invasion of Manchuria, so perhaps the message had got through. Jamie was being allowed to finish his project on his own.

The more I heard about it, the more incredibly complicated World War Two sounded. World War Three, on the other hand, was far more straightforward. World War Three was simply 'My Family versus Rest of The World'. Whereas the 1940s had been 'all pull together', 'everyone in the same boat', now it was me and my children pitted against everyone else: Alice, Molly, Jamie and Alfie versus Britain, France, United States, Germany, Japan, Russia and Ffion. (I hadn't decided which side David was on; he seemed to keep switching sides – he was Italy.) Of course, various superficial alliances were made along the way. If our embassy had to issue a sleepover invitation or present a birthday gift, then diplomatic channels could generally be found. But it was all part of the overriding objective: my children *über alles*, the permanent geopolitical battle for full-spectrum dominance for my precious offspring.

And now my mission was to go undercover, as a secret agent on behalf of my daughter, and so we set off for the King's Road to try on suitable children's outfits. Inevitably David was keen to be involved and scurried about Gap Kids finding glittery pink sweat-tops which he held up against me. He seemed oblivious to the fact that we had started to attract the attention of the staff; it never occurred to him that it might strike some onlookers as a little bit suspect to see a man trying to persuade his wife to try on various items of young girls' clothing. I came out of the changing room in a pre-teen T-shirt and his voice boomed across the shop, 'No, your bosoms look too well established. We should get you a training bra so your breasts look like they're just budding . . .' I had to send him home in the end before he was put on some sort of national police register.

I stood alone in the changing room, facing the full-length mirror dressed in 'aged 10–12' spangly jeans and a pink *sk8er gal* sweatshirt and feeling like some sort of zany fancy-dress nut. These clothes so clearly did not match the maturity of my face or the grey-streaked haystack on my head. I tried everything: baggy tracksuits, long flowery dresses, and a green skirt and tights that made me look like I was playing principal boy in some provincial pantomime. I stayed locked in there getting crosser and crosser as each item looked more ridiculous on me. Despite what the T-shirt claimed, I did not look like one of the *Koool Kidz*. Why did I have to have these crow's feet and these great big bags under my eyes and this little hammock chin and liver spots on my forehead? I couldn't remember any point at which I'd been happy with my age. I seemed to have spent my entire childhood wishing I was older and my entire adult life wishing I was younger. I'm not sure when the crossover happened but there must have been a period when I thought: This is just the right age, I'm happy being exactly the age I am now. I think it was one weekend back in the 1980s.

There must be a way of covering up this ageing face, I thought. David and I had toyed for a while with the idea of making me a devout Muslim girl. For a moment this had seemed like the perfect solution. I could walk into the examination hall at Chelsea College with just my eyes visible through the narrow slit in the yashmak and dark make-up around my eyes and on my hands. Who would have the courage to tell me to take a Muslim headdress off? Who would dare appear racist and say, 'You can't wear that in here, young lady, you might not be who you say you are.' And then I realized that *I* would have to say who I was in order to register for the exam, and that the name 'Molly Chaplin' didn't sound particularly Saudi Arabian.

I had hung the last of the girly tops on the back of the changing-room door and was studying my face close up in the mirror, checking that my tongue didn't have any wrinkles—

'No, darling, you don't want clothes with words all over the front, do you, darling, hmm, it's not very cool to be a walking advert for Gap, is it, darling, I mean they're not paying you, darling, are they, so you don't want that one, darling, do you, darling, do you?'

I recognized the oppressively persuasive voice immediately.

'That's a nice top, isn't it, Bronwyn, darling, try that one on, you like that sort of thing, don't you, that's your favourite colour, isn't it, no, not that one, the one underneath, you like that, don't you?'

What was Ffion doing in Gap? I thought she got all her children's clothes hand-made in Milan. I couldn't come out of the changing room now with piles of children's clothes but no child. She'd start asking herself all sorts of questions.

I resolved to sit it out in there until they had wandered off. That way I'd be completely safe. Suddenly the handle of my cubicle rattled.

'Oh, there's someone in there, darling, don't you have any other changing rooms for goodness' sake . . .'

'There's more downstairs,' said the assistant, coming to my rescue.

'It's all right, we can wait. Just stand here with me, Bronwyn, so that no one else jumps in front of us.'

I lifted my feet off the ground, thinking that if my shoes were visible it might give me away. I was trapped. Ffion was going to wait outside and I couldn't possibly come out – it was an impossible situation. Then I heard some tourists outside the door and I thought maybe the path was clear.

'*Il fait beau aujourd'hui, n'est-ce pas?*'

'*Oui, il fait très beau.*'

No, they weren't tourists. It was Ffion taking this opportunity to practise talking to her daughter in French.

'*Quelle heure est-il?*'

'*Il est onze heures et demie.*'

My Molly barely knew any French. She did know the French for 'yes', but only in the context of a joke that ended '*Oui?*' 'No, poo!'

The oral exam continued outside: '*Qu'est-ce que tu as mangé pour petit déjeuner ce matin?*'

'What?'

'Don't say "what?", darling, say "*comment?*". We're speaking French, aren't we?'

'You're not.'

'Well, I'm not now, because you started speaking English.'

'*Il fait beau aujourd'hui, n'est-ce pas?*'

'All right, that's enough now. Anyway, I already said that.'

The handle was rattled again, and I realized that there was no way that Ffion and Bronwyn were giving up and that I had no choice but to brave it. I had a plan to front it out. It might work, it might not, but there was nothing else for it. I unlocked the door and marched straight out.

'At last . . .' I heard Ffion say to me. 'Oh! I think you've got that on the wrong way round, dear,' she added, seeing me stride out of the cubicle wearing a top back to front with the hood pulled up covering my face. 'She's wearing that back to front,' she reiterated to the assistant. But the strange child wearing the hood over her face completely ignored her, carried on walking and crashed into a pillar a few yards further on.

'Cool,' said Bronwyn. 'Can I try on one of those?'

In the end I selected a couple of dresses, a glittery light blue sweatshirt and some trainers that lit up when you ran along. But the experience made me realize that the clothes weren't the main issue. It was the head that stuck out of the top that counted against me. I had my teeth polished and then shelled out the most money I had ever spent on myself to have my hair coloured blonde at the best hairdresser in the West End. In the salon the stereo was playing 'Teenage Dirtbag' and I tried to feel like a film star in the transformation scene where they stick in a song to liven up the pace a bit.

I got home and shouted to David to stay in his office. I put on the most appropriate outfit and stood in front of the mirror. I thought I looked years younger: no grey hair, my waist slim, I looked at myself from every angle in the mirror and attempted an immature giggle.

'OK, cover your eyes . . .' I said at the doorway to David's office. 'Ta da!'

'Wow. You look beautiful . . .' said David as he gazed upon his child bride.

'Thank you,' I said, spinning round and pretending to take a swig from my *Simpsons* water bottle.

'It's amazing. You look slim, young, healthy – just gorgeous.

It's an incredible achievement, really.'

'Well, I've worked pretty hard at it . . .'

'Yeah, and well done. You look fantastic. Except . . .'

'Except what?'

'Except I fancy you.'

'What?'

'I'm really sorry but I fancy you. And seeing as there is no way I could fancy you if you looked eleven, it simply can't be working. You're obviously a woman. A gorgeous, slim, healthy young woman, but there is just no way that you could ever pass for eleven. It's just not going to work. I'm sorry.'

I felt totally deflated. Either our plan for my daughter's future was fatally flawed or I was married to a paedophile. From where I stood both possibilities looked pretty grim.

The Ape-Man in Your Kitchen

By Simon and Sally Marrable   Sunrise Books £6.99

In the 1930s the British anthropologist Dr Walter 'Wattie' White did a groundbreaking study of the behaviour of African mountain gorillas. He discovered that male gorillas that were robbed of their food and all their possessions displayed significant levels of RESENTMENT towards their human tormentors, but, interestingly, male gorillas who were given lots of fruit and chocolate showed less antipathy towards the research team. Tragically Dr White was killed when he was attacked by an incensed 400-pound male gorilla, but his work remains valuable today.

When your 'ape-man' returns from 'the jungle', respect his need to grab hold of food, drink and his status symbols. For some primates this DOMAIN ASSERTION might involve clinging to a big stick to bash against the ground, for others it might be the TV remote control. Most female primates have learned not to monkey about with these trophies; show respect and understanding for the gorilla in your love life and your primate partner won't go ape!

— 5 —

David and I had argued at length about another school for Molly. I was already angry because he'd said I looked old; he kept saying, 'I didn't say you looked "old", I said you didn't look eleven.'

'So you're saying I'm just a wrinkly old pensioner and I should only wear knitted bedjackets and fluffy slippers, is that it?'

'No, for God's sake. I'm just saying we need a back-up plan if you get turfed out of the examination hall for impersonating an eleven-year-old.'

'You know what this is, don't you?' I said. 'It's called *Domain Assertion*. I've read about it; you get this with all the male primates. If a female has a plan, the male has to take control of it in order to feel that he is still the dominant partner.'

'I am her father . . .'

'It's like the TV remote control is the same as a stick.'

'What?'

'Gorillas have to have the TV remote control, no, hang on, they have sticks, but they use them for the same purpose.'

'What, changing channel?'

David was so ignorant sometimes – it was hard to understand how he ever managed to win the school quiz night that evening he kept disappearing to the toilets with his mobile phone. But he remained so unconvinced by my plan to disguise myself as a child, he eventually persuaded me to at least consider the boarding school option. It was either that or we start knocking on doors trying to sell copies of *Watchtower* in the hope of getting Molly into that new Jehovah's Witness convent. But even though I offered to accompany David and Molly on a tour of St Jude's, I was determined not to abandon her to some faraway institution, to leave her loveless and alone and forced to develop a crush on the captain of the lacrosse team, only to turn bulimic when her hourly text messages went unreturned.

My husband's own formative years had been at an all-boys minor boarding school in Yorkshire, where he had been admitted despite failing to demonstrate an aptitude for talking too loudly or masturbation. He always said that he'd been miserable there. But in the same way that some victims of child abuse grow up into abusers, David convinced himself that boarding school would be good for Molly.

'But you hated it.'

'Yes, but it made me what I am,' he said.

As if this was a good thing.

'Welcome to St Jude's,' intoned our deadpan teenage escort. 'We'll start in the main block and then I'll take you across to the swimming pool . . .'

'Wow, a swimming pool, Molly, how about that?' said her overenthusiastic father.

'Pah! Swimming pool,' I tutted. 'Imagine being forced to jump into a freezing-cold school swimming pool!'

'No, it's heated,' corrected David glancing at the school prospectus.

'Oh yeah, they say that in there, obviously. But as soon as the last parents' cars disappear through the gates, the boiler's switched off and the girls are made to rub cooking fat all over their skin before they break the ice and get thrown in . . .'

Molly looked in amazement at the way in which this famous old institution managed to combine classical grandeur with the very latest state-of-the-art digital technology.

'This is where we have our Spanish lessons . . .' narrated our tour guide in a flat monotone.

'Wow, this looks nice, doesn't it, Molly?' said her father.

'Oh dear, look at that bull-fighting poster, Molly. I think that's really cruel, don't you?'

David had volunteered to take Molly round on her own 'just to see what she thinks', but there was no way I was leaving my daughter for a whole afternoon of intensive lobbying from her father. He'd have her signed up on the spot and Molly would be taken away from me and condemned to a lifetime of believing that rowing was an interesting sport and being given some stupid nickname from a character in *Winnie the Pooh*.

'Through here is the gymnasium . . .' droned our thirteen-year-old guide, avoiding eye contact and constantly pushing her glasses back up her spotty nose. I had presumed that the gymnasium wouldn't have very much to excite my daughter, but as we walked in we were confronted by trampolines. Trampolines! Damn, why didn't they go the whole hog and have water chutes and a bouncy castle?

'Oh, this looks fun, doesn't it?' enthused David.

'Wow!' said Molly.

'I don't suppose you get very long on the trampoline?'

'We have to take turns.'

'I bet. Shame. So you'd mostly be watching other girls on it, Molly . . .'

The dispute between her parents had handed all the power to Molly. She was suddenly the empress and we were two fawning courtiers persuading her of the merits of our contradicting counsel, knowing that if either of us was too obvious about our intentions it might count against us.

'Hmm . . . it's a beautiful old building, isn't it?' said my opposite number.

'Very old. Is it haunted at all?' I asked.

'I don't think so.'

'Wouldn't be surprised. A lot of these old buildings are packed with ghosts.'

Our guide looked uncertain as to what to say, and it was quite possible that she would now lie awake all night trembling in her dorm. Although, by the look of her, the night-time would be when she normally climbed out of her coffin. This was something of a lucky break. The girl who was showing us around, the example who was supposed to make our daughter want to come to the school, was some kind of weird androgynous Addams family reject and I could see Molly staring at her strange thick spectacles, over-ripe pimples and joined-up eyebrows. Occasionally a child is so musically gifted that they become completely unaware of their appearance or lack of social skills. On that basis this girl was the next Mozart.

Next we were shown into the dormitories. Rather disappointingly, they did not remotely resemble the huts in a World War Two prisoner-of-war camp. I had expected to see rows of metal beds in a long, cold Nissen hut, preferably with a frail girl in her vest and knickers cowering nervously under one of the frames while some bloated bully strode up and down the centre aisle flexing a riding crop in anticipation of administering yet another thrashing. But the dorm into which we were escorted was a warm and cosy boudoir with only four beds in it. There was a view across the hockey pitches where the entire school seemed to be out huffing and puffing in the wintry air.

'Oh, this is *very* nice, isn't it . . .' said David over-emphatically.

'Hmmm, very compact . . .' I observed. 'Very little room for your things in here, Molly, once all the other girls are crammed in.'

'Look, Molly . . . Beyoncé . . .' whispered Dad conspiratorially, pointing to a poster that unhelpfully declared its allegiance to Molly's favourite singer. Knowing that this was the sort of deal-clinching evidence upon which an eleven-year-old child would decide the entire basis of her future education, I urgently pointed out a tiny Kylie Minogue badge pinned on the notice board.

'Oh dear, Kylie Minogue. You can't stand Kylie, can you, darling. Imagine sharing a room with someone playing that song over and over again. Nah, nah-nah; Nah, nah-nah-nah-nah . . . it would drive you up the wall.'

'Oh, I'm sure they put you with girls you have things in common with. Best friends probably. Imagine that – pillow fights and midnight feasts, it would be like having a sleepover every day of the week.'

'Don't tell her what to think, David, let her make up her own mind . . . It's really very poky, isn't it, Molly?'

David raised his eyebrows at me, and then almost under his breath just said, 'Cosy.'

'Poky,' I reiterated, as if correcting him on an established point of fact.

'Cosy.'

'Poky.'

I was about to add: And imagine not having Mum and Dad around all the time, darling, when it occurred to me that this might now be the factor that finally swung it in the boarding school's favour.

Molly was smitten. Here was a child raised on Harry Potter suddenly being shown round her very own Hogwarts. I could see the years stretching out in front of me, my precious first-born sent a hundred and fifty miles away, leaving me to turn on my computer every morning in the vain hope that she might have sent her lonely mother a brief email. David knew the balance was tilting his way and was excited at the prospect of his daughter following in his footsteps.

'Of course, there are some day girls,' I said, clutching at straws. 'She wouldn't have to board. I could drive her in every morning.'

'Alice, it's in Wiltshire. It's two and a half hours each way.'

'I could get a camper van, and she could sleep on the way there. And do her homework on the way back . . .' I implored, my voice trailing off as David strode along the corridor ahead of us, urging us to come and have a look at some of the excellent artwork on the walls. 'Or we could see if they have any nice schools in Lundy?' I pleaded, more to myself than anything.

'Come and see these, Molly. Very impressive.'

'Wouldn't you rather have your old bedroom at home, darling?' I said quietly to my daughter.

She looked at me as if she knew her answer was going to hurt my feelings.

'Because I was thinking of getting you your own telly and DVD and everything to have up there.'

'Really? My own telly? With a DVD?'

'But, of course, you wouldn't be allowed to bring those to boarding school . . .'

'But like, when I asked before, you and Dad were like *absolutely not* . . .'

'Well, that was to make it an even bigger surprise for your birthday. And a mobile. You can have a mobile phone if you stay at home.'

'Oh cool!'

'Although, don't mention it to your father yet, because I'm still working on persuading him.'

'Wow, thanks, Mum.'

David returned and I tried to make Molly's delighted hug appear like comforting reassurance. '. . . You'd still see us at Christmas, darling . . . but if you would really rather sleep here with some strange girls instead of in your room at home with all your *own things* then that would be your decision.'

'No, I think I would rather be at home.'

'What?' said David, dumbfounded. 'But we haven't even looked at the music rooms yet. And that's what the school does best – you could be in the orchestra and everything.'

'We said we'd let *her* decide, David.'

And then the irritating little thirteen-year-old guide piped up, 'We do have televisions here. And a DVD library.'

'Who said anything about DVDs?' I said to her as if she was profoundly stupid. And the odd child pushed her glasses up her nose again and stared at the ground.

Molly had to go to the toilet and Morticia's younger sister took her across the green. I hoped that Molly wouldn't come back with two tiny teeth marks in her neck.

'She has to come here,' implored David. 'She's not going to get into Chelsea College, Alice.'

'She might still get in . . .'

'Get real. This is Molly's only chance. A musical scholarship to St Jude's.'

'She doesn't want to come here, David – you heard her yourself . . .'

'Then we're left with nothing. No school whatsoever. Or we just send you into the examination hall anyway and pray the invigilators are all completely blind.'

'Well, it would be better than sending Molly here and letting her turn into a weirdo like that one. That girl hasn't smiled once since we met her. Look at her with her greasy hair and her blank expression. Thirteen years old and going on forty.'

David went silent. His thoughts were suddenly elsewhere.

'Well, it's true.' I laughed. 'She looks like she was born in the war, and has been held back a year fifty times in a row.'

'That's it!'

'What?'

'That girl. *You* look like *her*!'

'Oh, thanks very much, David. My day is now complete. I do not look anything like her.'

'No, no, you don't understand . . .'

'How dare you. She's plain and ugly and geeky and spotty.'

'Yes, yes and you just said it. *Thirteen, going on forty*. We can't make you look like a pretty little eleven-year-old, but we can make you look like an ugly one.'

'What?'

'For the exam for Chelsea College. You need to look like "Odd-kid". One of those weird children whose age is imperceptible. But like *really* freaky so that people look away immediately.'

'So I'm not just old, I'm ugly as well now, am I?'

'And we can make you geeky and spotty and greasy and put you in really square, ugly clothes.'

'I'm sorry, but I don't think I look like her . . .'

'Maybe we should give you a great big port wine stain down the side of your face? Or you could eat Tippex or something? No, it might draw too much attention to you . . .' He was really excited now, running away with this idea.

'I'm sorry, David, but this just won't work. I do not look anything like that. Sarah said she'd never seen me looking so young and attractive,' I said indignantly.

'Yes, yes, you look nice *now* . . .' he said dismissively, as if it was easy. 'But imagine if you dyed your hair black and put half a tub of margarine in it? Imagine if we gave you thick chunky glasses with a bit of Elastoplast holding them together. And you had spots, lots of them, really big red shiny spots all over your face, and you were so self-conscious that you bit your nails the whole time so half your face was obscured anyway? No one's going to think, Well, she's obviously not eleven. They are all going to think, Poor child, I wonder what her home is like?, and then they'll look away quickly in case you thought they were staring and because it's much nicer to look at the pretty smiling children from Spencer House.'

It was a brilliant idea. Inside I had to concede that it sounded infallible. The rest of the tour was conducted at lightning speed, especially since our guide was becoming increasingly uneasy about the way the two of us spent the whole time looking her up and down, studying her clothes, her mannerisms and the way she wore her hair. On the way home I wondered if part of the appeal of pretending to be eleven had been because I was attracted to the idea of making myself look young and beautiful once more. Well, now I had to face up to it: to put my children first meant sacrificing my own looks and vanity. Nothing new there.

My first attempt at zits had looked like cartoon spots, a few dabs of red lipstick speckled randomly across my face. Any examiner would have taken one look at me and rushed me out of the hall before I infected someone else with the comedy measles I appeared to have caught from Tom and Jerry. But after a visit to a stage make-up shop in the West End, I taught myself how to stick on the latex base with spirit gum, how to use foundation to help it blend in with the surrounding skin, how to colour it and shade it. The final touch was a film of olive oil on my face: the greasy sheen on my skin somehow made the acne look particularly authentic. I decided that no two zits should be the same. Some would be emerging, others would appear to have been recently popped, while here and there was the faded crater of some long ago seismic eruption. Each spot would be carefully constructed over several layers so that there was a tangible three-dimensional swelling that changed subtly in shade from its yellowing peak to the pinkish aureole. The final touch was to resurrect my old thick-rimmed glasses from the days before I wore contact lenses.

'Urgh, you look horrible,' said David.

'Thank you,' I said sincerely. It was actually quite fulfilling, creatively speaking – making myself this hideous gave me a real sense of achievement. I'm spotty, I'm greasy, I'm ugly; I haven't felt this proud of myself in ages.

If only the maths could have been as easy, but my brain was even less clear than this teenage complexion. *Peter is tiling his bathroom wall. The black tiles are 20cm wide, and the white tiles are 15cm wide. If he alternates the colours, how many tiles will he need to cover exactly 120cm?* Well, I don't know, can't Peter just call Balham Bathrooms? They have a Polish decorator who's very polite, even if he does smoke roll-ups out of the window and leave the butts in the toilet. Come on, Alice, concentrate . . . try three of each, that would make 60 plus 45 . . . 105, which is just 15 short of what they want, so add in one more 15cm white tile and that's the answer! It's seven! Four small tiles, three big ones, yes, I did it, yes! I am Einstein! I am Pythagoras! I am, um . . . another famous mathematician . . . can't think of any. Wouldn't have chosen those tiles myself, though – they're a bit 1970s public toilet for my taste.

Through continual practice and endless tutorials I got better. Finally I felt I had the confidence to tackle any mathematical challenge that confronted me, as long as it wasn't correctly estimating the right amount of pasta for three children without ending up scraping a ton of the stuff into the swing-bin.

We bought two copies of each practice paper, though Molly left so many of her answers blank I could have used the same one. We had to keep up appearances and keep her practising, but now the panicky atmosphere had lifted; when she didn't do very well, she didn't have to listen to her fretful parents arguing through the bedroom wall all night. I still spent time helping Molly with her homework, but now I didn't care *far too much*, now I didn't have to suppress anger that she wasn't getting 100 per cent after spending half an hour staring resentfully at a sheet of questions. *Molly has two parents. If you take away one panicky mother and one highly competitive father, what does Molly have then? Answer: skin growing back around her fingernails.*

But just as one worry receded, another reared up to take its place. Now that Molly's next school no longer consumed me, I became increasingly aware that something wasn't quite right with Jamie. A mother just instinctively knows when something is up – we have these hypersensitive antennae that can detect a slight shift in mood or morale. And the fact that on Monday morning he burst into tears when I said it was time to go to school might have been the final clue.

Bullying is a very common phenomenon that most children are likely to experience at some point, and childcare professionals have developed very clear strategies and step-by-step policies for tackling this complex problem. However, when it was my child being bullied, I still felt that the most appropriate response would be for me to go into the playground myself and smash the little bastard's face in.

It was like a random illness. I had heard about other children being bullied at school, never imagining that the dreaded victim virus would strike down my own child. There was no obvious reason why this disorder should suddenly befall Jamie; I hadn't dyed his hair ginger or made him wear white ankle socks with sandals. He was very reluctant to talk about it at first and between his half-sobs rather unconvincingly attempted to deny that there was anything the matter. But eventually it was teased out of him that a boy called Danny Shea was tormenting him from the moment he walked in the gates until the end of the school day. Only now did I discover that the reason he didn't want me cutting his sandwiches diagonally was that Danny Shea had been teasing him about them. The reason he had wanted packed lunches in the first place was because Danny Shea had been waiting for him in the lunch queue. Danny Shea kicked him when he walked past his desk, pinched him in the changing rooms for PE, tracked him down every playtime and pushed and slapped him until the playtime supervisors finally intervened to dutifully tell them that they were both as bad as each other.

Part of me was indignant that one of my children should be a target for bullies *and* need so much help with his school project. I mean, that wasn't fair – surely the deal was that if your child was victimized in the playground at least there was the consolation that he sailed through all his A levels at the age of thirteen. But the strongest sensation was anger, the primitive fury of the mother wanting to protect her young. Because I didn't just want to frighten off Danny Shea, I wanted to really hurt him. I wanted to pull his hair back until he cried, I wanted to grab him by the throat and shout in his face to never touch my son again, I wanted to make him so frightened of Jamie Chaplin that he would hide behind the piano while Mrs Soames was playing 'When I'm Sixty-four' rather than so much as brush past him.

Deep down, of course, I knew that it wasn't acceptable to take things into my own hands; I knew that these things had to go through the proper channels. OK, I couldn't remember exactly why it would be totally inappropriate to take on a nine-year-old bully on my own, I just knew that it was. It's a bit like assassinating evil dictators; David would patiently explain to me why this is not a viable United Nations policy and I'd finally understand and agree. Then after a couple of days I was back to saying, 'But why didn't they just plant a bomb under Saddam Hussein's car? Why did they have to invade the whole country?'

Jamie begged me not to tell the teachers at school, claiming this would make it worse, and in an attempt to reassure him I foolishly promised I wouldn't. And so I was left feeling totally powerless. Watching him reluctantly traipse into school every morning like a lamb to the slaughter, thinking about him every moment of the day, wondering if it was happening right now, I'd fret the hours away until I'd got him safely home. Then I would anxiously ask how school was that day and he would parrot a neutral 'fine' and without wanting to be too direct I would say, 'No problems of any sort or anything or whatever as it were?' and he would say nothing, instead voluntarily opt to practise his piano and I would know then that something was very amiss. I knew it would have to be tackled head-on eventually. If you don't stand up to a bully when you are young, you will be bullied for the rest of your life. Ffion told me that and I didn't dare disagree with her.

That week I was the victim of Ffion's most direct assault to date. Or perhaps 'offensive' would be a more appropriate word.

Dear All,

Alice commented that the table that I emailed everyone after the girls' mock exam wasn't fair because it didn't take into account all the other things that the girls do, like Molly's violin etc, which I thought was a fair point!!! So Philip and I have had a bit of fun adding in everything else!!! I think it's interesting to see where their strengths and weaknesses lie!!! Enjoy!!

Ffion.

Attachment: revised league table

I clicked on the little icon and my computer asked me if I was sure I wanted to open this attachment, which was probably quite a wise question. The first thing that struck me about the document that popped up on my screen was how complex it was, how much work this elaborate new league table must have involved. No, that's not true, the first thing I noticed was Molly's position on the list. Just as a seal can hear its own pup on a beach of thousands, a mother can instantly spot her own child's name on a whole page of text. Molly was fourth. The only girl to reach grade 5 at violin and she was still only fourth. But Ffion had taken all sorts of other attributes and achievements into account and my daughter's musical supremacy had been qualified by shortcomings in other areas, from 'sporting achievements' to 'ballet grade' and, rather incredibly, 'manners'. And looking at the public-speaking scores, I thought Ffion might have made a little more allowance for Jemima's stutter.

	Test Results	Sporting Achievements	Number of School Merits	Public Speaking	Swimming Level	Music	Foreign Languages	Ballet Grade	Horse Riding	General Smartness & Appearance	Manners	Overall Rating of Child
Bronwyn	87%	90%	92%	75%	77%	55%	93%	82%	83%	92%	97%	84%
Henrietta	70%	89%	83%	75%	76%	75%	79%	81%	82%	83%	76%	79%
Druscilla	63%	76%	89%	78%	72%	80%	74%	70%	80%	82%	72%	76%
Molly	38%	12%	90%	86%	74%	95%	62%	80%	0%	54%	88%	62%
Kirsty	51%	61%	58%	71%	74%	60%	61%	32%	68%	69%	69%	61%
Jemima	59%	59%	57%	0%	74%	80%	71%	60%	68%	51%	70%	59%
Fleur	62%	57%	63%	41%	76%	50%	9%	72%	69%	70%	36%	55%
Eliza	78%	40%	60%	74%	1%	17%	85%	42%	55%	60%	5%	47%

So where had Ffion and Philip's complex system for grading all these children left their own daughter? Where in a league table of eight girls could Bronwyn possibly have ended up? Ooooh, there she is, look, right at the top, well done, Bronwyn, what a clever girl! It was there on the computer screen. Who could possibly argue with Ffion that her child was the best when her specially created computer spreadsheet had proved it?

Looking more closely at the scores I saw exactly how she

had contrived to persuade the computer to make her daughter champion. Bronwyn got 83 per cent for horse riding, for example, whereas Molly, who did not ride, scored 0 per cent. 'Well that's just ridiculous!' I said out loud; this is all complete nonsense. Then for sporting achievements I noticed that Molly had scored a dismal 12 per cent and my heart sank on recognizing this bitter truth about my precious darling daughter. In fact, 12 per cent was probably generous. She wouldn't catch a ball in twelve attempts out of a hundred because she was terrified of them. If anyone so much as tossed a little beanbag at her she would duck and cower in fear. 'Worse than an England cricketer,' as David had said.

However, I was gratified to see that Molly had merited an excellent 88 per cent for manners, second only to Bronwyn's 97 per cent. Eliza Rhys-Jones managed 5 per cent for manners. Yes, well, that was probably about right, I thought to myself. In fact, looking at all the grades in more detail, I had to concede that many of them were pretty fair assessments of the children concerned, with the exception of Bronwyn's scores, which were patently much too high, and Molly's, which were much, much too low. I mean, fourth out of eight, it was so insulting! The more I stared at it, the more incredulous and indignant I became. And Ffion's emails had a really annoying habit of using exclamation marks to sugar an outrageous message. I suppose the next stage would be for us to start using those smiley-faced emoticons that our kids put on the end of their messages, in the hope that we could get away with being even ruder: *get stuffed ffion you fat cow :)* or *drop dead yourself alice, you anorexic flat-chested bitch ; -)*

This file had been sent to every parent on the email list on Ffion's computer, nearly every parent I knew would see that Molly had only scored 54 per cent for 'general smartness and appearance'. (Although I noticed that Eliza's parents, whose dreadful daughter was bottom, were wisely omitted from the list of recipients.) It was insulting nonsense, it was preposterous, and yet I knew some less judicious mothers might take it seriously. Where was the A+ for Molly's Mother's Day poem entitled 'My Mother' that I kept in my handbag? And she had given her own daughter 55 per cent for music, which was way too high. (Bronwyn was being taught the piano; they were using the Suzuki method. On a Yahama keyboard. And she sounded like a knackered old Kawasaki.)

Examining the league table in more detail, I wondered what would happen if you discounted the rather arbitrary criterion of horse riding. Using David's calculator, I discovered that if you took out the stipulation of being expected to be able to ride a horse in London in the twenty-first century, Molly would move up the table two places, so really you could say she should have finished second. Second out of eight was pretty impressive, though if you deducted 15 per cent from Bronwyn's score for 'manners' for that time she asked me if we couldn't afford an au pair, then Molly would have been top.

And at least Molly didn't go round to other people's houses and then neglect to flush the toilet after doing number twos, like Bronwyn, but I didn't see 'ability to flush toilet after doing a poo' listed among Ffion's criteria. No, I mustn't resent little Bronwyn, I thought to myself, even if I had wanted to buy her a 'lack-of-charm' bracelet for her last birthday; she's one of Molly's best friends and she's not to blame for her over-competitive mother. Even if she did cheat in the school's egg-and-spoon race. No penalty for that on the league table, I noticed; no points deducted for the tell-tale traces of Blu-tack discovered on the winner's teaspoon. The whole thing was farcical. It showed how pitiable Ffion now was, how pathetic and insecure a mother she had become. And then when David finally came in late that night to find me sitting up in bed popping bubble wrap: 'David,' I asked, 'do you think that Molly should maybe start riding lessons?'

When I moaned about Ffion to David he always asked me why I remained friends with her, but you can't just cancel a friendship like a monthly direct debit. Come to think of it, I never got round to cancelling my direct debits either. I think I was still paying for membership of a gym I had only ever visited twice in January 2003. Lasting friendships are forged when people are thrown together under extreme duress: comrades in the trenches, cell-mates in prison or middle-class new mothers reeling in shock from giving up careers to be kept awake and puked on for twenty-four hours a day. Once you have shared the hell that was the Mothers and Babies Aqua-aerobics, you feel a profound bond that is hard to break. Both my parents had died before I became a mother and so I had been desperate for some support during those early days. And we had kept finding we had new things in common. When to my shock and amazement my baby daughter started growing teeth, it turned out that Ffion and Sarah's children were growing teeth as well. When she turned five, their children turned five as well; it was uncanny.

But on a deeper level I think I didn't want to give up on Ffion because I didn't want to *lose*. I was scared of dropping out of the race. Besides, the last mums to disappear from our group had given us someone new to badmouth for years after. It's human nature – as soon as someone walks out of the room you want to bitch about them. I'm sure it was the same in that Antarctic snowstorm when the frostbitten Captain Oates staggered out to die in the blizzard rather than be a burden to his comrades: 'I'm just going out. I may be some time.' A very brief pause and then, 'That bloody Oates, he's so bloody worthy, isn't he?' 'God, yeah, what a martyr, *oh don't worry about me, leave me to die, blah, blah, blah* . . . I'm glad to see the back of him quite frankly.'

So every time Ffion won a battle like this it made me all the more determined to win the war. Molly's entrance examination to Chelsea College required me to pass two tests. But while I had practised countless mock exams, not once had I actually attempted a dummy run in the more difficult of the two tasks. Not once had I gone out there in disguise and seen what sort of reaction I got as I tried to pass myself off as a girl about to leave junior school.

'Youth club?' said David in astonishment. 'What if one of Molly's friends is there?'

'We'll go somewhere else, somewhere miles from here.'

'But, then, how do we find one? I mean, where do we . . .'

'We make a few calls. Honestly, David, you're supposed to be the adult here . . .'

Since he'd had the idea that I disguise myself as 'Odd-kid', I had felt the need to reclaim the initiative on this project, and so I made the most of the fact that he was struggling to keep up with the next part of the plan. A vicar in Putney said that our daughter would be more than welcome to come along to their youth club on Friday evening, and promised to tell the young chap who ran the club to look out for her. 'Whereabouts in Putney do you live?' he asked David. 'Er, just about to move in . . .' improvised David, rather impressively I thought, though I didn't say so. 'And we thought it would be nice for Molly to come along to the youth club so that she'd know a few children before she arrived . . . Yes, that's it.'

'Super. So which road are you moving into?'

There was a pause.

'Sorry. You're breaking up . . .' said David, his hand half covering the mouthpiece. 'I'm on a mobile and we're just going into a tunnel . . .' he croaked, casually twiddling the flex on his office phone before placing his finger over the button to cut off the call.

I sat in the back as we drove west. We had left early, before the kids were picked up from school by our babysitter so that our children wouldn't be permanently scarred by the vision of their mother wearing geeky kids' clothes and a baseball cap with spots all over her face. David thought I had rather over-done it on the acne, but I maintained that it had to make people look away, this had to be a 'rude-to-stare' face; that come D-Day, the decoy explosions on my skin had to be sufficiently alarming to distract the lookouts from spying on the secret infiltrator slipping behind enemy lines.

We were so early that we went for something to eat. I'd never allowed the children to go to McDonald's, but now it just felt right, and in any case it was nice to be somewhere where the staff had worse spots than I did. I asked for a Happy Meal. In all the acting that I was going to have to do, surely nothing would be as demanding as pretending to relish every bite of that disgusting burger.

'Finish your chips, Alice.'

'It's Molly,' I hissed. 'My name is Molly, *Dad*. And they're called "fries" . . .'

'Right, of course. Finish your fries, Molly. Um, do you like the little toy?'

'What, a plastic Disney figure? I'm eleven years old; not a *loser*.' And I made a letter 'L' with my thumb and index finger and stuck it to my forehead in the way that Molly and her friends did. On a nearby table sat a slightly bewildered-looking father of teenage children, who looked like he had just picked them up for his occasional weekend of legal custody. He gave David a look of long-suffering sympathy, as if he recognized a fellow divorced dad making the best of it.

By now I was enjoying this role of the hypercritical preteen exasperated by her dozy father. 'Daa–addd!' I moaned as he got up to leave. 'You're supposed to empty your tray into the bins!!!'

David apparently wasn't sure whether to enjoy my satirical impression of Molly, or whether his wife had just found another voice in which to tell him he was doing everything wrong. 'Oh well, not everyone does, though, do they?'

'No, right, just leave it for your slaves to clear up all your disgusting mess *as usual* . . .'

'All right, that's enough now, Molly!' he said firmly as the other father looked on. 'Or I'll hide your zit cream again, you spotty little ball of pus . . .' and the empathetic smile of the other dad suddenly dropped away.

I felt a flutter of nerves as we approached the church hall and pulled the brim of my baseball cap lower over my face. Other children were arriving in twos and threes, excitedly chattering about what had happened that day at school, swapping gossip and catchphrases that were unfamiliar to me. At this moment part of me would have happily turned round and walked back to the car, but for Molly's sake I forced myself to go on. I realized that my nerves were completely appropriate. I was a weird-looking geeky new girl with a skin problem being sent into a youth club full of strangers. Of course, I would let my greasy hair fall in front of my face and bite my nails and stare at my sandals.

'Hello, this is Molly Chaplin . . .' David told the young man who met us at the door. 'She's not been before. I spoke to the vicar on the phone about her coming along tonight . . .' The young man's smile almost didn't crack when he looked across at me and saw this strange-looking child. 'Hello, Molly!' he chirped enthusiastically. He was about twenty years old with an irritatingly contrived friendliness. This must be where they train the *Blue Peter* presenters, I decided.

'She's very shy . . .' David explained, when I mumbled some inaudible reply.

'Don't worry, I'll keep an eye on her.' My 'dad' paid my 50p, left a contact mobile number and then I was alone. I fiddled with the grubby Elastoplast on my glasses. 'My name's Simon,' said the *Blue Peter* presenter, 'and I've got a very important job I need you to help me with, Molly . . .'

Oh pur-lease, I thought, not that old chestnut, *make child feel important by giving her a task*. We stopped doing that with our kids when they were about seven. I followed him through to the kitchen, picking my way past children playing board games or table tennis, who didn't even notice my arrival.

'I really need you to help me set out these paper cups for when we all have some squash, Molly.'

Great, we were going to have some squash. Next time I'd bring a couple of vodka miniatures to help get me through this.

If I say so myself, I made a pretty good job of setting the paper cups out on the sideboard. Disappointed that this job had not taken the new girl more than about forty seconds, Simon then sat me down with some craft materials. 'This is Molly, everyone.' The other children looked at me un-certainly. 'Molly doesn't know anyone here, so will you look after her, Ellie?'

'Er, OK . . .' said Ellie, rather reluctantly I thought.

'What school do you go to?' said Ellie.

'You wouldn't have heard of it, it's not round here . . .' I mumbled. She shrugged and got on with attaching pipe cleaners to her bit of cardboard, while inside I felt a triumphant euphoria that she hadn't added, 'Yeah, but how come you're still going to school when you're so obviously nearly forty?'

I had thought I should avoid getting into extended conversations, but the occasion didn't seem to arise. The boys ignored me completely, and though one or two of the kinder-looking girls attempted a friendly question, they soon gave up when I failed to give them anything but one-word answers. But I was getting away with it. No one questioned my right to be there. They may not have wanted to be my best friend, but I was tolerated in their midst: a child. A strange one, but a child.

My efforts at artwork were 'abstract' to say the least, but Simon praised them with the patronizing dishonesty that a care worker might use to applaud a senile old lady who'd finally managed to get a spoonful of trifle into her mouth. There were, in fact, two play leaders at the club, both about twenty, but although I guessed they were supposed to work separately in the two rooms, Simon seemed to be needed far more in the other hall where the attractive female worker was preoccupied. It was so transparent; Simon must have thought I was born yesterday. Or eleven years ago, anyway.

It was around then that I heard Ellie groan and say, 'Oh no . . .' as a younger boy came into the room. I was used to Molly taking an automatic dislike to boys but this seemed stronger, this was the level of loathing reserved for extra maths lessons or taramasalata.

'He's horrible . . .' she whispered. It seemed a harsh summary of a child's entire personality, though it rapidly proved to be right on the button. The boy started to grab bits of cardboard that other children were already using. He said his was the best model; he boasted that his parents had the biggest house and that he was the best skier at the youth club – a difficult claim to disprove in the middle of Putney.

'And I'm the best ping-pong player at my school,' he bragged. 'I could beat you twenty-one nil, Ellie. Come on, who wants to play me at table tennis?'

The other children were unattracted by the proposal of getting thrashed by the precocious champion and then being endlessly reminded of it ever after. 'Come on, losers, who'll take me on?' he repeated. The defeated silence was embarrassing to behold.

'I'll give you a game of table tennis,' I heard myself say. I don't know what made me volunteer. I suppose I was just irritated at the way he was dominating the other children. Deep down I think he reminded me of Ffion. I must stay in character, I said to myself as I picked up the frayed and peeling bat; I must play like a nervous, unconfident child. He announced that he'd serve first and smashed the ball over the net five times in a row, while I did my best to look nervous and overwhelmed on the other side of the table.

'Yes! Five nil to Danny!' he broadcast, telling me that this meant it was my turn to serve. I patted a pedestrian, high-bouncing ball over the net to him and he smashed it back at a hundred miles an hour. 'Yes! Six nil to Danny!' he said loudly, looking round to check that everyone else had heard. Seven love, eight love, nine love – his delight increased with each point. Until I became too irritated to tolerate him any more and decided to hit a shot back. He launched a fast low smash to the end of the table and I sent it hurtling back to the other side with a little backspin just to throw him. He missed it completely. There was a pause.

'Lucky fluke!' he said, leaving me to pick up the ball even though it was nearer to him.

What young Danny didn't know was that I was an extremely good ping-pong player. We had a table at home and only last summer I had reached the dizzy heights of the Corfu Club Med final. I could have beaten this spoilt arrogant little boy twenty-one love if I had wanted to. Except now I had decided to beat him twenty-one nine.

'Ellie, hold my glasses, would you?' I said solemnly.

It was his serve again but my return shots whizzed to the edge of the table, sending him jumping from side to side. A crowd started to gather.

'The new girl's beating Danny Shea,' I heard someone announce when I went ahead, and I saw him start to really sweat. It was then that I suddenly broke off.

'Danny Shea?'

'Yes?'

'From Spencer House school in Clapham?'

'Yes. Why?'

Here he was, the boy who had ruined my son's school life this term. Standing on the other side of a table-tennis table actually looking a little bit pathetic. The boy I had imagined as a huge muscle-bound thug was not particularly big or scary, just massively over-confident and aggressive.

'Oh, no reason. I just wondered why you don't go to a youth club in Clapham?'

'Because I don't live in Clapham any more, stupid. We moved to Putney. It's twelve nine to you.'

'No, thirteen nine . . .' corrected Ellie.

'I'm not bothered.' I shrugged. 'Twelve nine is fine by me . . .' and the other children looked as if they had never encountered a child like this before.

'You've got the best bat,' he announced with the scores at fifteen nine to me.

'OK, you can have this one,' I said, showing, I feel, a confidence and maturity well beyond my eleven years.

'Go on, Molly . . .' whispered Ellie to me as I passed her. I saw she had her fingers crossed.

Danny might have been quite a decent player if he hadn't been so determined to go for a dramatic macho smash every single time it was his shot. It was as if all this child's anger and frustration were being vented on this table-tennis table. Where did all this rage come from, I wondered. Perhaps it was important for his development that I allow him to continue to be the best table-tennis player. Perhaps he should be permitted to continue to excel in one legitimate pursuit so that he might be less inclined to bully and torment the other children like mine. And then I thought: Sod that, I am going to smash the vicious little bastard right off the table.

With the score at twenty twelve, Danny was now serving to stay in the game, when suddenly he put his bat down.

'I don't want to play any more. It's boring.'

'That means you lost,' said Ellie.

'Shut up, Smelly Ellie,' said Danny. 'And go and play with your spotty new friend.'

'You lost. Molly beat you . . .' said Ellie.

'Smelly Ellie loves Molly. Smelly is a lesbian,' quipped Danny.

'Don't call Ellie Smelly, Danny,' I said, calmly putting my glasses back on. 'And whether people are gay or not isn't something they can be expected to know or understand until after they have reached puberty. Then if Ellie decided she was a lesbian or you realized you were homosexual, there would, of course, be absolutely nothing wrong with that.'

This made the others laugh at him and I felt that my rejoinder should have closed the society's debate on 'Whither Sexuality?' but the erudite young man opposing my motion had another rhetorical trick up his sleeve. I felt a sharp tug at the bag of my hair.

'You calling me a gaylord, you spotty lezzy?'

'Let go of my hair, Danny . . .'

'Why's your face like that? Have you got AIDS?'

'Let go of my hair, Danny, you are actually hurting me now . . .'

'Stop it, Danny . . . someone get Simon . . .' said Ellie.

'Ow, you little bastard, I'm warning you – let go!' I said, but he tugged harder, pulling my head down and nearly causing me to topple backwards. In a flash of anger my elbow flew back into Danny's stomach, probably harder than it should have done, and he yelped in pain and doubled up. Then I span round, grabbed his arm and forced it right up his back till he cried out in pain.

'And listen carefully, Danny Shea,' I whispered into his ear. 'If you ever, EVER, EVER, lay another finger on Jamie Chaplin in your class at Spencer House, if you so much as say something horrible to him, let alone hit or kick Jamie Chaplin, I swear I will come and knock your teeth into the back of your fucking skull, do you understand?' and I shoved the arm further up his back for good measure.

'Yes, ow, yes, please let go . . .'

'Molly, get off him!' shouted Simon sternly, striding into the room.

Danny was openly sobbing, crouched down on the floor. I think his arm was hurting, though I hadn't really pushed it that far.

'I will not have you bullying people in my youth club.'

'He was pulling my hair.'

'Don't tell tales, Molly.'

'I'm not telling tales. I'm explaining the context. He was pulling my hair and refused to let go.'

'I'm not interested in who did what to who.'

'Whom.'

'What?'

'It's who did what to whom,' I said, perhaps stretching the characterization of my chronically shy eleven-year-old. But I was angry that he was taking Danny's side, and perhaps I was angry at myself for having lost control in the way I did. 'And these children should not have been left totally unsupervised. The Childcare and Children's Supervision Act of 1994 specifically includes youth clubs and summer camps in sub-section two, stating that children under fourteen may not be left without adult supervision, and what is worse your absence was a transgression of the trust placed in you by these children's parents,' I barked. Ellie and her friends stared open-mouthed at me.

'How old are you, Molly?' said Simon.

'Er, eleven?'

'Come on, what's your game? What are you, some kind of undercover reporter or what?'

'I'm eleven, really. I was born in, er, 1994. You remember – that really hot summer? Oasis, Blur, um . . . Live Aid?'

'Either you leave now or I am calling the police and informing them that you have assaulted a child.'

David looked surprised to see me half an hour before he was supposed to come and pick me up. He was sitting in the corner of the pub, reading a newspaper and sipping a pint when I dejectedly plonked myself down opposite him and announced that it hadn't worked.

'What do you mean?'

'The supervisor rumbled me; he threatened to call the police.'

'The police? Shit! Did he think you were trying to kidnap a child or something?'

'Worse – he accused me of being a journalist.'

I felt totally exhausted; the intense mental effort involved in sustaining my subterfuge had finally hit me. 'Shit! I can't believe it – it's not going to work. All that effort, all that study and it's not going to work! What are we going to do? I mean, that's it, isn't it? We'll have to take Molly out of school altogether and teach her ourselves, or we'll have to sell our house to pay for another school and we'll have to live in a mobile home that we can park right outside the gates to make sure we live close enough to get in and all our children will be teased and bullied for being trailer trash.'

'Calm down, calm down. We'll think of something.'

'Oh great! That's your solution, is it? *We'll think of something*. You're about as much help as Microsoft Help.' I was devastated. I felt utterly miserable and negative and defeated. 'I need a drink. Do you want another half?'

'No, I'm all right, get yourself a large one – I'm OK to drive.'

The stout and bearded landlord was chatting with a regular and seemed to do a strange double-take as he saw me approach the bar.

'Vodka and tonic, please,' I said with a long-suffering sigh. 'And make it a large one.' My body ached for alcohol, like chocolate after swimming lessons.

'Sorry, but I wasn't actually looking to lose my licence this evening,' he said in exaggerated sarcastic tones.

'I beg your pardon?'

He pointed to a number plate behind the bar with the registration *RU 18*. 'Can't you read? Or have they stopped teaching you that at school these days? Go on, out! Come back in a few years when it's not way past your bedtime.'

I was dumbstruck. 'Oh, thank you!' I cried. 'You have made my day!' I could have leant over the bar and kissed him full on the lips, except that he was hideous and smelt of stale pipe tobacco. 'David! David!' I shouted excitedly across the bar. 'He won't serve me, he says I'm too young!'

'Oh yes!' declared my husband. 'What a result!'

On the way home I told David all about the youth club.

'*The Childcare and Children's Supervision Act of 1994*? How did you know about that?' he said, laughing.

'I didn't. I just made it up. Do you think he might contact the police?'

'No, because then it will come out that he was flirting with the other play leader instead of keeping an eye on you lot.' When David had heard a full account of the evening he put it to me that I had indeed got away with being a child up until the point that I'd decided to take on Danny Shea at table tennis. His newfound excitement persuaded me that he was right. I had done it really. I had just blown it at the end by coming out of character. But I wouldn't do that a second time. I had learnt my lesson – that was what this evening was supposed to be about. David persuaded me that it followed that there was no reason why I shouldn't get away with it at Chelsea College, so long as I managed not to hit anyone.

'Not even if I see Ffion?'

'Oh yeah, Ffion excepted. If you see Ffion, you can punch her as hard as you like. But you're ready, Alice. The exam is just a few days away and you are ready.'

I felt a surge of excitement and trepidation as I faced the prospect ahead of me.

'Why are we stopping?' I said as he pulled up at a petrol station.

'The final touch for your exam,' he said enigmatically. 'These places always have a few soft toys. We are going to buy you a lucky gonk . . .'

Feng Shui Your Mind

By Rohan Jayasekera   Sunrise Books £6.99

*Your mind has various compartments, or 'chambers',
just like the rooms in your home. There are passage-
ways that are cluttered and untidy, there are little
nooks and crannies that you'd almost forgotten about.
Most of your everyday thinking is done in the central
part of your brain; this is your mind's 'Living Room'.
Go upstairs from there and you come to the chamber
that is used for dreaming – let us call that the
'Brain-Bedroom'. And through a little door in here is
your psychological 'Attic', that dark space where we
put all the things we don't want to think about any
more. And just as in a building you can redirect and
concentrate the positive energy flowing through a
space, so using meditation and positive thinking can
you harmonize the 'chi' within, letting energy and
light flow through the windows of your mind!*

NEUROENDOCRINOLOGY LETTERS

including Psychoneuroimmunology, Neuropsychopharmacology, Reproductive Medicine, Chronobiology and Human Ethology, www.nel.edu/25_4/NEL250404R01_Esch_Stefano.htm

With regard to specialized brain compartments involved in motivational processes, the physiological substrate for appetitive or aversive motivation primarily lies within the limbic system. The limbic lobe surrounds the corpus callosum and consists of the cingulate gyrus and the parahippocampal gyrus. The hippocampus, which is in the floor of the temporal horn of the lateral ventricle and is closely linked to memory processing, is also included in the limbic lobe. Additional structures incorporated in the limbic system are the dentate gyrus, amygdala, hypothalamus (especially the mammillary bodies), septal area (in the basal forebrain) and thalamus (anterior and some other nuclei). Functionally, the 'hippocampal formation' consists of the hippocampus, the dentate gyrus and most of the parahippocampal gyrus.

— 6 —

I re-read both explanations of the brain's compartments, and decided to go with the Feng Shui one. I mean, if you're worried about your mind's ability to concentrate, it doesn't help to have your husband print out some advanced medical guide to your brain that has you giving up at the end of the second sentence.

The time to put my brain to the test had finally come; it was my mental D-Day, as David put it. We'd been looking at a picture of the Normandy beaches that Jamie had drawn for his project: hundreds of stick soldiers wading ashore, grenades going off, ships sinking and planes exploding in the sky. June 1944: the greatest invasion force ever unleashed. However, this was nothing compared with the onslaught being faced by the staff of Chelsea College on the Saturday morning of their school's entrance exam. Hundreds of middle-class mothers and fathers, all pushing to the front of the reception desk at the back of the examination hall to explain that their child had woken during the night because of the neighbour's car alarm and could this be taken into account when their child's exam was marked:

'This is Edina Symes from Thomas's Preparatory School – she has poor circulation. I have a doctor's note here saying she needs a seat near a radiator, look, you can read it, that's from an actual doctor saying she needs a seat near a radiator, she has to do the exam near a radiator, this letter proves it . . .'

'Excuse me, my wife knows the deputy head Mr Worrall? Yes, well, you see we were under the impression that the exam was two hours, not three hours; we've been practising two-hour tests, so he's not really geared up for a three-hour test, I mean it's hardly his fault, will this be taken into account during marking? As I say, my wife knows the deputy head Mr Worrall . . .'

'My son will need to go to the toilet during the exam, won't you, Henry, can he go to the toilet during the exam, he always evacuates his bowels at exactly 11.30, don't you, Henry, he's very regular but it does take him about ten minutes, can he have ten extra minutes at the end because it wouldn't be fair if pupils were penalized for having regular bowels, you should get *extra* marks if anything . . .'

Was this what I was like? Surely I could never be as aggressive as these mothers; I didn't have the fanatical certainty of these *über*-parents. David says I always worry too much about doing the wrong thing or appearing rude – just because I still put 'yours sincerely' at the end of text messages.

The teachers behind the registration desks seemed to age several years during this frantic twenty minutes. They tried to reason that only genuinely 'exceptional' factors could be taken into account, but this only seemed to reinforce the very point that every single mother was making. The teachers had suddenly transformed into monstrous authority figures who dared to try and drive a wedge between their child and the word 'exceptional'. The parents had, in fact, been told not to

come into the building at all but to drop off their children outside, but this ruling didn't apply to them, any more than the
double yellow lines outside the school gates where rows of
4x4s were all double-parked with their hazard lights flashing
(which apparently makes it acceptable to block all traffic going
in both directions).

I felt curiously detached from the whole manic experience.
Like my war-artist son, I was an invisible observer. Perhaps
this was because I seemed to be the only student to have no
adult fussing over me, crouching down to give me last-minute
guidance or checking yet again that I had my back-up fountain
pens with spare cartridges. My invisibility was no doubt aided
by the retiring persona I had adopted. I wore my baseball cap
pulled low over my face, and I stared at the ground and
hovered inconspicuously at the back waiting to be ticked off.
Such was the chaos inside the school that I wondered if after
all my efforts I could have just turned up in my adult clothes
and sat the exam as I was without anyone noticing. One or two
of the other children glanced at the spotty strange girl for a
moment, but soon found their chins being yanked back to face
their parents who were manically gabbling '. . . and-don't-
forget-to-have-a-drink-from-your-water-bottle-but-don't-
drink-too-much-because-you-don't-want-to-have-to-waste-
time-going-to-the-toilet-during-the-exam-blahdy-blahdy-
blahdy-blahdy-blah-blah-blah . . .' but by now the children
seemed so cranked up with endless conflicting tips and advice
that they were just nodding blankly as if they'd been plonked
into the middle of a teeming Arab souk after five years in
solitary confinement.

Honestly, why can't these parents just leave their children
to it? Why can't they let their kids put out their own pencil
cases and choose their own desks and find their own way of

doing things? I mused as I prepared to take the entire examination on behalf of my daughter. In the urgent competitive atmosphere engendered by so many desperate parents I felt strangely serene and prepared; I may have had only one spare pen, I may not have brought a cushion for my chair or a glucose energy drink but I felt that I did have one advantage over many of the other entrants to this exam: I was thirty-six rather than eleven. This factor, I thought, could well be decisive.

However, as a mother I had found it very hard to leave the house that morning, what with my daughter being so unwell. 'Gosh, Molly, you look pale . . .' we had both said to her the night before. 'You're white as a sheet; you look like you're going down with something . . .'

'I don't feel ill,' she had countered brightly.

'Ah, you see, no, you wouldn't do; not with this particular virus that's going round,' David added. 'What incredible bad luck – and just before you're supposed to be doing the test for Chelsea College . . .'

'But I feel fine . . .' she protested as I popped a thermometer in her mouth. David fetched her duvet down for her to lie on the sofa in front of the telly and gradually Molly seemed to be persuaded that this might be what was required. A few minutes later, frowning severely at the 'normal' reading that shimmered in the glass, I announced that her temperature was very high and she couldn't possibly sit the exam the next day; we'd have to arrange for her to take it later at home.

With David ensuring that the attention of all three children was diverted by the fail-safe hypnotist that is television, I proceeded to execute the now well-rehearsed transformation into Odd-kid. Locked in the bathroom, I applied the constellations of zits that even made me want to look away. I stuck on the baseball cap, pulling the peak down low. With the clothes came the whole persona. I found myself naturally hanging my head slightly as I stood in front of the mirror, picking nervously at my nails: timid, self-conscious and awkward. There had been a girl just like this when I was at school. Always on her own, alternately laughed at and despised. I spoke to her only once. When three girls had emptied her bag in a puddle, I helped her pick her things up. 'Thank you,' she had whispered without daring to make eye contact.

'That's all right,' I had said. 'They're horrible.'

And then I didn't think about her for another twenty-five years. Until suddenly there I was, back at school, remembering her mannerisms and the way she stared at the ground, as I stood alone in the queue at Chelsea College awaiting my turn to whisper my name at the registration desk. Having no grown-up to push into the queue on my behalf meant that I was going to be one of the very last children to be ticked off the list. I could see only one other girl who was also un-accompanied. A neatly dressed young girl with tightly braided hair and a shy face, who stood behind me looking a little bewildered. It was only when I saw her that I realized I had not seen another black child in the whole hall. Apart from a Japanese child and one or two Asian kids, every child here was white and looked just like Molly and her friends. A whole hall full of children who would all have had their comfortable lives documented in tasteful black and white photos up the stairs of spacious Victorian townhouses like ours.

I was wondering if any of Molly's friends would be taking their entrance exam on this particular Saturday when I spotted Bronwyn, and then, striding out a few yards in front, her mother, completely bypassing the registration desk to claim the best spot for her daughter before anyone else had even thought about the next stage of the arrangements. The chair was tested and deemed to be unsuitable. While Bronwyn was instructed to place both hands on the table to prevent any-one else making any territorial claims ('No, *both* hands, darling'), her mother tried out a couple of other seats, finally taking a seat from a desk a few rows back where a nervous-looking man was just settling his child. Bronwyn was clearly embarrassed by her mother's chutzpah, particularly now that she noticed that the whole episode had been observed by that strange spotty girl with the thick glasses. For a split second she seemed to have the impression that she had seen me some-where before, but once our eyes met she looked away and continued to scan the room in vain for the real Molly.

I sensed that the black girl in the queue had somehow gravitated towards me; maybe something in her perceived that I too was an outsider, I was alone and different like her. It wasn't just her skin that was different; her clothes were different from those of the other children around us. The shoes were the giveaway. They betrayed the guilty secret that she alone in this room did not come from a family that could afford to spend forty pounds on a pair of child's shoes every six months. She was trying to catch my eye but I'd learnt my lesson about saying as little as possible and so I stared hard at the floor, hanging back, letting the last few harassed parents push past us in the rush to register their children. Finally it was my turn to be ticked off as I found myself looking at a rather shell-shocked teacher.

'Hello, and your name is . . . ?' he sighed.

'I'm . . .'

I was frozen. I could say nothing. Standing right beside me was Ffion, waiting to register Bronwyn now that she had settled her daughter in the best possible spot. How could I say

'Molly Chaplin' with Ffion standing right there?

'Sorry, your name please? I have to tick you off our list . . .' said the teacher staring at me. I felt myself shaking. I bit my nails, trying to cover my face, praying that Ffion wouldn't engage me in conversation.

'I'm . . . um . . .'

There was a period of silence, somewhere between two seconds and a decade.

'You have to tell him your name . . .' said the black girl. 'What's your name?'

'Excuse me, my car's on a double yellow,' butted in Ffion. 'Can I just register Bronwyn Russell who's seated in the far left corner at the front there?'

'Russell . . . Russell; Bronwyn, yes, got her, thank you, see you at one o'clock . . .' said the teacher scanning his lists, and then Ffion was gone. I looked round to watch her sweep out of the double doors with one last glance towards her daughter and finally I blurted: 'Chaplin. *Molly* Chaplin.'

'All right, Molly, yes, there you are; find yourself a desk and just listen out for the instructions . . .'

I managed a half smile at my fellow examinee and whispered, 'Thank you, sorry,' to her.

'Don't worry, it's OK, you're gonna do just fine . . .' she whispered back.

I heard her give her name, Ruby O-something, and then the pair of us were placed beside one another in the last two available desks at the back of the hall. Ruby O-something gave me a brave smile and I managed a shy smile back.

Now the parents were gone and their abandoned children were left to cope all alone at these desks for the rest of the morning. The only adults left in the room were the in-vigilators. And me. One exasperated teacher was despatched outside to tell a lingering handful of mums and dads that they were not permitted to watch their children through the hall window, nor could they mime encouragement from the other side of the glass for the next three hours. 'Yes, the children do get a break halfway through. Yes, they will be offered fruit juice. Yes, I mean, no; oh look, I don't know if the bloody juice is pectin-free or not.' I listened to the instructions as the test papers were placed face down on our desks. The duplicated sheet smelt of offices and jammed photocopiers. A life before children. I followed the instructions extremely carefully; as clearly and as neatly as possible I printed my name in the box at the top of the paper as I had been told. I looked at it with a little pride, paused, then hurriedly rubbed out the name 'Alice' and replaced it with 'Molly'.

The written comprehension was very straightforward. It was a piece of writing about Columbus sailing to America. Contained within the text were phrases like: 'The largest of the ships was the *Santa Maria*, which often left the two other ships struggling to keep up', and then I just had to answer questions like, 'How many ships were there on the trip altogether?' It was so simple it felt like there must be some kind of catch, as if I was missing something. But I just wrote a rather ungratifying 'three' and restrained myself from show-ing off that I also happened to know that the trip took place in 1492 although the Vikings had actually discovered America hundreds of years earlier. I finished in half the time allowed and checked and rechecked but could not see any mistakes.

The non-verbal reasoning paper was less straightforward. You couldn't be so sure that you were definitely right with these perplexing rows of abstract shapes and lines and dots. But in the past few weeks, while every other pupil in this room had been busy at school, I had spent hours and hours practising these papers, learning the different ways in which they tried to trip you up, spotting sequences and odd ones out. I methodically worked my way through them all with the sort of patience and thoroughness that I would never have sustained when I was eleven years old. I felt confident and in control: here inside the worst possible exterior was the brain that would get the highest score in the whole room.

During the break I stood alone sipping my squash from a paper cup and nibbling my one permitted biscuit. If I'd had my phone I would have rung home to give David an update on how it was going, but we were under strict instructions not to bring mobiles into the exam hall. There had been an incident a year or two earlier in which a boy had been caught exchanging text messages with his mother about one or two of the trickier maths questions. The giveaway was when the child dutifully reported that the square root of 81 was '9 – CU L8R'.

Bronwyn was standing just a few yards away, still scanning the crowds for a glimpse of Molly. Then she began to wave enthusiastically in my direction – I even began to raise my hand to wave back but realized my mistake and scratched the back of my head with it instead. She was waving at Kirsty, who came bounding right past me to talk to who I maintained was still only her second-best friend. I edged closer to eavesdrop on their excited chatter. What had they made of the exam so far? Would they wonder why Molly wasn't here? Were they aware of the life-changing importance of this test?

'Did you get a biscuit?' said Kirsty.

'Yeah, but like, you're only allowed one?' said Bronwyn.

'I know, but I like managed to get one of the ones with like the sugar on top?'

'Oh not fair, those are like my favourites.'

And to think if I had never gone to all the trouble of adopting this disguise, I would never had been privy to this secret conversation.

I had watched these two girls growing up ever since Bronwyn had been the first child to walk in our mothers and toddlers group, and today they were on the threshold of going off to big school. Of course, I wanted them to get into this exclusive college as well, but not if it was at the expense of a place for Molly. In fact, deep down I knew the main reason I wanted them to get places was so that Molly would move on to the next stage with her best friends; if Molly had failed, I would have wanted her friends to fail as well. If I'd ever displayed such a level of personal selfishness I'd have felt ashamed of myself. Strange that such egotism on behalf of one's offspring is seen as acceptable. All is fair in love, war and secondary transfer.

The chatter in the hall slowly faded as we were summoned back to our seats for the final paper. Maths. No problem, I told myself; you have practised this, you do not have an irrational fear of maths. In any case, I had been to the toilet in the break and I'd be very surprised if they asked me to convert numbers into binary while standing on top of the desk.

'You have forty-five minutes. You may turn your sheets over . . . now!' On reflection, it was incredible that I never got any sort of apology from my maths teacher for that humiliation when I was thirteen. My eyes scanned the questions and I felt my heart fluttering at the prospect of this final hurdle. I still felt angry about it; would I have passed my maths O level if Miss Torrance had allowed me to go to the toilet when I'd asked?

The first question looked fairly straightforward: 'Which value does the 9 in 14,971 represent? Circle the correct answer: a) 9 b) 90 c) 900 d) 9000 or e) 12.' I circled answer 'c', double-checked it and moved on. Next came a bar chart representing the popularity of boys' names: 125 were called James, 50 were called Bill (unlikely, but never mind) and 25 were called Kevin (poor things). How many more Jameses were there than Bills? I wrote 75 in the box provided and then felt a momentary pang of guilt that we had given Jamie such a stunningly unoriginal name. That was David's fault. In the 'it's-my-turn-to-name-the-child' argument, he'd even gone as far as to say that the biggest favour we could do our new son was to give him the most popular boy's name in London that year. He backed down when this turned out to be 'Mohammed'.

I looked at the clock and I realized that my thoughts had allowed ten wasted minutes to slip by. I wondered if old Terrible Torrance was still alive. And then I had another flashback to the sensation of humiliating defeat I had felt in her lesson, physical and mental surrender, my only thought at that moment the desire to die. I tried to concentrate again. The third question was multiplying fractions, my old bête noire, the one topic that my husband-tutor had retaught me so many times that I'd had to overcome a mental block about it. But I'd mastered it. You multiplied both the top figure and the bottom figure, so $\frac{1}{4} \times \frac{1}{4} = \frac{1}{16}$. Definitely. But then my confidence wobbled. So what was the next question: a quarter *divided* by a quarter? Surely that must be one sixteenth? The alternative would be to multiply a quarter by four, giving me *one*, but there was no way that dividing something could make it bigger, so where was I going wrong? I stared hard at the figures for a while – I was now looking at them without seeing them. I shook my head out of my numb trance and attempted a slow step-by-step conversation with myself.

'So you've got one quarter, right?' I stated patiently and clearly.

'A quarter; one over four, yup!' I replied confidently.

'Yeah. And you *divide* that by a quarter?'

'Divide, right . . .'

'So, what have you got?'

'Hmm?'

'Are you listening to me?'

'Yes?'

'No you weren't, you were looking over there.'

'I was listening, honestly. Er, what was the question again?'

My chances of scoring a perfect 100 per cent seemed to be evaporating, and I decided I had better leave this one tricky sum and come back to it at the end. I turned over the sheet. There staring up at me was a whole page of dividing and multiplying fractions. I felt flushed with panic and tried to put all thoughts of binary numbers and standing on a school desk out of my head. I glanced round expecting to see all the other examinees sharing my sense of outrage and injustice at this insidious trap, but everyone else seemed to be methodically working through the paper. Admission to Chelsea College demanded that I excelled in all three papers, and so now this one gap in my numeracy skills seemed like it would be enough to make the difference. That was one bit of maths I certainly could do. 'If you have three girls, and one gets 98 per cent and one gets 45 per cent and the other one's already got a place because her bloody mother's got a job at the school, which child's life is ruined because her brain-dead mother can't get her head round dividing and multiplying stupid sodding fractions?'

Come on, Alice! Come on, I told myself. Think about it. A quarter divided by a quarter? A sixteenth. It must be. So what was a quarter multiplied by a quarter? One? No, how could it be . . . I looked at the next sum, and the one after that, and the

one after that and I felt cheated and stupid, it wasn't fair, I'd
come all this way and now I was going to fail, I was a bad
mother, I had let my children down because I couldn't
multiply and divide fractions because of bloody Miss
Torrance, and then the next sum was blurred by a tear landing right on top of it. It wasn't fair, it just wasn't fair. The
tears were falling freely now, but I didn't care, and so what if
my earlier correct answers were being smudged into in-
distinguishable inky blobs, it didn't matter now.

'Shhh!' said the invigilator, and I jumped slightly as I saw
him striding towards me. I hadn't realized I was crying out
loud. Now he was crouching right beside me and I stared hard
at the ground between my feet.

'Try to be quiet, you're disturbing the other students . . .'
he whispered, slightly more sympathetically. He passed me a
folded tissue from a little polythene packet, and I dabbed my
eyes with extreme care in case I knocked one of the spots off
and made him think I had leprosy. Actually he was rather
gorgeous, but I was a married woman and also a hideous
eleven-year-old schoolgirl; frankly, it was never going to
happen.

'Just answer the questions you can and leave the rest, there's
nothing to worry about.' Oh no, nothing to worry about, he
says. Nothing to worry about at all . . . no, things couldn't be
better! I nodded but I tried not to look at him, keeping my
head in my hands, continuing to stare at the desk in front of
me.

'Do you want us to talk to your parents?' he whispered.

Talk to my parents? I thought. What, we're going to have a
seance now as well, are we? I shook my head.

'If we let you out of the examination hall we can't let you
back in, do you understand?'

I nodded. I just wanted him to go away now. I could sense the other children nearby looking round at me, staring at this strange girl who had cried like a big baby under a bit of pressure.

'So you're all right to carry on?'

'Yes. Sorry,' I whispered almost inaudibly, desperate that he stop making me the centre of attention.

I was alone again and I tried once more to make any sense of the page of sums before me. It was useless. I stared across at the Ruby girl, confidently dashing through her sheet. She saw me look at her, gave me a brave smile and I looked away. Then I waited a minute or two, and keeping my head facing directly forwards I directed my eyes slowly to my left just to see if it was possible to make out the figures on Ruby's sheet of paper.

The invigilators strode up and down with ponderous heavy steps while occasional coughs and sneezes echoed around the hall. I took my glasses off and rubbed my temples as if I had a headache. Her answers were clearly visible. Question 5: answer ¾. Question 6: answer ½ – for every mathematical door that I'd found impossible to unlock, here was a set of duplicate keys. She looked up at me, and a split second too late my eyes moved to stare at the space above her head, as if I was concentrating really hard and sought inspiration from something in the near distance beyond where she sat. She went back to her work and then immediately looked back at me, catching me craning my neck to get a better view. Oh I was tired! How tired I was: look, look at me stretching and yawning! No, no, I hadn't been craning my neck to look at someone else's work, certainly not; she had merely caught the beginning of a particularly demonstrative yawn. I pointedly rubbed my shoulder muscles and head and lowered my arms again as my big stretch petered out. Damn, I must've really blown it now, I thought – caught red-handed trying to cheat by the only girl whose paper I could see to copy. Now she would block my view to prevent me from stealing her answers, now I'd never get the chance to see those solutions she was confidently and methodically working out. Or perhaps I was giving her too much credit. Because when I attempted one last desperate look over at her desk she wasn't attempting to shield her exam sheet with her arm at all. In fact, her paper actually happened to shift slightly, which gave me a better view. What incredibly good fortune, I thought to myself. Then as I began hurriedly copying down her answers, she pushed the sheet closer towards me, right to the edge of the desk at an implausible 90-degree angle to herself. Without making eye contact with me, she was subtly but deliberately allowing me to copy all her answers.

Oh Ruby, I love you! Thank you, thank you, thank you! When she could tell that I had finished copying one sheet, she turned over the page of her booklet so that I could see all the answers to the next section, and I quickly scribbled down the solutions to a couple of questions I hadn't even attempted yet. She was canny enough not to look directly at me during any of this, coolly staring ahead waiting until she could sense that I had got everything I needed. At one point she skilfully swivelled the sheet back to face herself without changing the angle of her head one iota and I realized that the invigilator was approaching. I stared into the middle distance, appeared to find the answer I was searching for there and so suddenly wrote it down on my page. Then he span on his heels, like an oblivious guard in a prisoner-of-war camp, and began his long slow patrol back down to the other end of the hall. By the time he had reached the end I had answers for every empty box on my sheet.

'Could you put your pencils down now, please!'

I had done so several minutes earlier – there had been nothing else left to check. After our sheets were collected up we were allowed to leave the hall one row at a time, with my row leaving first. As I brushed past Ruby's desk I mouthed 'thank you' and she gave me a half smile, and that was it.

Heaving themselves to their feet, the children all looked so drained and tired. Their faces were pale and there were bags under their eyes. Many would have more tests still to do, other entrance exams for other schools, more evenings spent with private tutors after hours of homework and cello practice and writing up their reading log before they collapsed exhausted into their beds. I wasn't the only adult-child there when I thought about it. These children had already reached adulthood in a way, putting on their ties, commuting across London every morning through the traffic to their desks, slogging through their forty-hour weeks, full-time workers by the time they were ten. It was the modern, white-collar equivalent of putting children up chimneys.

This was the last of the three weekends of tests for Chelsea College and there was a perceptible sense of relief among the teachers there. The registration desk was now abandoned and in the melee of chatting children and concerned inquisitive parents, I helped myself to a spare copy of the test papers I had just sat. If we were going to get Molly to pretend to sit an entrance exam for Chelsea College at home, she might as well do the real thing.

With David having three children to look after, we'd decided it would be perfectly believable if this particular odd child were expected to make her own way home. However, I felt it was important that I should remain in character right up until I walked through my front door, so I opted to take public transport rather than simply hail a taxi. I went and stood at the bus stop for twelve minutes. And then I hailed a taxi.

'Well, how did you get on?' said David as I crept through the front door, having checked the coast was clear.

'What's a quarter divided by a quarter?'

'Well – one. Obviously.'

'Oh, thank God, that's what she put.'

'Who?'

'Er, the little girl . . . I was pretending to be. That's what she put. A quarter divided by a quarter is one.'

'So how did you do?'

'Pretty well, I think, pretty well . . .' I said modestly. 'The fractions were the only thing I was briefly unsure about and there were loads of them, but I got them all right in the end . . . So a flawless performance all round, I would say.'

'Right – and no one suspected you were cheating?'

'Cheating?' I said indignantly.

'Hello? You're thirty-six years old?'

'Oh that. No. No, I think I passed both tests with flying colours.'

'Dad? Is that Mum?' came a voice through from the lounge.

'Shh! Get back to watching television,' admonished their father and I slipped upstairs to the shower.

I peeled off my spots and scoured my face and watched my brief second childhood wash down the plughole. I knew I'd done something pretty extreme, but that was it – I resolved that from now on my children would have to do things for themselves. I was not going to proceed to the next stage and live out the whole of Molly's secondary school career on her behalf. It might get a bit weird when I started being asked on dates by fourteen-year-old boys after netball practice.

I looked at myself in the mirror as I dressed. I felt strangely deflated now this project was all over. I was still anxious about the school place for Molly, but for myself I felt a sense of loss. A new-found sense of purpose had been abruptly taken away from me. I wondered aimlessly into the children's rooms and just stood there looking at all their possessions. So many toys and books and games and things to occupy themselves with and barely time to play with any of them. On top of Jamie's wardrobe was a football on a thick piece of elastic. Our London garden wasn't big enough for a normal game of soccer, so I had bought my son a special ball that could never stray further than a few yards from where it was firmly staked into the ground. Even the football was kept on a lead.

I went downstairs to find that David had turned the television off and had Molly seated at the kitchen table to finish off her school homework.

'But I'm ill . . .' she was protesting.

'No, you're better now,' he announced. 'And you haven't practised your violin today and, Jamie, you've got to do some work on your project . . .'

Their faces fell, resigned to the grim fact that the work didn't stop at the weekends.

'Oh well, no hurry,' I said, to my husband's obvious annoyance. 'Here, David – I bet I can get a higher score than you on the dance mat!'

'The dance mat? What are you talking about?'

Although it was one of our children's favourite toys, neither of us had ever had a turn on the PlayStation dance mat ourselves. But suddenly I thought the kids might think it enormous fun to see their parents try it out.

'Yeah, Mum and Dad on the dance mat!' clapped Alfie delightedly.

'You know if we leave her violin practice to the end of the day she gets grumpy about doing it,' he whispered.

'Oh, what's one day missed! Come on, it'll be fun . . .'

'Alice . . .' he whispered crossly. 'We agreed we'd always back each other up. I've said they have work to do. It's not fair if you undermine me.' The children looked up expectantly. 'I know, Alfie,' said David. 'You could dance to Molly's violin practice! But why don't you get changed, son, because that Cinderella dress is very restricting.'

It was a whole ten days before we received any form of communication from Chelsea College. I had tried to restrain myself from calling the school too often. Indeed, on the fifth day I didn't ring them once after David said I should add their number to our list of BT friends and family. The information vacuum was quickly filled with all sorts of nonsense in my head. Maybe they knew what I was up to all along and it was taking this long for them to prepare criminal proceedings? What if Ffion broke into the office at night and stole Molly's entrance paper? Maybe the biology department has a tank of African termites that have escaped and eaten their way through Molly's paper before it was marked?

David sensed that I was worried when I came back from the shops. 'Oh what did you get in Ryman's?'

'Oh nothing, just bits and bobs . . .'

'It's a whole roll of bubble wrap.'

'Yes?'

'What, you're buying it specially now, are you?'

'I just thought we might have to send some valuables through the post.'

'Yeah, right. I think I may sleep in the spare room tonight . . .'

Finally after a week and a half I came home to see a significant-looking envelope sticking out from under the usual half a hundredweight of clothing catalogues, pizza leaflets and free local papers full of muggings and murder. The envelope was neither heavy nor embossed, as you might hope when you were paying several hundred pounds just to take the exam, but the historic crest of Chelsea College (est. 2001) had been respectfully printed with as much upper-class polish as their franking machine could muster. My heart went up a gear, my mouth felt cold. Right, this is it. It was addressed to both David and me. Hmm, is that a good sign? But then even before the envelope was opened I could see the first few words printed underneath the address. 'Dear Mr and Mrs Chaplin, I am pleased to inform you . . .'

That was it, that was all I needed to know. Molly was into the school we had set our hearts on, she had made it, she was safe, there would never be anything as important to worry about ever again; a huge valve of stress was suddenly released and I disintegrated into tears. 'Drug dealer found murdered in council flat' said the headline on the local free sheet lying on the mat. Yes, but not anywhere between here and Chelsea College, I thought.

'Oh my God, that's fantastic!' said David, actually taking the trouble to read the letter. 'A scholarship! Look, you got a scholarship!'

'What?'

'Look, here . . . "exceptional examination performance", blah, blah, blah, "the governors invite you" . . . blah blah – they're going to pay all our fees in full!'

'A scholarship? What you mean, we don't have to pay for her education? A scholarship!' I kept repeating. 'God, that just never even occurred to me . . .'

'Didn't it really?' said David incredulously. 'I'd been secretly hoping for this right since the outset. I didn't want to mention it and put you under any more pressure, but you did it! You got a scholarship; Molly's got a place and we don't have to pay . . .'

I strode into the living room and began to busy myself, plumping up the cushions with slightly too much force, picking up empty video boxes, returning stray bits of Lego to their rightful place under the sofa.

'What are you looking like that for? Aren't you pleased?'

'Of course.' I shrugged. 'Just rather taken aback, that's all. I hadn't reckoned on, well, committing fraud . . .'

The Karma Accountant

By Maurice Edelston BCG   Sunrise Books £6.99

Are you overdrawn? Are you spending more than you are
earning? Or perhaps you haven't even stopped to do the
math? I'm not talking about dollars and cents here, I
mean is your 'karma account' in credit? Karma is the
universal currency of world spirituality, the legal
tender that will pay for your place in the next life.
Get seriously into karmic debt and you'll get worse
than a rude letter from the bank. You get to come back
as a dung beetle.

But by using the 'lama life ledger'™ that may be
purchased at www.karma-accountant.com you will learn
to enter your every action as a spiritual credit or a
debit. And with the Dharma auditing software™ that
may also be purchased online, you will come to understand that money is not important, it is the spiritual
energy that flows towards your fellow creatures that
counts. All major credit cards accepted.

— 7 —

David persuaded me that Molly had as much right to a scholarship as anyone else. We had less money than Ffion and Philip or Sarah and William, so why shouldn't it be our daughter who got help with her schooling? After all, she was very bright. 'Well, that's true,' I conceded, 'she just doesn't do well in exams.'

'Exactly, so she's precisely the sort of pupil who should be given a chance . . .'

I had been sitting in the office, going through my dormant in-tray, sorting out that pile of charity letters that had worked their way down to the bottom of my pile of outstanding correspondence. They always seemed to be the last bit of admin to receive my attention, with the possible exception of the postcard I was supposed to send off to activate the guarantee for the yoghurt maker. But tonight I felt the vague need to do something for someone else.

'Do you think we should send some money off for that Mexican earthquake appeal?'

'What's suddenly brought this on? The disaster was weeks ago – they must have dug everyone out by now.'

'They probably still need money . . . Or there's these . . . we ought to send something to both, it's just so hard to choose. What do you think: Rainforest or Donkey Sanctuary?'

'Um, I dunno, send a few quid for the rainforest but ask if they could set a bit aside for the retired donkeys.'

I had an erratic relationship with various charities. I posted them occasional guilty ransom payments and they sent me cheap biros and small change sellotaped to letters. The 5p coins made it much harder to just throw the letter away. You had to fiddle around taking the coins off and then throw the letter away. But it was rare that an appeal went straight into the bin without a decent interval during which I at least intended to send off a cheque.

I went to squash the pile of charity letters down in the wastepaper bin, but then decided that I might not feel quite so guilty if I at least recycled all the paper.

'Of course, Chelsea College is a registered charity,' David pointed out, 'and we'll be supporting that by sending our daughter there.'

'Though not actually giving them any money, as it turns out . . .'

'No, well, anyway, it's not a proper charity. That's just a scam that the government go along with to help keep school fees down . . .'

It was good to have the principled lodestar that was my husband to guide me through these complex ethical issues.

For me, the most uncomfortable moral predicament had involved deceiving Molly. As parents you lie to your children all the time. I had told Alfie he was really, really clever to sit on his potty, when really it's not that clever, it's pretty basic when you think about it. I had left a pound under Jamie's pillow and told him it was from the tooth fairy (though by the time he grew up the government would probably decide that coins from the tooth fairy were only a loan and had to be paid back out of his taxes). But even though it was in Molly's long-term interest, this little white lie felt different; it just didn't feel that white. Not even a calming pastel off-white like Ice Storm or Jasmine Dawn, not even Apple White or Magnolia; in the soothing colour scheme of all our little white lies, this one clashed terribly.

We had sat her down to do the test the day after I had sailed through it on her behalf. 'Do they let you just do it at home then?' she asked as she took her seat in the office.

'Only in exceptional circumstances, darling, like if you've been ill or whatever.'

'But it would be so easy to cheat. I mean, your parents could help you with some of the answers . . .'

David and I looked at one another with shock at such a suggestion.

'I suppose it would be possible, yes. But what sort of parent would do a thing like that?'

'Ffion,' she had whispered to herself, and then glanced at us as if this had been a slightly naughty thing to say.

'Yes, well, the school are making a very special exception for you,' explained David, 'but they don't want people making accusations or having suspicions, so one thing they did ask is that you don't mention this to any of your friends or their mums or dads or whatever.'

'OK,' she chirped.

'No, I mean seriously!' I said perhaps too emphatically. 'You must never tell anyone about this, not your friends or teachers or anything, that's really important.'

'OK, OK, you said . . .' she pleaded, as David cast a worried look in my direction.

'Sorry, darling, but parents can start acting very strangely when it comes to getting their child into a certain school.'

She didn't feel the need to question that statement. This was despite the fact that the pressure on Molly had eased up considerably since I'd ceased to worry about her school tests. While her ashen-faced school friends were becoming irritable or waking in the night, and in one case developing a pronounced nervous twitch, Molly had become almost care-free. I didn't have to tell her to stop biting her toenails any more. It made meal times slightly more civilized.

Now, finally confronted with the challenge itself, Molly did her best to make this examination a big deal, but neither of her parents seemed particularly willing to play along any more.

'Oh no! My favourite pen isn't working!' she declared dramatically, expecting us to rush to her in total panic.

'Oh, there's a little disposable biro tied to the downstairs phone – you can use that if you want.'

'All right then,' she said just sitting there.

'Well, you'll have to fetch it yourself, dear, I'm sorting the washing out . . .'

When her three hours were up, we ostentatiously placed her completed sheets in an envelope before her very eyes, which was to be sent straight to the school to be marked along with all the other papers.

'Well?' she demanded.

'What?'

'Aren't you going to ask me how I got on?'

'Oh yeah . . . how was it?'

'It was hard. There were loads of multiplying and dividing fractions. I'm rubbish at those.'

'Oh, they're quite easy once you get the hang of them,' I informed her casually.

I had noticed that Molly had left quite a few questions unanswered when I'd popped the exam paper into the envelope, which made it all the more impressive now Molly had managed to get a scholarship. She was genuinely delighted when we told her the news, not just by the prospect of going to the school that everyone thought was best, but also the realization that she had done well in a test, that she had excelled at something at last. I found it impossible to disagree with everyone's verdict that my daughter really was a very clever girl.

Telling Ffion about Molly's scholarship never really happened in the way in which I had fantasized. 'Did Bronwyn get the result of the entrance exam for Chelsea College?' I casually enquired over Sunday lunch at Ffion's house.

'Oh yes, we got the letter days ago. She passed *with distinction*. We're so delighted for her. I mean, distinction is about as high as you can get . . .'

Without actually getting a scholarship, I thought, but I didn't say it. Though it would be dishonest of me to keep Molly's result from Ffion when she asked about my own daughter's performance in a few moments' time.

'Yes, it's very gratifying, though thoroughly merited, of course. Bronwyn worked very hard and I always thought she would get in but you can't help worrying about it, can you?'

'No, I was very worried about Molly . . .' William cast me a mischievous smile; he could see exactly what was going on.

'Yes, but she's such a clever little girl . . .'

'Hmmm, I suppose she is,' I admitted modestly.

'I don't know whether she gets her intelligence from me or

Philip; both of us, I suppose,' continued Ffion, 'but it's good for Bronwyn to see that if she really works for something, she will actually get it.'

'Yes, that's what I told *Molly*,' I said, waving a big placard saying, *Conversation, this way . . . Diversion: please follow signs marked 'Molly' . . .*

'. . . But then Bronwyn's always been advanced for her age, but that's because Philip and I always felt her education was important. I mean, I remember the book saying that by the time they were two they should know their primary colours, but that seemed so unambitious to us, so we made up flash cards for all of the secondary colours as well, you know, turquoise, olive, indigo, yellow ochre, cerise, teal . . .'

'Teal? That's a sort of duck, isn't it?'

'Well, it's a colour and a species of duck. But we didn't confuse her by teaching her all her ducks till she was five.'

Molly had been awarded a scholarship to the most sought-after school in London and Ffion had made me feel anxious that my daughter was eleven years old and still didn't know her ducks.

Lunch was a culinary triumph. Philip did three courses and then we sat back and relaxed as their Croatian au pair played Swingball with all the kids in the back garden. Four-year-old Gwilym got a ball in the face and angrily repeated the strongest swear word he'd ever heard: 'INDICATE!'

He ran to his father who was enjoying a relaxing smoke on the patio.

'Is there no cream for the coffee, Philip?' called his wife.

'I'll have a look,' he said, stubbing out his cigarette on the bird table. There were so many fag ends on there it looked like the sparrows were on forty a day.

'No, no, Philip, let me go,' I said, leaping up from the dining table, 'you've just cooked.' And then as I went to the kitchen I wondered why Ffion couldn't have got her own cream for the coffee. Somewhere along the way Ffion had hijacked the cause of feminism as a moral justification for simple laziness. Philip staggered through the front door every evening and then proceeded to cook dinner and wash up and tidy away the children's toys, and then brought his wife a cup of tea and was still made to feel guilty that he had chosen to absent himself from the family home all day, selfishly doing things like earning all the money that paid for everything. He was so liberated he was a slave. Perhaps that's why he couldn't give up smoking, because it would mean being inside the same building as Ffion every evening.

As Sarah and I carried a few dirty plates through to the kitchen, I told her that Ffion hadn't even asked whether Molly had got in to Chelsea College or not. 'Oh, that's because she already knows Molly got a scholarship. I rang her as soon as you told me. I hope you don't mind. I just thought it was such exciting news.'

Incredible, I thought to myself. She had known but she just couldn't bring herself to refer to it. She's totally obsessed with her own children. I hope my kids don't grow up to be like that. I was about to head back through to the kitchen, but then added, 'Sarah, do you think when they arrive at Chelsea College they'll be expected to know their ducks?'

'Sorry?'

'I was just a bit worried that Molly might go on a field trip or something and end up being teased for mixing up a teal with . . . with a um, you know, another sort of duck.'

'Is there more than one sort of duck then?' Sarah said brightly.

In the back garden the game of Swingball seemed to have

developed into some sort of knockout championship. I watched Ffion's au pair deliberately missing shots to allow an easy victory for her employer's daughter. So that's why the last one was sent back to Poland. Kirsty had already been knocked out, not helped by Sarah wincing and saying, 'Ooh, mind out, ooh, careful!' every time the ball came in her daughter's direction.

'Bronwyn's rather good, isn't she?' said Ffion, catching me watching them through the window. I don't know why but I just didn't reply. I gave her a forced half smile, and we rejoined the others round the dining-room table, where a surreal conversation had developed that I struggled to comprehend.

'Value of car,' said David.

'Got that; I just put *car*,' replied Philip through the open French windows.

'Golf handicap,' continued my husband.

'Good, golf handicap,' said Philip waving his smoke away, 'or batting average or whatever.'

'Value of home *or homes*.'

'What on earth are you talking about?' I interrupted.

'It's Philip's big computer idea,' explained Ffion. 'He's got it at last! You remember that league table I sent round of the children measuring their all-round achievement?'

'Oh yes, I think I glanced at it . . .'

'Well, everyone thought that it was such fun that Philip decided to develop it a little further and now he's got a buyer for it as a commercial piece of software . . . Isn't that fantastic?'

'Only not just for kids, for adults too!' added Philip. 'David and I are just designing some example league tables for adult males to adapt.'

'You're letting in smoke again, darling . . .'

'Adapt?'

'That's how it works. You judge yourself by what *you* think is important. Say Mike Tyson was chatting with Stephen Hawking – he wouldn't immediately feel a failure because he didn't understand how the universe worked, he'd be content in the knowledge that he'd probably beat Hawking in a fight.'

'Probably. Over ten rounds . . .' said William.

'See, everyone measures his self-worth by the things that he excels in. That way, everyone is near the top of their own personal league table.'

'Except Prince Edward. Surely he *must* put himself somewhere near the bottom,' William added.

'Oh yeah, all right, except Prince Edward. But once you have set out the criteria by which you and your colleagues are measured, you can keep a running tally on your position. If you get promoted, or your work rival gets a new car or whatever, you enter the appropriate value on the computer and the table changes automatically.'

'The software company are very excited about it,' added Ffion.

'What about "salary"?' David continued. 'Or is that just the same as job status?'

'No, I think you could have a separate column for that . . .' mused Philip. 'Mind you, if this takes off like they think it might, we'll be scoring 100 per cent in both columns.'

'Penis size,' suggested William, to laughter around the table.

'It might be a tough one to measure. But I suppose it would liven up a dull board meeting.'

'OK. What about "beauty of wife"?' suggested David, rather provocatively smiling at me.

There was a pause in which I saw Philip half glancing

towards his spouse. 'No, I don't think that's a particularly important one,' he said, making no effort to prevent his exhaled smoke coming into the dining room. Ffion bristled very slightly, her wispy moustache just twitching in the afternoon sunlight.

'Is it particularly good for one's mental health to be so ultra-competitive all the time?' I volunteered into the embarrassed silence.

There was no time for anyone to give an answer. At that moment, Bronwyn burst into the room sobbing in anger while my son followed behind looking a little anxious. The Swingball championship had ended acrimoniously: Bronwyn had just lost the final.

'Jamie was cheating,' she wailed. 'He was hitting it too hard.'

'Really, Bronwyn!' exclaimed Ffion. 'Jamie's two years younger than you . . . You're going to have to learn to be a slightly better loser . . .'

'But he was hitting it too hard on purpose.'

'All right, but don't cry just because you lost, Bronwyn. Now, why don't you make the final best out of three? Go on, off you go. But Jamie, try not to hit the ball quite so hard,' she added as an aside. Whether Bronwyn's eventual victory in the Swingball championship was ever entered in a specially designed league table I never discovered.

My chance to check out some of the other parents at Chelsea College came sooner than I expected. A letter came asking me to bring Molly to the school for an opportunity to meet the head teacher for a little one-to-one chat. This was wonderful, I thought. Such a charming letter, such a lovely thought – this was exactly the sort of extra pastoral attention that made

Chelsea College worth every penny that other people were paying. The letter did, however, list the items we would be expected to provide ourselves: sports kit (summer and winter), hockey stick, indoor PE kit, apron (woodwork), apron (food technology), tennis racquet, fencing mask, lacrosse stick, small tiara . . . it just went on and on. When David added up the total he was thrown into a blind panic; he put the war project to one side and started ringing back prospective clients saying he did have time to take them on after all. So it was just Molly and I who walked up the grand steps to the school's entrance feeling like we were going to Buckingham Palace to collect our knighthoods.

Chelsea College looked different now that I wasn't staring nervously at the polished floor. It felt grand and important, it flattered you with its imperial columns and panelled walls, it assured you that you'd gone up a notch on the social scale by getting your child in there. I found myself walking past other visiting parents and teachers with an exaggerated benevolent smirk. 'Hello, yes, we'll be starting here in September . . .' said my munificent nodding grin, and passing teachers smiled hesitantly back wondering whether they were supposed to recognize us. I was directed towards the office where we were to have our individual chat with the head teacher. 'It's for my daughter, because she passed the entrance exam you see . . .' I wonder if we'll become friends with them, I thought as I passed other adults bustling down the corridors; I wonder which prep school that lady's daughter goes to; I wonder if Sarah has an appointment today?

But then I did recognize someone. Sitting in the open-plan waiting area outside the head's office I suddenly spotted Ruby, the little girl whose exam paper I'd copied. She was perched awkwardly on the edge of one of the large low chairs as if she shouldn't really be there, shiny plastic shoes locked firmly together on the floor. Beside her was an elderly woman, her grandmother I presumed, who sat clutching a defensive handbag in front of her while swivelling her head hawk-like, looking for someone to talk to. Ruby's grandmother wore a coat with polished gold buttons and a big hat that made her look as if she was going on to a wedding. Seeing this little girl again unsettled me. My memory had succeeded in burying the particular details of how Molly had won her place here. In fact, recently I had felt a growing sense of pride in Molly's academic achievement – the stunning exam result had gained her a certain amount of kudos at Spencer House. 'Well done on getting the scholarship!' her form teacher had said to me. She looked a little puzzled when I snapped, 'It wasn't *me*, it was Molly . . .'

Ruby glanced briefly at me but gave no reaction and I told myself to stop worrying. We took our seats opposite them and the girls briefly eyed one another.

'Excuse me, do you work here?' said Ruby's grandmother in an accent that I found hard to locate.

'No, no. Prospective parent!' I said, adding a long-suffering phoney laugh. I looked away. This was uncomfortable. I didn't want to get into a conversation.

'My granddaughter passed the entrance exam.'

'Jolly good. Well done.'

'Thank you,' whispered Ruby and for a split second we had direct eye contact for the first time since she had given me her maths answers. I quickly looked back to her grandmother, smiled, and found something inconsequential to mumble to Molly. Though I would rather not have encountered the accomplice to remind me of my crime, the fact that Ruby had also got into this highly sought-after school made me feel somehow exonerated. No harm was done.

A rather gangly and flustered teacher struggling to hold a pile of exercise books to his chest popped into the waiting area to check his pigeonhole.

'Excuse me, sir, do you work here?'

Although he clearly did, he appeared cornered by this question, as if committing himself to any sort of answer might be a mistake.

'Er, yes, yes, I do.'

'This is my granddaughter Ruby.'

'Right, um, hello, Ruby. Are you waiting to see the head?'

'Isn't she lovely?'

'Yes. You must be very proud.'

'She's very polite; always says please and thank you, isn't it . . .'

'Glad to hear it.'

'So can she come to this school then?'

He paused, unsure of how to respond to the old lady's novel idea of an admissions system.

'Um, well, you know the college has an entrance exam? She has to take that.' The books still threatened to burst from the volatile pile pressed against his chest, and he bent his body awkwardly to try and keep hold of them all.

'She passed the exam.'

'Oh splendid. Well, look forward to seeing you in September then, Ruby. I'm Mr Worrall, deputy head.'

'So she can come to the school?'

'Yes, if she passed the entrance exam. You should have got a letter. I'm sure the head will be out in a minute.'

'Can she have a scholarship please?'

'I'm sorry?'

'Please can she have a scholarship to pay for her to come to this school?'

'Well, that depends on how well she did in the exam. Look, admissions isn't really my department. Why don't you wait until the head is finished and speak to her?'

'She's very clever, you know.'

'I bet she is.'

'And she can play the recorder . . .'

'Jolly good . . .'

'So can she have a scholarship?'

'Well, you see, that's not how it works. You have to get an exceptional mark to get a scholarship, and you'd have been told if Ruby had done that well.'

'She very good at her internet. She practises every night . . . Look at her, isn't she lovely?'

'Why don't you have a word with the head when she's finished . . .'

'Can you just tell me please, Mr Worrall, is the scholarship related to how much money you have?'

'Er, no . . . it's just how gifted the child is.'

'Ruby is gifted. She can send emails and everything, isn't it? But her mother doesn't have any money. She has three jobs, she's working all the time, but it all goes on the children.'

This conversation had now strayed into the uncomfortable territory of money, an area that Mr Worrall seemed not to want to accommodate into his imaginary universe of the happy high-achieving school where fees were an unspoken minor detail, a slightly embarrassing fact of life that one knew about but didn't need to refer to, like going to the toilet or one's parents having sex.

'Um, well, I can't really, um, as I say, I'm just one of the deputies and I teach English here. Have a seat and I'm sure the head will be happy to explain how it works as soon as she's free . . .'

'How much does it cost if she doesn't have a scholarship?'

'It's in the prospectus there – oh, there's normally some on the table . . .'

All this time Ruby had been watching this teacher as if she was reading his face, her brow slightly furrowed as she struggled to comprehend his embarrassment. As Mr Worrall made his escape, Ruby's grandmother turned her attention to me.

'Excuse me, madam, do you know, how much does it cost to come to this school?'

'Oh, well – at the moment it's about three and a half thousand pounds a term.'

'Oh my lord! That's a lot of money.'

'Yes, yes it is.'

'We don't have three and a half thousand pounds a term . . . oh my lord, so how much would that be till Ruby went on to Cambridge University?'

'Well, if she was here for seven years, um, that would be three times three and a half thousand times seven, which is, um . . .'

'Seventy-three and a half thousand . . .' said Ruby quietly.

'You see how clever she is? Just like that! Can these other children who got the scholarship do sums in their head like that? I'd like to see them try.'

I could feel Molly's eyes boring into me. Don't you dare suggest it, said the silent laser glare.

'How much did you say, Ruby?'

'Seventy-three thousand and five hundred pounds.'

'There's no way I could ever find that sort of money.'

'No, it's madness, isn't it? It's like they expect us to sell the house or something just to pay the school fees . . .'

'We don't own a house.'

I felt my face flush with the warm glow of embarrassment and Molly finally whispered her first words since we had sat down.

'Mum. Shut up!'

'No, well, that would make it even harder, I suppose . . .'

'Seventy thousand pounds to spend on each child! I've never met anybody with that much spare money in my whole life.' And then she gave a little laugh and added, 'Apart from you, I suppose!'

I hadn't wanted to say it, but now the alternative seemed worse.

'No, well, actually we don't have that sort of money either. Molly here got a scholarship.'

'Mum. Shut up.'

'She did? Oh my lord, you must be a very clever girl!'

Molly managed a half smile and then asked me how much longer we would have to wait. Almost on cue, the headmistress came out of her office and Ruby's grandmother stood up and said, 'Hello, we have an appointment. I am Mrs Osafo and this is my granddaughter Ruby . . .'

'Hello, Ruby,' said the headmistress. The head was younger than I had expected; in contrast to her surroundings, she had a modern, friendly air about her.

Mrs Osafo gestured to her granddaughter to stand up and held her arm out to direct the head teacher's gaze. 'Isn't she lovely?'

'Er, yes. She must make you very proud.'

'She's very polite. And she can play the recorder. I have it in my bag, would you like to hear her?'

'Another time,' she said, ushering them into her office and casting me a brief smile as she closed the door.

Five minutes later the door opened again and I heard a

fairly competent recorder player racing through the concluding notes of the theme tune to *EastEnders*.

'Very nice, Ruby, and thank you for coming in. And best of luck elsewhere . . .'

The old lady looked dignified but couldn't hide her disappointment. She addressed me directly: 'You have to try, isn't it?' then headed past me with Ruby scurrying along behind staring at the ground.

The inside of the head's office was a shrine to Achievement. There were silver trophies on the shelf, plaques on the desk, framed newspaper clippings of children holding up science projects, all underlined by several long school photos showing hundreds of healthy smiling children, all with that uniquely rosy complexion that comes from generations of good diet and skiing holidays.

'Well!' said the head teacher as she closed the door behind her. 'I've never had anyone ask for a place on the basis of a private recorder recital before!'

'It must be very difficult. I expect you wish you could give a scholarship to everyone.'

'Actually that girl came very close, one hundred per cent in maths, just let down by a couple of mistakes on her English paper . . . It's a great shame. We would have loved to have her here.'

I paused uncertainly, not wanting to presume to take a seat until offered. The last time I had been in a head teacher's office was for writing 'Duran Duran' on my arm in biro.

'Anyway, I'm Miss Reynolds, and you must be . . . Molly Chaplin! Ah yes, one of our new scholars! Well done on your splendid exam result!'

'Thank you,' said Molly.

'Were you surprised you did so well?'

'Well, I was, what with being ill and having to do it at home and everything—'

'No, darling, that was the mock exam I set you, you're getting confused!' I said, correcting her more sharply than might have been appropriate. 'No, we weren't too surprised because Molly's always been a very bright girl and, as I say, always been a very bright girl, so we weren't surprised at all, we did a few dummy runs at home, the *mock exams at home*, as it were, and she scored very well in all of those and jolly good, jolly pleased to be here, jolly good!'

Molly stared at me and I attempted the tiniest imperceptible shake of the head at her, hoping the intensity of my glare might warn her off saying anything more.

'A straight one hundred per cent in all three papers. We don't get many of those. I hope you are not going to let your standards slip from there, Molly?'

I looked expectantly at my daughter, willing her to perform as she managed a nervy shake of the head. After that I think the rest of the interview went very well.

'Do you have any hobbies, Molly?'

'Oh yes, she has lots of hobbies, don't you, darling, she plays the violin, and she likes drawing and swimming and she goes to ballet and she loves to read; Molly and her friends even have their own book group.'

'Have you travelled much, Molly?'

'Oh yes, she's been all over the world, haven't you, darling? France, Italy, America, Kenya, um, Center Parcs . . .'

I had desperately wanted to like Miss Reynolds and I was not disappointed. Her warmth and interest in my daughter filled me with excitement and optimism; she was more liberal, friendly and unstuffy than I had dared to hope. At the interview for Spencer House, the head always wandered back to the car park with potential parents to see what sort of car they drove. Here there was no sense that we were being judged or pigeonholed – it was the child that interested her, she said, not the bank balance or social standing of her family. Miss Reynolds would never send a snotty letter home asking that mothers refrain from picking up their children wearing jeans. Not that I had taken any notice of that letter from Spencer House. Those jeans were a bit unflattering anyway.

It was raining when we got outside, so we postponed our planned walk round the site. As Molly skipped over the puddles in the car park, I asked her how she felt about going to her new school.

'Mmm,' she said nodding, doing her best to provide the answer I was hoping for. But as she waited for me to unlock the car I could sense there was something troubling her.

'Mum, you know I got this scholarship? Well, how can I have got one hundred per cent in all three papers if I didn't answer every single question?'

I struggled to find the right key.

'Oh, I think they probably must allow for leaving one or two questions unanswered, don't you? Or maybe they rounded it up, yes, that'll be it I should think, they rounded it up,' I stammered, finally realizing that the house key was never going to unlock the car. 'Though, as I said, it's important that you don't talk about the exam any more. We don't want some jealous person trying to question your result, do we?' At that moment I managed to set the car alarm off. The siren wailed and the lights flashed and I suddenly felt panicky and stupid.

The rain turned into a downpour as we climbed into the sanctuary of the 4x4. I switched the hot air up to maximum and the windscreen wipers began their eternal rhythmic game of tag: 'Got you, got you back; got you, got you back.' I steered my urban tractor out of the school and turned down the road. The rain was so heavy that the street lights had blinked awake, confused at the sudden darkness in the middle of the day. In the distance I could see two figures standing by the side of the road, sharing a damaged foldaway umbrella. As I got closer I could see through my half-misted windows that it was Ruby and her grandmother, still waiting for a bus. They must have been there twenty minutes. I steered the car out away from the kerb as I passed them, not wanting to send any spray too close, but my eyes stayed firmly locked ahead. I didn't see if they looked directly at me or not. I turned the wipers up to double speed. Then I glanced in my rear-view mirror: the two figures standing in the rain began to shrink into the blurred distance. I wondered where that little girl would end up going to school, what she would do with the rest of her life, where the bus would take her now. And then I stopped the car.

'Mum, what are you doing?'

I slowly reversed the 4x4 back up the road, pulled up beside them, lowered the electric window and said, 'Hello there. Er, I'm sort of going in the same direction as the bus route. Can I offer you a lift?'

Meditation on the Move!   *Sunrise Audio £24.99*
Ayurvedic Audio Tapes for Busy People
Read by Yogi Shree Deva Prem (with an introduction by
Carol Vorderman)

*In our demanding modern lives it is not always easy
to make the time to attain inner peace and harmony
through the ancient practice of transcendental meditation. Until now, entering into the truth of Zen
could take an entire lifetime, but with the Ayurvedic
Audio Tapes you can become Awakened to the Absolute
in a matter of hours, and all without interrupting
your hectic daily schedule!*

*Whether you are busy doing the ironing, jogging in
the park or simply driving to the supermarket, these
vedic exercises are designed to allow you to transcend
to a higher level of consciousness quickly and effi-
ciently. And once you've crossed off 'Achieve Total
Inner Harmony' from the top of your to-do list, you'll
be free to get on with the 101 other things you still
have to do each day.*

*Erratum: It has been pointed out that on Tape Three, the
Yogi Shree instructs us to close our eyes and focus on*

being fully present in the moment. If you are listening to the tape while driving, we ask that you keep your eyes open for this part of the exercise.

— 8 —

It turned out that Ruby and her grandmother lived about five hundred yards away from the end of our road.

'Oh, we live in Clapham as well, don't we, Molly,' I'd said brightly, when she told me where they were headed.

'Really! Well, you know the Wilberforce Estate?'

'Yes . . .' I lied. I had vaguely heard of the Wilberforce Estate, but I'd never have been able to place it. Those roads didn't feature in my mental A–Z; there were just a few invented hills with the legend 'Here be monsters'.

'We live in Gisbourne House.'

'Oh right. Lovely.' And then not knowing what else to say I heard myself ask, 'Do you have a nice view from up there?'

A little voice in my head was saying, 'Alice – shut up!' but this was drowned out by the louder voice of my daughter saying, 'Mum – shut up!'

'No, our block is only three storeys high. We look out onto Thornton House.'

'Oh yes . . .' I said, as if that had helped me place it.

'What about you? Where do you live?'

'We live in Oaken Avenue?'

'Oh, that's a very nice road. So she can hop on a 137 and that'll take her all the way to Chelsea College!'

'Mmm, although the school lay on a special bus, don't they? It picks them up from the Old Town.'

'Yes, I read about that in the prospectus!' Ruby's grandmother hooted with laughter. 'Why would anyone pay seven hundred pounds a year for a private bus when the 137 goes from door to door for only 40p?'

'Well, quite!' I laughed, tutting at the madness of some people. Because it felt safer . . . I thought. Because we are frightened of the idea of letting our precious children travel alone on the white-knuckle ride of a public transport bus. Of course, even using the private bus is still a worrying prospect – one mother I knew let her son travel on it, but then manically cycled alongside every day to make sure he got there safely.

'I expect Molly will just get the 137 . . .' I mumbled.

There was a minute's silence in memory of my honesty as we waited for the lights to change at Chelsea Bridge.

'You have a very nice car.'

'Thank you. Do you, um, have a car?'

'No.'

'Good for you. I mean, well, they're very bad for the environment, aren't they?'

'Ruby's mother used to have a Metro but it died.'

'Oh, I'm so sorry . . .'

I was shocked by how self-conscious I felt, by my nervousness at making small talk with an elderly black lady. Despite the fact that I lived in south London I didn't know any black people at all. Obviously there are occasions when one finds oneself in conversation with smartly dressed elderly black women, but since Ruby's grandmother was not offering me a copy of *Watchtower* I didn't know quite how to react to her.

'So, er, did you grow up in south London?' I finally enquired, having decided that this sounded better than: 'So where are you from?'

'No, I'm from Accra.'

'Right . . .' I nodded. I'd heard the name but couldn't place it. 'My husband and I went to St Lucia for our honeymoon.'

'Oh really? Accra is the capital of Ghana. In West Africa.'

'Yes, of course, but you just reminded me of St Lucia because, well, it was quite sunny there. Um, like Africa is . . .'

My face changed to red, the lights changed to amber. I switched on the cassette player, hoping some pop music might puncture the embarrassing silence.

'Only through sharmatha can you enter into the truth of Zen . . .' said an eastern-sounding man as wind chimes tinkled mysteriously in the background.

'Oh not that one, let's see what other tapes we have here . . . Avril Lavigne, Dido . . . Ah, perfect, *Motown's Greatest Hits*. . . . Oooh baby love! My baby love . . .'

'Mum, why are you singing along? Just shut up!' said Molly.

'Ooh miss kissing you . . .' I crooned. 'We love Motown, don't we, Molly? And soul music. I've got some James Brown somewhere . . . I like all black music, actually: Motown, soul, reggae . . . Except rap, I don't like rap, but not because it's black because I don't like Eminem either and he's white, isn't he?'

'Mum, which bit of *shut up* don't you understand?'

In the rear-view mirror I saw Ruby's face register shock at my daughter's rudeness and for a moment I was embarrassed by Molly's privately purchased overconfidence.

As we approached Clapham I wished I hadn't casually claimed to be familiar with their estate. 'So what's the best route to your block exactly?'

'If you just take the main entrance into the estate, it's on the left,' she said unhelpfully.

'Right, OK . . . so just remind me, which road is the Wilberforce Estate off again?'

'Wilberforce Road.'

'Of course, Wilberforce Road . . . which is . . . up here on the left, isn't it?'

'Third right.'

'Third right. That's it, yes.'

The council estate might as well have been on another planet. Except I imagined if Captain Kirk beamed down into this estate, the moment he flipped open his communicator he'd probably be mugged for it by some fifteen-year-old hoodie. 'Wicked mobile! You can text, send pictures and be transported through antimatter.' We pulled up outside their block, a utilitarian postwar build combining concrete and Lego, where the architects had decided the first thing you would want to see were a couple of huge steel sani-bins. The patches of grass were all worn and there was the stripped skeleton of an old bike pointlessly locked to the railings. Kids who had wanted to make a name for themselves had graffitied the doorway, though their names were completely illegible, which seemed to me to rather defeat the object. The rain had eased up but I still made an effort to get as close to their door-way as possible.

'Well, thank you very much for the lift.'

'Yes, thank you for stopping,' said Ruby.

She fumbled for the door handle, but I hadn't released the child lock yet.

I pulled on the handbrake. 'So, where will Ruby go to school now, do you think?'

'I don't know, she's got one more exam to try and get a scholarship for Barnes Girls. They do their exam later, isn't it?' Mrs Osafo didn't say 'innit?' at the end of each sentence like most of the indigenous population of south London. She was far too well spoken. She said, 'Isn't it?'

'Oh good, yes, there's one or two girls from your school hoping to go to Barnes Girls, aren't there, Molly?' Molly gave an affirmative surly nod, which would have been undetectable in the back seats. 'But what if she doesn't get in there, what will you do then?'

'Well, tell me, what do you think of Battersea Comprehensive?' said Mrs Osafo.

'Oh goodness no!' I blurted out. 'I mean, none of Molly's friends would have been going there, so it would have been completely unsuitable for us . . .'

'I like the headmaster. And the new art block, isn't it?'

'Well, I've not actually been there as such, myself, but you know, one hears about various schools and it was just never a place we even considered . . .'

'Her mother says Ruby will probably go to Battersea Comprehensive. We can't afford private school without a scholarship. But Chelsea and Barnes get more children into Cambridge University, where Ruby is going, isn't it?'

'Are you going to Cambridge then, Ruby?' I said with a smile.

'Yes,' she said flatly.

'And what are you going to study?' I chuckled.

'Pure Maths.'

'Oh. All right.'

She was deadly serious. Eleven years old. *My* daughter wanted to be a pop star.

It was now that a sense of gloom descended over me about the chances of Ruby's obvious potential ever being realized. She was never going to get a scholarship without intensive one-to-one coaching from one of the handful of private tutors who specialized in getting children through those exams. I had been there, I'd learnt what was required, I knew the hoops that the children had to jump through. I turned off my engine.

'Those private tutors are very expensive, aren't they – has Ruby had any one-to-one sessions or anything?' I asked tentatively.

'I sit with her while she does her homework . . . She always does extra.'

'Right, and what about practice papers? Has she done any of those?'

'What do you mean, practice papers?'

'To practise doing a test so you can see where she needs help before the exam proper?'

'Oh yes, they do tests at school – sums and spelling and all that, isn't it? She always comes top . . .'

This lady had no idea of what she was up against. Parents who would have arranged private tutoring for their children while they were still in the womb if they'd possessed the technology. Kids who'd spent the last six years at a *preparatory* school specifically designed to *prepare* them for getting into the top private schools. Parents with the time and money to make sure that their children reached the peak of their mental and physical condition at the exact moment that they hit the Exam Olympics. I stared straight ahead, where a young Alsatian, locked out on a first-floor balcony, was frustratedly pacing back and forth.

'Look, I have some spare practice papers left over at home

– we don't need them any more. I could let you have them, if you like . . .'

'Well, that would be very kind, wouldn't it, Ruby?'

'Er, OK, I'll drop them round then,' I blurted out carelessly.

'We live at number 23.'

The Alsatian gave a long low howl at nothing in particular.

And so it was that I found myself agreeing to return to the foreign country that was the Wilberforce Estate. I didn't think it was even worth mentioning to David. Anyway, he was busy failing to get the children to play football in the back garden, repeatedly suggesting to little Alfie that he might like to put on his new Arsenal shirt. 'No, darling, the referee wouldn't let you play dressed as Pocahontas.' I would just pop round and give Ruby's grandmother the test sheets and that would be that. It was no big deal. I looked at myself in the hallway mirror before I left. And then took off my Nicole Farhi coat and swapped it for the old anorak I wore when we went black-berry picking in the countryside.

I walked down Oaken Avenue, now struck by the sheer volume of wealth on show all around me. Every car on my street must have cost over twenty thousand pounds, with many couples having a car each. The big four-wheel drives would breed at night and a few weeks later there would be a little two-seater BMW sports car in between them. The homes were all tall Victorian townhouses arranged over four floors, expensively refurbished with kitchen extensions and incongruous conservatories bolted onto the back. And despite all this room and expense, most families spent all their time in the basement; the poorly lit subterranean kitchen area that was originally intended for the servants. You could have the prettiest Aga-heated oak-floored designer kitchen that money could buy, but the view was still out onto a damp stairwell which all year round filled up with an urban pot pourri of dead leaves, sycamore seeds and discarded burger cartons. The basement windows all had bars over them, of course, which seemed a perverse way to solve the problem of crime. It was as if we had all decided we were never going to be able to put all the burglars behind bars, so instead we all shelled out to create individual private prisons where we would stay locked inside. On the doorstep were vulnerable-looking terra-cotta pots that would just have to take their chances on the other side of the security zone. The general presumption was that it was the kids off the estate who stole the window boxes and the holly wreaths at Christmas, but on reflection I was not convinced about this. It was hard to imagine teenage boys sidling into the pub carrying a neatly clipped bay tree in a big glazed pot and trying to get a fiver for it. 'No way, bro', bay leaves are a pain, you always have to pick 'em out of the casserole.'

Within a couple of minutes I was at the top of Wilberforce Road, and already the parked cars were older and tattier, occasionally attempting to cheer themselves up with semi-humorous car stickers in the back window. 'Mafia Staff car – keepa da hands off!' Unless of course that really was a Mafia staff car, and that's how people knew not to cut it up at the traffic lights. I had to confess I felt a little ignorant of London working-class culture. I imagined things had probably moved on a little since they all dressed up as Pearly Kings and minced round singing hits from *Me and My Girl*. My kids would never do the Lambeth Walk – they'd expect me to drive them.

Now I was entering the estate itself. There was no official frontier as such, no Checkpoint Charlie where you were quizzed by border guards about your reasons for wishing to visit the proletarian zone. Was I unwise to venture in here without a guide? Should I have brought an interpreter? Then I decided that the locals must surely be used to the occasional middle-class person wandering onto their patch, even if I wasn't asking for their votes or making a disturbing documentary for Channel 4. The Wilberforce Estate seemed to have been chosen as the venue for the Bored Teenagers Conference: a group of boys, some of them as young as my own children, were hanging round by a doorway just doing nothing; barely summoning the enthusiasm to talk to one another. One of them had a big Nike tick shaved into his scalp. It was not a hairstyle I could imagine the salon doing for my children; we were far too middle-class to worship the brand of Nike. Maybe Jamie could have the John Lewis logo shaved onto the back of his head.

The feral kids chose not to notice me as I walked past and once I was clear of them I realized that my muscles had tensed up and that my heart was beating faster. The exam sheets were clutched tightly to my chest, as though the kids might rob me if they realized what I had: 'Forget the iPods and video mobiles – she's got secondary transfer practice papers!' At the big steel door of Gisbourne House I pressed the buzzer for number 23 but no voice came out of the speaker grille. Instead there was just a loud discordant buzz from the door, which now opened without resistance. Uncertainly I ventured in, hearing the heavy door clunk behind me as I inhaled the faint scent of cement and boiled cabbage. I decided I would forgo the uncertain claustrophobia of the lift and headed up the echoey concrete stairwell. On the third floor a sign directed me towards the appropriate flat number and I walked along the external walkway. One front door had a glittery sticker on the front saying something in Arabic. Another had a big metal plate over the entire door. Then I stood outside number 23 and paused for a while.

I could just slide the envelope through the letterbox and slip away, I thought. But then I would never know what happened to Ruby. And it was then that I realized I hadn't just come round to drop off the practice papers. I had to be sure that Ruby was going to do these tests; I felt a need to go through them with her, pointing out the pitfalls, passing on some of the secrets and techniques I had learnt. I wanted to give her the tools to go on and achieve things for herself. It's like that saying – give a man a fish and you feed him for a day. But teach a man to fish, and you – well, actually you condemn him to endless weekends sitting by the pond on Clapham Common looking bored out of his skull.

Over the past year my own eleven-year-old daughter had become increasingly hostile to me, instinctively rejecting my maternal advice and encouragement. But here was a child I could still really help, who would appreciate what I had to offer. It's like those letters from third world charities in my in-tray: 'Sponsor a child in Africa'. I was sponsoring a child on the council estate, I thought, blushing at such a patronizing notion. 'With just a few minutes of your week you can make a real difference: help them get a basic education, provide them with the tools to help themselves and maybe ask them not to eat McDonald's sitting next to you on the underground.'

I gave the knocker three loud bangs and listened to approaching footsteps, but was surprised to see an elderly black man smoking a rolled-up cigarette open the door.

'Yes?' he said lugubriously.

'Oh hello, is Mrs Osafo in? I've brought round some exam papers I promised for Ruby.'

'Constance! Someone here to see you . . .'

Mrs Osafo came out of the darkness, looking older in her everyday clothes despite the fact that she was carrying a baby on her hip, a little white boy.

'Oh hello again,' I said, smiling. 'I've brought those practice papers for Ruby . . .'

'Well, thank you very much,' she said taking them. 'Very kind of you to drop them round.'

I hovered there for a moment. 'OK. Well. Just thought they might be useful.'

'Much appreciated.'

'Lovely baby.'

'Yes, isn't he?'

'Is he yours?'

I don't know quite how such a stupid question escaped from my mouth. She was at least sixty years old and black. Of course this little white baby wasn't hers.

'No, I'm looking after him for a neighbour,' she said with a gentle smile.

'Right. Well, OK, hopefully Ruby will understand them. Is, um, is she in at the moment?'

'She's practising her internet . . .' she said a little proudly.

'Right, I see.'

The baby stared at me, a dummy lodged firmly in his mouth. He had an expression that suggested he was permanently startled by the world. 'Because if you like I could just explain the format of these tests to her . . .'

Mrs Osafo gave me a smile, which in my paranoia I imagined as somehow knowing. 'Well, that's very kind of you; come in. Ruby! Turn off the world-wide-webs now, there's someone here to see you, isn't it.'

Ruby's flat was what estate agents would describe as

'compact'. 'A bijou apartment, situated in the increasingly popular "Wilberforce village", comprising three bedrooms, lounge – oh, hang on, the lounge is one of the bedrooms – kitchen, TV room, well, the kitchen is the TV room, bathroom and balcony-cum-dovecote. Well, doves, disease-ridden pigeons, it's all the same.'

Ruby said a polite hello and then her grandmother explained why I was there. I felt excited by the possibility of having so much I could offer this child, a sponge who would eagerly soak up all I could teach her. She was my own little Pygmalion, except in this version . . . actually, I had never seen or read *Pygmalion*, but I knew it was by George Bernard Shaw, and it was adapted into the musical *My Fair Lady* starring Audrey Hepburn and Rex Harrison, and that was enough to get by if the subject happened to come up at a dinner party. Oh, and George Bernard Shaw had a big beard, there, that was another thing I bet Ruby didn't know about English Literature. Really, there's so much to tell her I didn't know where to begin.

I was less nervous about chatting with Mrs Osafo than I had been that first time in the car. I made casual conversation about whether she ever went back to Ghana, or if she'd ever visited the neighbouring countries, such as Ivory Coast to the west, Togo to the east or Burkina Faso to the north (at least I think that's how it was pronounced, Jamie's atlas hadn't given any guidance). I enquired about where Ruby usually did her homework. 'Does she have a little desk in her bedroom or anything?' I asked, casting a hopeful glance down the corridor.

'No, there's no desk, no. You sit yourself down there,' said Constance. 'I can lay the table later . . .' and she indicated the tiny kitchen table, where Ruby's grandfather sat watching a televised football match through the nicotine fug of Golden Virginia.

'Right . . . we wouldn't maybe be better off in the lounge perhaps?'

'Lounge? No, I don't think so. Is it the television you don't like?'

'Well, it might make it a bit hard to concentrate . . .'

'Yes, I understand. Lloyd! Turn down the television, isn't it . . .'

And without looking round Lloyd picked up the remote control and very slightly lowered the volume on a TV set that was far too big to look comfortable on a kitchen sideboard. It was actually a rather expensive-looking set, I found myself thinking admonishingly, as if they didn't have the right to have as good a set as ours.

Ruby had hopped up onto a stool and sat there expectantly. She was a model of respect, politeness and good behaviour, like a parody of a character from some 1950s British film in which all the upper-class children wore clean, white, pressed clothes and only spoke when they were spoken to.

'Right, Ruby, I just thought that since I was dropping these papers round I might as well point out one or two of the pitfalls that you need to look for—' I began.

'Did you hear that, Ruby?' chipped in her grandmother. 'You've got to look out for pitfalls!'

I turned round and acknowledged the unsolicited assistance with a weak smile.

'So first of all, when you did your exam for Chelsea College, was there any of the three papers that you felt you were weaker on than the others?'

'I think my maths was OK.'

I decided to take her word for this, particularly since the head of Chelsea College had told me that Ruby had scored a hundred per cent in mathematics.

'All right, what about the non-verbal reasoning: how did you feel you did on that?'

'OK. I like those; they're like puzzles.'

'Good, good. They *are* like puzzles, aren't they, but sometimes they trick you by giving you false clues to try and make you put down the wrong answer . . .'

'Offside!' said Ruby's grandfather. 'By a yard, at least.'

Ruby glanced up briefly while I persevered, pulling out a perfect example. 'Um, right, you see on this sequence of pictures, they are all shapes within shapes, and at first sight you think, well, they're all circles except the last one, so the odd one out must be the square.'

'You listening, Ruby?' interjected Constance. 'The square is the odd one out.'

'No, no, it isn't the square!' I said hurriedly. 'I was just saying it looks like it is . . .'

'Got that, Ruby? It's *not* the square.'

'That was a foul, definite.'

'Which one do *you* think it is, Ruby?'

'The second one: b.'

'Yes. Clever girl. Why is it the second one?'

Ruby looked at me as if I was completely stupid. 'Because you've put a letter "b" in the answer box.'

I let out a sigh as the football commentator became increasingly excited.

'Did she get it right?' said her proud grandmother.

'Well, yes, but—'

'Well done, Ruby! Did you hear that, Lloyd? She got it right!'

'Well done, Ruby. Square! Square!' exclaimed Ruby's grandfather at the television.

'No, it's not the square,' said Constance, 'it's the second one, number b,' she explained with a smug nod to herself.

Then one of the teams on the television scored a goal and Lloyd shrieked so loudly that it made the baby cry and Constance passed it to Ruby to hold while she warmed up some milk in a pan. Ruby stood in the kitchen rocking the baby expertly back and forth and I didn't know quite what to do.

'So the answer isn't always the first thing that strikes you, see, Ruby?' I said over the din. And she nodded at me but both of us felt unable to ignore the action replay on the huge screen that dominated the room.

The answer certainly wasn't the first thing that struck you. I had thought this would be so easy. That I could just go in there and give Ruby a private tutorial at her little desk, leave her some practice papers and maybe come back to check her score a few days later. But the answer was no longer apparent to me; the puzzle got harder the closer you looked. After just a couple of questions explained against a running commentary from Ruby's grandmother – 'Clever girl, Ruby!' she said. 'Yes, that really was excellent!' agreed John Motson – I had left the papers with them and suggested she try and look at them when she had a bit more time. It had been impossible. How could I have been so stupid to think that I could walk in there and duplicate the precious study periods I had set up with my own daughter? I had thought I could dispense spare learning in the same way that I dropped off old clothes at the charity shop, expecting thanks and perhaps the odd compliment on my taste in pashminas. But a simple truth struck me as I walked back to my own comfortable house. The one in need of education was clearly me.

I have no idea of how most people live, of the obstacles that people face, of how little money people have. I thought we were relatively hard up because I was comparing myself to

Ffion and Sarah. But Ffion's idea of poverty is someone who buys their nanny a second-hand car. Her idea of stress is having to sack her eleven-year-old's personal trainer. And I'd thought life was a battle because I couldn't find the right Hoover bags for Carmen, our cleaner. What must it be like for Ruby's mother, leaving her children in the care of her mother while she went out as sole breadwinner for all three generations, juggling several different jobs to make sure that her children had all the things they needed? What must she think when she looks at the clock at their bedtime, and wishes she could be with them instead of out earning a few extra quid to make sure they were as smartly turned out as all the other children? Ruby had been eager to work but just didn't have the space or peace, while a few hundred yards away our house had special children's study zones sitting there empty.

Apart from David's office, which doubled as family work station and Allied command centre for the D-Day Landings, our children each had their own bedroom with their own private desk laid out with sharpened pencils and crisp new stationery. Their work stations were a shrine, places of reverence and respect; glasses of milk would magically appear beside them, grown-ups would whisper on the landing if children were trying to concentrate – all hail the mighty god of *Study*.

That night I could not help but notice the contrast when I tried to sit down with Molly to go through her maths homework. The setting was perfect yet the very suggestion of work prompted weary sighs from the pupil; Molly's body flopped onto the chair like a tangled marionette, her head suddenly so heavy as she stared blurry-eyed at the page that an elbow was needed to prop it up.

'Some children would relish a chance to have this much time to study . . .'

'Where? *In Africa?*' she said contemptuously.

'No, in Clapham actually.'

'Oh yeah, right . . .' Then almost immediately she got up.

'Where are you going? Sit down!'

'The toilet – durr! Aren't I even allowed to go to the toilet any more?!'

'No, do one question and then you can go to the toilet . . . "Jane's mum buys a new dress at half price. The original cost of the dress was £9.50. How much change does Jane get from a £20 note?" So what are the two sums you have to do here?'

But Molly's body was doubled up in agony; in the space of about ten seconds some sort of bizarre internal flash flood had clearly deposited several pints of urine into her bursting bladder and now only by rocking back and forth and clutching her tummy was she able to hold off wetting herself and David's new office chair.

'Go on then, quickly!'

Five minutes later I was knocking on the toilet door.

'Come on, I thought you only needed a wee?'

'No. Both.'

At least if she ever suffered from constipation in later life she would have an instant cure. *Problems with constipated children? Give them Extra-Math™, the natural laxative that will have them locked in the bog for hours.* I was losing the battle of wills but I was determined that Molly was not going to get out of doing maths just by taking too long to go to the toilet.

'Molly!' I shouted through the door. 'What's seven times nine?'

'What?' came the muffled reply.

'Come on, we can practise your tables while you're in there. What's seven times nine?'

'I'm on the toilet.'

'I know, but you're not getting out of it that easily. Seven nines are . . . ?'

'What are you doing?' said David, standing at the top of the stairs.

'Oh hello. It's extra maths.'

'Can't it wait till she's out of the toilet?'

'No, because then she just stays in there. Come on, Molly, you should know this by now. Seven nines are – actually, what are seven nines, David?'

'Sixty-three.'

'Seven nines are sixty-three, Molly! So repeat, what are seven nines?'

Silence.

'Molly?' shouted David, feeling obliged to take my side in this power struggle. 'Molly!' he repeated banging on the bathroom door. 'Say "sixty-three" to your mother when she asks you.'

'Sixty-three,' mumbled a weary voice from the other side of the door.

'OK . . .' I said, pretending to myself that I had won a victory of sorts. 'That's probably enough maths for today.'

In contrast to his sister, Jamie had become a whirlwind of enthusiasm since he had been allowed to finish his project on his own. He spent hours drawing tanks, gluing down pictures and writing captions with such painstaking care that he made one side of his mouth sore by sticking his little tongue out of the side in concentration. But despite all the hours that Jamie put into it, the project clearly wasn't good enough for the sulking, jilted father. A couple of days later David plonked a fat scrapbook on the kitchen table. It was obvious from his manner that my intervention had ruined his precious History of World War Two.

'Well, I did what you said. I let Jamie do it himself.'

'Good. Ah, bless him, he's worked so hard . . .' It was beautifully presented with photos from the internet glued on every page and brightly coloured captions scrawled underneath.

'But he can't give it in like this . . .' said David indignantly.

'Oh, don't be so possessive. I know you might have done it differently, but we have to learn to let the children do things for themselves.'

'It's *wrong*.'

'Look, it may not be perfect in your expert eyes, but this is Jamie's history of the Second World War, not yours.'

David raised his eyebrows at me. 'The Germans win.'

'What?'

'In his project on World War Two, the one you said I should let him finish on his own? The Germans win.'

My knowledge of the war was not as encyclopaedic as David's, but one detail I had gleaned was that the German army were definitely on the losing side.

'How did they win?'

'I don't know, on penalties? Look at his caption for the last picture: "The German people celebrate their victory in the war."'

'Ah, look how neat his writing is, bless him . . .'

'That's not really the point, is it? When Admiral Doenitz signed the unconditional surrender in May 1945, his mum wasn't standing over him saying, "All right, so we lost, but look how neat my son's writing is . . ."'

I skimmed through the lovingly glued maps and pictures and felt a surge of pride.

'These Germans do look quite happy, though – was Goering lying to them about the result or something?'

'It's a picture of a Berlin crowd celebrating the fall of France. He's five years out.'

'OK, so he wrote "celebrating their victory" instead of "celebrating a victory" – it's only one word. It doesn't matter.'

'What, it doesn't matter that our son's history of World War Two has Germany winning? Well, call me a pedant but I'd say that was quite an important detail myself. I mean, you know, historians disagree about some aspects, but all the primary sources I've read seem to concur on that particular historical detail. Let me think . . . A.J.P. Taylor, Alan Bullock, Richard Holmes, Simon Schama? Nope, I can't think of a single historian I've studied who has the Third Reich triumphant at the end . . .'

'Yes, but Jamie has worked hard and must be really proud of this. How's he going to feel if we now say, "You know that one bit you did on your own, well, that's complete rubbish, start all over again"?'

'Hang on – so you're saying that for the sake of our nine-year-old's feelings, Hitler wins. All Europe is subjugated by a brutal genocidal dictatorship for evermore, but our little boy doesn't have to endure any criticism from his parents and that's the main thing . . .'

'It's only one mistake,' I said. 'Admittedly, quite a big one.'

'It's not just one mistake – look at this . . .' David skimmed back a couple of pages. '"Germany occupies Romania": correct. "Germany invades Bulgaria": correct. "Germany invades Narnia": incorrect.'

'Narnia?'

'Yes, Jamie's project lists Narnia as one of the countries invaded by the Wehrmacht.'

'Blimey, I'd have put the Snow Queen on the Nazis' side myself. Does he describe the invasion? I mean, there must have been a bit of a bottleneck at the wardrobe . . .'

'He can't give it in like this.'

'It'll prove it's his own work . . .'

'Oh right, well, let's make it really obvious it's his own work, why don't we? We can have Vietnam win at the end. After Rommel and a load of fawns beat Hermione Grainger to secure the vital bridgehead at Pooh Corner.'

'It's not that bad.'

'I'm embarrassed by it.'

'Well, that's the test for us as parents, isn't it? Can you bear to let your son give in a piece of work knowing that it is wrong, or do you write the correct answer in yourself and pass it off as all his own work?'

David's astonishment could not have been greater if I'd let the kids go to bed without flossing. 'Er, hello? So helping Jamie with his project is going too far, whereas taking Molly's exam for her is normal parental support, is it?'

'That was a one-off.'

'No – when Molly did her project on "Endangered Species in Nature" you wrote the whole thing from start to finish, then bribed her with Kinder Eggs to copy it out in her own writing.'

'I did not.'

'Yes, you did. And you got that handyman who was fitting the kitchen units to assemble the free toys. Why are you suddenly so against doing the same for Jamie?'

'Because we won't always be there to assemble their Kinder Egg toys.'

'Or to get the handyman to assemble their Kinder Egg toys . . .'

'Whatever. Eventually they will have to assemble their own Kinder Egg toys.'

'Or pay someone to assemble their Kinder Egg toys.'

'I didn't pay him.'

'Yes, you did – he was working on an hourly rate . . . He even put the stickers on. Surely Molly could have done that.'

'Exactly. That's my point. We can't do everything for them for ever. That's what I realized in the exam hall. And is it any surprise that Molly is so reluctant to do any work on her own when we hold her hand over every obstacle, telling her how clever she is because she managed to write down the correct answer that we just gave her? Is that what we are going to do for Jamie as well?'

David tried to form a sentence in reply but the words didn't come. He knew I was right, and I pressed home my advantage.

'Which is better for your son? A project with mistakes that *he* wrote, or a perfect project that *you* wrote?'

There was a pause and he looked away, possibly at his complete boxed set of *The World at War* videos. 'So the Germans win?'

'The Germans win.'

He shuffled uneasily and finally mumbled, 'All right. But if he ever does a project on the World Cup, they're not winning the 1966 final as well.'

Jamie's fervent enthusiasm for his project had made me all the more determined to make Molly learn to sit down and study like any other child. I made a deal with her. I said she could have someone round to play on Sunday while the boys were off visiting the Cabinet War Rooms if she and her friend did a little bit of study together for just half an hour. She readily agreed. 'Can I invite Bronwyn?' she added excitedly.

'Um, they're probably going to their cottage for the weekend . . .' I said doubtfully.

'OK, can I invite Kirsty?'

'I'm not sure what they're doing . . . I know, what about that nice girl we gave a lift to on the way back from Chelsea College?'

Molly's little turned-up nose wrinkled in confusion.

'But . . . but I don't know her.'

'But she seemed nice, didn't she? And she only lives round the corner.'

'But . . . but we don't know their telephone number or anything.'

'I already looked it up. Osafo, 23 Gisbourne House. It's surprising how many Osafos there are . . .'

It seemed to me the perfect arrangement. I could suggest to Ruby's family that she came round to play with Molly, and we could use the opportunity to have a quick look through any spare practice papers I happened to buy in the bookshop before Sunday. Ruby would have the space and peace she couldn't get at home, and Molly would see what it meant to sit still and study. And apart from anything else, Ruby seemed like the nicest, most unprecocious child I had met for a long time. It would make a pleasant change to serve lunch to an eleven-year-old girl who wasn't having a month off carbohydrates. 'No mash potato for me, thank you,' Bronwyn had said last time she was round for tea. 'It goes straight to my hips.'

On Sunday morning the doorbell rang and I tried to gee up Molly at the imminent prospect of having Ruby round to play. I had been hoping that this might be my chance to meet Ruby's mother, but through the frosted glass of the doorway hovered a giant silhouette. Either Ruby was standing on her grandmother's shoulders or there was someone else at the door. I must confess I leapt back slightly at the sight of Ruby's enormous brother standing on my doorstep. I'd seen a photo of him at Ruby's house, but the picture didn't convey the Manhattan scale of the boy. He must have been six foot six or six foot seven, though his bony frame seemed ashamed of his height: his shoulders were hunched and his head hung low, hidden inside its grubby hooded top.

'Brought Ruby round,' he mumbled, and his little sister smiled shyly from somewhere near his waist.

'Oh thank you. Tell your grandmother I can drop her back after lunch.'

He managed a mumbled affirmative. And then I realized I had seen this boy before. He was one of the youths at the bottom of the road I had imagined were going to mug me that night I was walking to Blockbuster on my own after dark. And now here he was on my doorstep, mumbling and shuffling and avoiding eye contact – it was *he* who was intimidated by *me*.

'See you later, Ruby. Be good . . .' he said, and then he was gone.

So he wasn't 'Scary Youth #2' but 'Ruby's brother, Kofi'. He had an identity and a place in the universe. He was seventeen years old, studying at Lambeth College with his friend Aubrey from Norbury; he was six foot six and he slept in the bottom bunk underneath his sister, where Ruby told me his legs stuck out the end of the bed. The more detail she imparted about her brother, the less frightening he became. That's why they don't let you get acquainted with the auks in *Lord of the Rings*. They're only terrifying while they're anonymous; they'd cease to be scary if Auk #3 turned to camera and said, 'Hi, my name's Malcolm and I'm just mad about macramé and Lloyd Webber musicals.'

216

I was relieved to see Molly being so friendly and welcoming to Ruby, even though I had taken the precaution of giving Molly strict instructions to be friendly and welcoming to Ruby. There was still the statutory period of awkwardness that was probably exacerbated by having me hovering over them clucking, 'Molly, why don't you show Ruby your bedroom?' or, 'Why don't you show Ruby your doll's house?'

'Oh yeah, my doll's house – like, I'm still six years old.'

It saddened me that my only daughter had already grown out of her doll's house. David and I had bought it when she was a baby; it had been as close as we could find to the big Victorian houses in Oaken Avenue, with the exception that the dolls didn't disappear off to a little doll's house in the country every Friday night.

Before long the two girls were jumping round on the dance mat, finding some deeper form of communication in the ancient leveller that is the Sony PlayStation. Molly claimed they were taking turns, though every time I went into the lounge it seemed to be my daughter's go. She had never had anybody so compliant round to play; everything that was suggested was politely agreed to, there were no arguments about which game to play next or who had won the last one. Molly chose the game, and then won it. And then I listened to them talking about which secondary school they were going to, and Molly said that she had got a scholarship into Chelsea College and Ruby said she had tried for a scholarship too but hadn't been clever enough, so it seemed that Molly had won that one as well.

I had decided that I'd let them have an hour or so playing together and then after lunch I would spend a little time with Ruby helping her prepare for her one last crack at a top-flight school. I had also been right when I had thought that Ruby might be able to teach Molly a few things. Over the course of the morning I overheard Ruby saying, 'Don't you know what "cuss" means?' And, 'You don't know what "dissin" is?' Ruby eagerly ate up all her lunch, and Molly felt less inclined to mime vomiting and follow each agonized mouthful with a hasty gulp of water to wash away the disgusting flavour. And then, incredibly, Molly did her English homework in silence while I sat at the other end of the kitchen table going over some test papers with Ruby. She was so keen to learn, and it felt rewarding to teach a child who listened and who I could almost see making progress. By the time I dropped her back at her flat, I felt like the day could not have been a bigger success. The whole thing worked perfectly and left me feeling vindicated and, if I admitted it, a little proud of myself. Ruby had looked up at me with such a quizzical gaze, with such wonder in her eyes. It was as if she was thinking: Why are you doing so much to help me? Why are you being so kind? At least, that's what I imagined she was thinking.

'She's a smart girl, isn't she?' said her grandmother proudly as she helped her off with her coat.

'Oh yes,' I happily concurred. 'A very smart girl.'

The Brain Allergy Cookbook
Are Wheat and Dairy Lowering Your Child's IQ?
By David Zinkin   *Sunrise Books £6.99*

*Many parents are becoming increasingly aware of aller-
gic reactions caused by our gluten-heavy Western diet.
Allergies to wheat, dairy, nuts and shellfish can
prompt highly visible physical symptoms such as skin
rashes, swellings and wheezing. Much harder to identify
are what nutritionists refer to as 'brain allergies' –
chemical reactions in the mind that can cause your child
to fall short of his or her intellectual potential.
Often the only symptoms are behavioural; you may have
punished your child for being naughty when the fault
actually lies with you, the parent, for feeding him nuts
or tomatoes. Try these simple tests to see if your child
is 'brain allergic'.*

- *Your child shows hostility to a sibling. This is
  a classic symptom of a cranial wheat allergy. Cut
  out bread, pasta, pastry, breakfast cereal and
  other wheat products.*
- *Your child has demonstrated a reluctance to do
  homework. Your child's brain may well be lactose-
  intolerant. Cut out milk, cheese, butter and yoghurt.*

- **Your child usually gets a cold in the winter.** Your child may well have an allergy to additives. Cut out all prepared meals, tinned foods, packet food and frozen foods.
- **Your child is pale, tired and listless.** You have not replaced the food that you cut from your child's diet.

— 9 —

It was the first really hot weekend of the summer, when millions of Londoners are spontaneously drawn by some genetic migration instinct that sees us all jump into the Land Rover and seek out the lush greenery of the natural world that lies beside the garden centre car park. Ruby's grandmother had invited Molly round to play, and with David and the boys off watching a display by the Bombing of Dresden Re-enactment Society or something, I found myself sitting alone in the queue of traffic with all the other garden makeover refugees, adding to the carbon monoxide haze and doing my bit to help warm up the city.

This new friendship has been good for my daughter, I thought, staring at the cosmopolitan mix of south London pedestrians. Ruby was always so grateful and well behaved, and with Ruby's family being from Ghana, it also gave me the opportunity to open Molly's eyes to a bit of African culture, so I'd recently taken them both to the theatre to see *The Lion King*. Ruby was mature in lots of ways, but unlike Molly's other friends, there was nothing phoney about it. She was just at ease with herself; she took everything in her stride and didn't seem to bear any resentment about not getting a pony for Christmas.

I had made real progress with her English and non-verbal reasoning, getting her scores up to scholarship level so that she was well prepared for the Barnes Girls' exam. Sometimes Ruby would walk round to our house on her own, though when it was time to go home I always felt I had to drive her back myself. Although her grandfather remained detached, I got to know her grandmother and her brother quite well. Kofi was an awkward boy, embarrassed by his enormous height. I began to think that he too must have enormous potential if only he was guided in the right direction. I had a bit of a brainwave about this. I made a few enquiries and then excitedly announced the way forward for him. 'Kofi, I was speaking to someone who runs a semi-professional basketball team and they would be more than happy to give you a trial.' He was nowhere near as excited by my idea as I had hoped. I'm not even convinced he ever rang them up.

The traffic inched forwards and teenage boys on BMX bikes weaved at speed between the pensioners on the pavement with as much care as it is possible to take while doing extended wheelies that jumped alarmingly from road to pavement to zebra crossing, all pedestrians and drivers obligingly giving way to the new emergency vehicles: urban teenagers riding with one wheel in the air. A red light commanded me to stop and the urgent beep of the crossing hurried people to the safety of the opposite pavement. Barely registering the faceless heads that streamed past on the other side of my windscreen, I flicked through the radio presets in search of whichever station was playing 'Mr Blue Sky'. But something made me look up again. Suddenly in the blur of the crowd, one face was sharply in focus. There crossing the road right in front of me was my daughter. Not sitting behind me strapped into her seat, with me at the steering wheel dictating her direction, but walking freely on the other side of my locked doors – she was just *out there*, meandering down the high street on a sunny day. In her hand was a McDonald's milk shake and she was chatting excitedly with Ruby and a couple of other girls as they skipped up onto the pavement and towards Woolworths. I glanced round, presuming that Ruby's grandmother must be a few paces behind, but unless the girls were under the care of that beggar sitting by the cashpoint machine, there was no adult near enough to be supervising them. No chaperones holding their hands or stressed teachers at front and back pointing them in the direction of the school coaches – just four eleven-year-old girls walking free. The other children were clearly friends of Ruby's because they certainly weren't from Molly's school. I think I would have remembered a girl with pierced ears and a Florida 'Gators Puffa jacket like that one. Molly broke off from her milk shake and accepted the offer of some chips from another girl, and I tried to press down the electric window to shout across to her, but the window on the wrong side went down and then the car behind me tooted impatiently because the lights had started to flash amber a good half a second earlier.

I looked frantically for a space to pull over, to park up and rescue her from this perilous situation, but buses were pulling out from the left and the side roads on either side were marked no entry. I was helplessly washed downstream with all the traffic, forced to drive straight ahead with Molly's head receding in my rear-view mirror. A tow-away lorry was just lifting an illegally parked car so I gratefully grabbed the vacated parking space and leapt out. Zigzagging between the traffic, I crossed the road, narrowly avoiding a potentially fatal and particularly messy pile-up with a pizza-delivery moped that was speeding between the crawling cars. But when I arrived at the spot where I had last glimpsed Molly, she was nowhere to be seen. There was a betting shop behind me – maybe they'd dived in there and were now blowing Molly's pocket money on the greyhounds at Catford? There was a pawnshop a few doors down – perhaps they'd just got 50p for Molly's friendship bracelet? Or what about the pub next door? Maybe if I hung round till closing time I could catch my eleven-year-old daughter as she spilled out of the pub with a Bacardi Breezer in her hand, staggering over the road for a kebab?

Then I saw them. A stranger that used to be my eleven-year-old daughter was being ordered out of Woolworths by a uniformed security officer for eating burgers on the premises. The girls were giggling as they scurried back out onto the pavement and then one of them threw a bit of burger bun at Molly, who laughed and threw a chip back. And then her face fell as she saw the thunderous face of her mother, striding up the road towards her.

'You realize you might have a brain allergy to wheat?'

'What?'

'Can't you just pick out the salad? Hello, Ruby . . . does your grandmother know you're out on your own?'

'Yes.'

Silence. What I really wanted to do was take Molly away there and then, and drive her home till she was behind our electric gates safe from cars, muggers and gluten, but I realized I couldn't just pull her out in front of these other girls.

'I've got a great idea. It's such a lovely day, I've got my car over there – why don't I drive you all to Battersea Park?'

The two girls I had never met before glanced at one another warily.

'We could go to the children's zoo maybe; you could take turns to have a ride on the pony. I don't mind paying.'

'We're not allowed to get into cars with strangers,' said the taller of the two girls.

'I'm not a stranger, I'm Molly's mum, aren't I, Molly?'

'No,' she said, and then rather undermined her case by adding, 'Mum, go away.'

'Or we don't have to go to the children's zoo, you could all rent a banana bike if you like, I don't mind paying, and I'll buy you all an ice cream, which is dairy, but that's fine, and, and, um, some chocolate biscuits, which are wheat *and* dairy, so there you are, see, completely normal. What do you say?'

The two girls who had never met me before just stared at the ground.

'We're not allowed to go off with strange adults.'

'I'm not strange.'

'Yes, you are,' said Molly firmly.

In the end I said that if they didn't want to come to the park then perhaps they should be getting back to Ruby's flat because her grandmother would be worried about them, and the four girls reluctantly turned back towards the Wilberforce Estate. And while Molly and her friends ambled down the pavement I drove along at walking pace twenty yards behind them, with other motorists tooting and flashing their lights and angrily overtaking me.

I was still contemplating whether to say something to Ruby's grandmother as I went to pick Molly up. I skipped confidently across the estate, saying good afternoon to the family who lived next door to Ruby, wondering how I might find the words to express the fear I felt about my daughter being allowed out down the high street. A tall Rastafarian was coming out of Ruby's block and held the door open for me. Ruby had pointed him out to me before; he worked with the infants in her school. 'The thing is . . .' I would say, '. . . is that there are a lot of strange people out there . . . and, well, it's different for Ruby because, er, well, she seems to know half of them . . .' Basically I had to explain that I hadn't planned on letting Molly out on her own until she was an age when I was completely comfortable with the idea. Say, when she was around forty-three.

Ruby's grandmother invited me in for a cup of tea, which I forced myself to drink despite it having about eleven sugars in it, while the girls sat there sipping a luminous squash that looked even sweeter. I made stilted conversation, seated on the edge of the kitchen chair. 'How's Ruby getting on with practising her internet?' I asked, not meaning to sound as if I was mocking her.

'Oh, our computer died, isn't it?'

'Oh dear, that's a shame.'

'No, it was our fault. We didn't get it inoculated against all the viruses.'

Constance said she felt very bad that she'd missed Molly's birthday and I dismissed this out of hand. But again she apologized that she had not bought Molly a present – 'after all you have done for Ruby'. 'Anyway,' she announced, 'I've got her something now . . .' and she headed through to her bedroom to fetch a little something as I offered up the standard token resistance, 'Oh you shouldn't have, really . . .'

I glanced around the kitchen. The food packets were from Lidl, the cash-only low-grade supermarket for the shopper whose only consideration was cost. On the notice board there were cut-out tokens that would entitle the bearer to 10p off their next bottle of washing-up liquid. Then Constance returned and this time when I said, 'You shouldn't have,' I really meant it. Into the kitchen Ruby's grandmother wheeled a brand-new girl's bicycle, gleaming metallic purple with a bell and a water bottle and spokes that glistened and sparkled in the sunlight streaming through the window. 'Oh my God, you shouldn't have . . .' I kept repeating. Molly's mouth hung open – she was thrilled but also amazed at the scale of this gift.

'Wow, cool!' said Molly. 'Thanks!'

I didn't know what to say. It was so excessively and in-appropriately generous that I wondered if I should refuse it or offer to pay half or something.

'You mentioned that Molly didn't have a bike?' she elucidated into the stunned silence.

'Yes, but I hope you didn't think that I was hinting . . . I mean, it's so very generous of you – I'm embarrassed.' I nearly added, '. . . and you just can't afford this . . .' but managed to stop the words coming out.

'It's a sort of thank-you from Ruby,' she explained and I thanked Ruby as well, but she said nothing. In fact, she seemed as surprised as I was.

'Did you know your granny was going to do this, Ruby?'

'Well, I saw the girl's bike hidden out on the balcony,' she said, 'but I didn't know it was for Molly.'

Molly hauled herself onto the saddle. It looked completely incongruous, my daughter sitting on a bicycle in this little kitchen with her podgy legs dangling awkwardly on either side. She really did look a little overweight. The trouble was there just never seemed to be the occasion for my children to get any exercise – there was so much else to fit in. We'd never managed to find a maths tutor who would be prepared to swim alongside them and explain matrices while the children practised their breaststroke.

'Jamie will be so jealous that I've got a bike and he hasn't,' said Molly.

'That's not the way to look at it, darling,' I said, giving Ruby's smiling grandmother a knowing look. 'In fact, maybe we should stop off and get him one on the way home,' I added quickly, thinking that if I didn't Constance would be round to our house first thing in the morning with a brand-new boy's bike and maybe a Harley-Davidson for David.

'You know, it's just occurred to me,' I said as I thanked her for the seventeenth time, 'I've got an old computer at home that we're not using any more. Ruby could have that one if you like.'

'Oh no, you have been too kind already . . .'

'No, it's my old laptop, just sitting in a drawer. Ruby could use that to practise her internet or whatever.'

As we loaded the bike into the back of the car, I wondered if I should have let them repay what they thought was their debt to me without trumping it with an even more expensive gift in return. Maybe I should have just let Constance be the richest lady for once. Or had this bike come from Ruby's mother, I mused; was it a guilt thing, repaying me for the time I had spent with her daughter? When I had arrived to pick Molly up, I had secretly hoped that this might be the day on which I finally met Ruby's mum, but again I'd been disappointed. I gleaned that she was a cleaner who also worked in a bakery in the early morning and then waited on tables in a posh London hotel, often until long after her children were all fast asleep. 'One of the best hotels in London,' Ruby had said proudly, as if it gave her mother status to be earning the minimum wage in such grand surroundings.

I must confess I was even momentarily attracted to what I imagined was the simple honesty of Ruby's mother's life.

Only one thing to worry about: earning enough money to keep the family going. Nothing else matters. What a luxury, I secretly thought, for life to be such a financial struggle that all that other mental clutter was swept aside. Of course, in my more rational moments I knew this must be nonsense, but I occasionally imagined myself struggling to pay for school uniforms, or working weekends to make sure my children had toys at Christmas, and it seemed unlikely I would have the energy to worry about whether my four-year-old's clumsiness was brought on by a brain allergy to Chocolate Weetos. Are we just programmed as parents to fear and fret, with our worry-dials turned up to the maximum level whatever the situation? Perhaps we were evolutionarily conditioned to be terrified about having our babies stolen away from the cave by packs of wolves or whatever, and now that there are no wolves in Clapham any more, we lie awake agonizing to the same degree about the fact that our child only got the part of second donkey in the school nativity. Among my circle of friends, so much time was spent fretting about our children's safety that every conceivable danger was removed from our homes. I'm surprised we didn't get old men knocking on the door saying, 'Have you got any knives you want blunting?'

Well, today it had been forced upon me: my daughter had been out roaming the big wide world without adult supervision, and I could see that her expedition to the high street had made her feel immensely proud. Then and there I resolved to allow Molly a little more independence before she headed off to big school. David agreed that she should be permitted to walk round to Kirsty's on her own at the weekends as long as she rang as soon as she got there. 'Yes,' he mused, just as I was falling asleep. 'I mean what's the worst that can happen?' And having left that thought in my mind he dozed off, leaving me to follow him three hours and two rolls of bubble wrap later.

While Ruby's mother never saw her children because she was earning every penny she could to support them, Kirsty's mum had just taken a major pay cut to be in the same place as her daughter for the next seven years. Sarah had now begun her job at Chelsea College, and I sensed there may have been one or two initial disappointments. As administrative assistant, Sarah discovered that she was expected to work in the school office, when I think she had been hoping she might be allowed to take her laptop and sit at the back of her daughter's class. Neither were they planning to let her out to watch over her daughter at playtime, nor to help her choose the right foods at lunch; in fact, they didn't really seem to understand the point of Sarah's job at all, but had some completely different idea that as administrative assistant Sarah should somehow assist with the administration.

'Guess what?' announced Sarah as she came to collect Kirsty one Saturday afternoon. 'I've got us all tickets to see the Chelsea College play.'

'Oh what a super idea,' said Ffion. 'Of course! You can get the tickets for free! We are lucky to have you there, to tell us all about the school and make sure the girls are all in the same class and get us tickets for the school play for free . . .' She went on with such enthusiasm that Sarah clearly felt it might seem a bit penny-pinching to point out that she hadn't got the tickets for free. This year Chelsea College were putting on *The Pirates of Penzance*, Gilbert and Sullivan's stirring Cornish operetta about extortion, robbery and revised charges at the Tintagel Visitors' Car Park. And so the following Wednesday evening we travelled in convoy across the river Thames and saw the massed gathering of the tribe into which our families would be initiated. David was completely inappropriately dressed. I don't think he even owned a pair of mustard-coloured corduroys.

Many criminals return to the scene of their crime. Some in the dead of night to remove incriminating evidence, others pretending to be casual passers-by just to confirm to themselves that it really had happened. But few can have returned quite as brazenly as I did when I walked back into the hall at Chelsea College. What's more, we would be taking my victim along too – because Sarah had casually offered her spare ticket to Ruby. Right in front of me, without consultation, she had just asked Ruby if she would like to come along to the play at Chelsea College since Kirsty's friend Eliza couldn't come now that Wednesday nights were Japanese conversation class.

'Oh, you probably wouldn't be interested in that, would you, Ruby, since you're not going to Chelsea?' I had prompted.

'Yes please!' Ruby said delightedly.

This wasn't my first time back at Chelsea College, but now we were returning to the very same room. I thought I might refrain from pointing this out as we all took our seats in the enormous hall.

'This is where we sat the entrance exam!' announced Bronwyn unhelpfully.

'Oh yeah, I sat over there . . .' said Kirsty.

'I sat at the back,' said Ruby.

'Where did you sit, Molly?'

'Oh, er, I didn't do the exam in here—'

'You did it somewhere else, didn't you, darling,' I cut in, 'not in this room but in another room on a different day to all your friends. I do hope the play starts soon. They're taking their time, aren't they? I am looking forward to it, have you ever seen any Gilbert and Sullivan before, it's sort of light opera, I'm very excited, aren't you?'

The girls politely waited for me to stop talking and then continued.

'I thought the exam was easy-peasy,' said Bronwyn.

'I thought the maths was hard,' confessed Kirsty.

'When I did the maths paper,' said Ruby, but then she broke off. 'Oh it doesn't matter . . .'

'What?'

'When I did the maths paper . . . the girl sitting next to me copied all my answers!'

'Really? Did she get caught?'

'No. I let her see them deliberately.'

'Mum! Mum!' said Bronwyn. 'Ruby says that when she took her entrance exam here, she deliberately let the girl sitting next to her copy all her answers.'

'Why did you do that, dear?'

'Because she looked so sad and worried.'

I was staring very hard at the programme. Then I turned it the right way up.

'Well, I'm sure you were trying to be kind, but you really shouldn't have done that, dear,' continued Ffion. 'That person was cheating. If you see her here you should point her out.'

It was only for a split second, but I was sure Ruby glanced at me. And then the overture struck up.

I did my best to enjoy the operetta. The story tells how the Pirate Apprentice was supposed to have been born into respectable society, and it was interesting to see how the young actor chose to convey this notion by affecting an extremely posh accent throughout. The singing was exceptional; the boy warbled like some angelic choirboy who might suddenly shoot to stardom with an unexpected Christmas number-one hit. The glossy programme notes recounted how he was in some grand choir that I think we were supposed to have heard of, and boasted that he had already performed in a number of professional concerts in Vienna, Paris and Bracknell. (I would have left out Bracknell.) There were thanks to parents who owned designer shops and had lent costumes. There were photos of the lead players taken by a well-known fashion photographer whose daughter was one of the stars. It was like the programme you would get at a West End show, right down to the little details, like it costing five quid. The whole thing was incredibly slick and professionally produced. 'Away to the cheating world go you, Where pirates all are well-to-do,' sang the Pirate King. Had I read too much into that glance from Ruby? I thought. Or did she know? Had she known ever since I'd first picked her up at the bus stop?

During the interval I glanced at Ruby for any clue as to her thoughts. She was looking round in amazement at all the people sipping wine at the back of the hall, at the slim and tanned women in Moschino tops and the men whose idea of chillin' was taking off their tie and wearing a cravat.

'Are you all right, Ruby?'

'Yeah. Are all the people who go to Chelsea College rich?' she asked me.

Once I would have instinctively fudged such an embarrassing issue but having been to Ruby's council flat and to both of Ffion's enormous houses, it was hard to bracket both families together in the middle somewhere.

'Well, yes, I would say that pretty well all of them are richer than . . . than the families on the Wilberforce Estate . . .'

'So are you rich then?' she enquired, as if this was like asking my star sign. Being English and middle-class, this was obviously something I preferred not to talk about. When our accountant had asked how much we had earned in the previous financial year, I had shrugged. 'Well, we get by, you know . . .' But Ruby deserved an honest answer.

'Well, I never would have said so before, but I suppose we are rich. Yes.'

'Before what?' said my daughter impatiently.

'Sorry?'

'You said you never would have said so before . . . Before what?'

'Before I got an education.'

The girls wandered off to get themselves a soft drink and Ffion smiled approvingly as Ruby followed her daughter and friends. I had been anxious as to how Ffion would react to Ruby. It was no accident that they had never met before.

'I think it's marvellous that you've been helping that little Ruby girl. You're a saint, Alice, you really are – everyone should do something for charity. Bronwyn has sponsored a donkey, hasn't she, Philip?'

'Well, it's not really charity. I'm just trying to give her a chance to realize her potential.'

'Yes, super. But I think it was probably for the best she didn't get in here, don't you, hmm?' she said looking round. 'She wouldn't really have fitted in . . .'

I followed her gaze. Nearby Sarah was trying to break into a circle where the headmistress was talking, but nobody seemed to be moving for her.

'I don't see why not – she's as clever as all the other children . . .'

'But we can't pretend she's not different, can we, hmmm? I mean, I suppose it must have occurred to you that her mother might be a, you know –' she lowered her voice – 'a prostitute?'

'OF COURSE HER MUM ISN'T A PROSTITUTE!'
I was a little too emphatic and a couple of other Chelsea College parents looked round. I attempted an upbeat smile at them.

'Think about it, Alice,' she whispered. 'You say she works in the evenings, and I mean we don't know who Ruby's father is, do we, hmm?'

'I have made a point of never asking. But lots of families have no father – it doesn't mean a thing. Listen, the hours that Ruby's mum works, if she was a prostitute she'd be a millionaire by now.'

'Unless she had a drug habit,' said Philip, checking the nicotine patch on his arm as his wife nodded sadly at that pertinent point.

'Cannabis . . .'

'Heroin . . .'

'Crack cocaine . . .'

'SHE HAS NOT GOT A CRACK HABIT!' I blurted out and a few more parents turned in my direction. 'I can't believe I'm hearing this. They are a perfectly respectable family – they go to church, they work hard, they just happen to be different to us, that's all.'

The girls returned with their soft drinks, plus a tub of ice cream each.

'Ice cream too! I only gave you a pound,' said Ffion.

'Ruby paid for it all. Her mum gave her ten pounds to buy us all something.'

And Ffion raised her eyebrows meaningfully at me. No further evidence required.

I knew Ffion was wrong. In fact, it was an incredibly liberating experience, because for years I had been nervous and unsure about so many things and so I'd allowed Ffion's total self-confidence to guide me. Now that I was sure that she was completely wrong about one thing, it opened up the possibility that she was misguided about so much else. Ffion's strident certainty had been a rock to cling to in the perfect storm of parenthood. But like the shipwrecked sailor in Alfie's picture book, I hadn't been clinging to a rock at all, but to a whale. A big fat killer whale with a facial hair problem.

For a while now I had been wanting to stop the fencing classes that Molly begrudgingly did with Bronwyn every Thursday, but I'd never quite had the courage to say so to her mother. Now I would just announce it – just tell her that Molly didn't have time for fencing.

'What, do you mean she's got too much on?' demanded Ffion, when I finally spat the words out the following weekend. We were all gathered in my kitchen as usual, but now I was shocked to notice my hands shaking slightly as I poured the coffee, knowing I was about to stand up to Ffion.

'What's she going to do instead of fencing?'

'Well, I just thought she might, um . . . do nothing . . .'

'Nothing?'

'Yes, on Thursdays between four and five, I'm time-tabling in nothing. Just being at home and, I dunno, having fun.'

'Fun? Fun? These children have nothing but fun. No, Bronwyn, if Molly bid hearts you have to put down hearts as well.'

Sarah bravely attempted to change the subject. 'Still not smoking, Philip?'

'Four weeks!' he said proudly. 'And I'm down to about forty nicotine patches a day!' He grinned, showing us the little sticking plaster on his arm.

'I think you should still have to stand in the garden,' said William.

Bronwyn picked up the card she had placed on the card table and replaced it with the two of hearts.

'No, clockwise, Kirsty! In contract bridge you always go clockwise!'

'Well, I know they're very lucky and everything to have so many opportunities,' I continued, 'and I'm sure fencing is lots of fun, but just not sandwiched in between their maths tutor and swimming lessons . . .'

'Swimming is fun. And horse-riding, and ballet and real-tennis and drama and fencing and piano – you have lots of fun, don't you, Bronwyn, hmmm, darling, don't you, you have lots of fun?' Her baggy-eyed daughter looked up from where she was being cajoled into learning bridge.

'Yes,' she nodded obediently before returning her furrowed brow towards the cards in her hand.

I didn't have a problem with any of these pursuits per se; if someone's passion was real-tennis or fencing, then good luck to them. But you can't load too many programs onto the computer or it's useless for anything. 'I don't know . . .' I mumbled. 'It's just that when Molly stopped studying hours every night after dashing from this lesson to that, she suddenly seemed a lot happier . . .'

'Well, that's super and I'm sure that Molly will be very happy watching television when the other girls are getting their fencing gold for Chelsea College, but fun doesn't pass exams, does it, hmm, does it? Fun doesn't make a child strive for excellence or get to the best universities, hmm? They have plenty of time to have fun at home. No! No! No! Bronwyn, don't put down the four of clubs if Molly has already led with hearts, for goodness' sake, concentrate, child!'

Sarah was looking a little anxious at Ffion's growing irritation. 'I'm sure they wouldn't mind if Molly just did fencing alternate weeks, Alice?'

'That's a lovely thought, Sarah, but I don't want Molly to do it all.'

'It's not always about what *we* want, though, is it?' said Ffion. A suppressed laugh escaped from William's mouth that turned into an affected cough. 'Our children are individuals, people in their own right, not extensions of our own egos,' she added, retrieving the card her daughter had just played, and choosing a better card from Bronwyn's hand.

Sarah's suggested compromise made me realize how totally Ffion had dominated our lives. A few months ago I would have agreed to the compromise of fortnightly fencing lessons just so as not to irritate Ffion, but now I felt ready to do what I was certain was best for my children. I'm not going to let Ffion's obsessive pushy parenting affect my own family any more, I thought as she hovered behind my nervous daughter to see which card she would play.

'I'm collecting nines,' Molly whispered, and Ffion pressed her fingers to her temples in exasperation.

'I said at the beginning, you don't collect cards of the same number.'

'Can we go and play in the garden?' said Bronwyn.

'Look, I don't have to do this you know,' snapped Ffion. 'A lot of parents wouldn't bother. So you better have a good think about the alternative. Do you want to arrive at secondary school not knowing how to play contract bridge? Is that what you really want?'

The children stared silently at Ffion, and tried their best to imagine just how great a social impediment this might be. Molly tentatively took a card from her hand and placed it on the pile, nervously looking to Ffion for some sort of reaction.

'Snap!' shouted Kirsty, and her mother tried to laugh as if she had been joking, though it was quite possible that she wasn't. Ffion seemed dangerously close to completely losing patience. She was determined that these children were going to learn contract bridge, and now set them up in the next room to play a few games on their own. Jamie didn't want to play bridge with the three girls. 'You have to. I already explained you can't play bridge with three people, weren't you listening, Jamie?'

The coffee tasted more bitter than usual. But the atmosphere lightened slightly as Ffion and Philip enjoyed being quizzed about the progress of their personal-league-table software.

'What about humility?' asked William. 'Can people give themselves a really high score for that?'

Ffion said she couldn't see why not and William cast me the tiniest of conspiratorial grins. Then Alfie wandered into the kitchen having done as his father had privately requested: he had refrained from cross-dressing in front of our guests. He came in disguised as Spiderman, a macho role model that would make any father proud of his boy. 'Look – Spiderman's got boobies!' announced our son, proudly jutting out the pair of oranges he'd stuffed under his costume.

We had expected the South-west London Junior Bridge Club to return after ten minutes declaring that they were bored, but without their parents to intimidate them it seemed that they had become genuinely absorbed. Half an hour later they were still in there. At one point I had suggested going to check on them but Ffion said that we should leave them to it and Sarah had agreed with her, which left me with no option but to sit down again. When Ffion had finally decided that they would have played enough hands, we returned to explain the scoring system to them. I was the first into the lounge to witness a scene of total and reverential concentration. All four of them were gathered round the television watching Bronwyn and Molly leaping about in front of the screen playing Wishy-Washy on the PlayStation Eye-Toy.

So engrossed were all the children in the computerized window cleaning that none of them even turned round as Bronwyn swung her arms about in front of the tiny camera on top of the telly, watching herself on the screen wildly wiping away the virtual suds on the TV while a distorted cover version of 'When I'm Cleaning Windows' boomed out of the speakers. 'Bird poo!' chorused the other children delightedly as a white smear appeared on the screen. It was then that Molly looked up and saw us standing there horrified. 'Mum, I beat Bronwyn at Wishy-Washy.'

By the end of the sentence I could see Molly was already sensing that this wasn't perhaps the point.

'Bronwyn, what on earth do you think you are doing?'

'Molly turned it on,' she squealed.

According to my script, this line is followed by that child's parent saying, 'Well, you should have said you weren't interested,' or, 'Don't blame Molly, it takes two people to play,' but to my astonishment I heard Ffion direct her fury to my own child: 'Molly, say sorry to Bronwyn for making her go on the PlayStation.'

'Sorry, Bronwyn.'

'Don't look at me, look at her when you say sorry.'

'Sorry, Bronwyn.'

I replayed this scene several times in my head afterwards and every version ended with me saying, 'Now just a minute,

Ffion. I'll admonish my own child, thank you very much . . .' but I'm ashamed to say that I was so shocked and her disappointment in Molly seemed so convincing that I found myself persuaded by it.

'Yes, Molly, you really should know better,' I concurred. 'Ffion goes to all this effort to teach you bridge and you go and fritter away all the chances we give you. There are children in Africa who would love to form a little bridge club, but they don't even have playing cards.' I didn't know what I was saying now, it was just nonsense, but you have to keep up appearances. The other grown-ups did their best to nod as if this was a well-made point. I looked at Sarah and she put on her best disappointed face at her own daughter, although I sensed that William seemed to think it was all quite funny. Deep down I suspected that if Molly hadn't beaten Bronwyn's high score on the PlayStation, then her mother wouldn't have objected quite so much. I suppose her daughter hadn't had as much practice at this particular game as my kids. If Bronwyn had tried to play Wishy-Washy at her house, Ffion would have got the Croatian au pair to clean the virtual windows for her.

'It really is very, very disappointing . . .' continued Ffion, as the children bowed their heads in shame while the upbeat ukulele theme tune continued strumming in the background. 'You really should know better, I'm very disappointed in you, Molly.'

Molly she had said again. Molly. Ffion had puffed just once too often and at that moment the balloon suddenly burst.

'Now hang on a minute, Ffion. It wasn't just Molly, they were all playing it. I've told Molly off – why don't you have a word with your own child?'

'Because Bronwyn was really looking forward to learning bridge. Bronwyn was hoping to join the bridge club at Chelsea

College but she won't be able to if your daughter keeps leading her astray and turning on Splishy-Sploshy.'

'Wishy-Washy,' Molly corrected her, perhaps unwisely.

'BE QUIET, MOLLY!' shouted Ffion. 'We've had quite
enough from you today, thank you very much.'

'DON'T YOU SHOUT AT MY DAUGHTER,' I
suddenly shouted back. '*I'll* tell her off, not you!'

'You have to admit—' began Philip in his best placatory
tone.

'No, I don't have to admit anything. This is my house and
she is my daughter and I will not have her taking all the blame
for everything.'

My anger had shocked everyone, including myself. Some
primal defensive instinct had kicked in and now I was tearing
up the ancient treaty under which adults had agreed to always
present a united front in the face of errant children.

'Why don't you have a word with your own bloody
daughter, instead of everyone else's? Why don't you face up to
the fact that your child is not, in fact, the only child in the
world that is one hundred per cent bloody perfect?'

'Because Bronwyn wasn't the one who turned on the Game
Cube, that's why!'

If Molly considered pointing out that it was a PlayStation,
not a Game Cube, she decided against it. The children were
staring open-mouthed to see the adults turn on one another
like this.

'And Bronwyn didn't start playing computer games, so
don't blame me for Molly's intellectual immaturity.'

'Intellectual immaturity? What sort of bollocks is that? You
think your child's so bloody smart just because she came top
of a league table that her own mother designed! Well bugger
me, what a surprise!'

'Please don't swear in front of Bronwyn,' said her mother. The language had taken the children's amazement to an even higher level. Their faces betrayed an uneven mixture of excitement rapidly being swamped by acute embarrassment.

'I'm sorry that you are so angry that Bronwyn is a higher achiever than Molly,' she continued, 'but perhaps that's what happens when your children start mixing with coloured children off a council estate. I don't mind you frittering away your own daughter's potential, but I won't have you letting it affect mine.'

'What are you talking about? They were playing a bloody computer game . . .'

'I'm sorry, but Molly is holding Bronwyn back academically, and I simply cannot have that.'

'*What?*'

'Your daughter is holding my child back academically. I don't think the friendship is benefiting Bronwyn.'

Suddenly my rage crossed a line and I felt possessed by some sort of serene calmness that came from no longer caring. I was furious without being volatile, incandescent but in control. There was a pause and then I just looked her up and down and said, 'Hey, F-f-f-fion? Why don't you just f-f-f-fuck off! Just f-fuck off and f-find something more worthwhile to do, like shaving off that hideous moustache, you big fat walrus.'

There was a stunned silence. And then William said, 'So, um . . . anyone fancy a game of Wishy-Washy?'

'Shut up, William!' said Sarah, but Ffion was already gone. We hadn't even set a date for the next bridge lesson. And out by her car I caught a glimpse of her husband taking a long slow drag of a cigarette.

Can Crystals Cure Cancer?

By Dr Henry Bagge   Sunrise Books £6.99

No.

— 10 —

The book didn't actually say 'No', but I felt able to make up my own mind about this without reading two hundred pages of what David termed 'bogus anti-scientific mumbo-jumbo'. I don't think I'd have been very comfortable if one of my children was rushed to hospital and the doctor said, 'I've just read this amazing book on crystology, so instead of giving him the usual cure for pneumonia I thought we might rest some agate on his forehead because that's the birthstone for Scorpio, although we might try some topaz since he's on the cusp with Sagittarius.' I'd always thought it was rather liberal and forward-thinking to be open to ideas about alternative medicine, spiritualism and astrology. But now I'd lost the faith.

I pulled *Can Crystals Cure Cancer?* from the shelf and chucked it on the pile destined for the Oxfam shop, and then decided it might be a bit tactless to give them *Think Yourself Thinner*. But they did get *Yoga for Toddlers*, *The Womb-man's Guide to Lunar Menstruation* and *Choose Your Child's Star Sign: How family planning and elective caesareans can help you pick the best sign of the zodiac for your baby*. Nor did I keep

Men Say Tomato – Women say Tomato, *Homeopathy for Cats* or the book that suggested I might use tarot cards to help me pick my child's GCSE subjects. Looking at the pile now made me feel there was something rather decadent and narcissistic about all these quasi-alternative bibles and endless self-help books. Funny how there isn't a market for 'help-other-people books'.

Ruby failed to get into Barnes School for Girls. Despite a planned programme of study sessions round at our house, despite mock examinations done in David's office while he tutted and huffed around in the kitchen, my adopted prodigy failed to make the grade. And it wasn't because I didn't give her any echinacea and nettle. Her grandmother rang me to thank me for all my efforts but to say that Ruby would be going to Battersea Comprehensive with all her friends after all. She didn't want to talk for long; when I asked how Ruby did in the interview with the head teacher, she mumbled something about them missing it because the bus had been late. There was a suggestion of embarrassment in her voice as if she now felt foolish ever to have harboured such social aspirations for her granddaughter. But I felt a personal sense of failure, as if I was somehow responsible for Ruby's fate. Her brother Kofi dropped round the practice papers that I hadn't wanted back.

'He really is very tall, isn't he?' said David. 'Do you know what occurs to me? That somebody should put him in contact with a professional basketball team.'

Sarah happily agreed to my suggestion that we take our girls out to buy their uniforms for Chelsea College together, and then her daughter let slip that this was the second set of school clothes they had bought; they'd already been out once with Ffion and Bronwyn. (Ffion and I had not been in touch since I had happened to allude to her striking similarity to an enormous whiskery sea-mammal.) Now with the kids all at school and David visiting a client, I sat at home sewing Molly's nametags on her Chelsea College blazer. I didn't use the whole space provided because Molly didn't have a triple-barrelled name. But I couldn't get Ruby out of my head. She would never wear a blazer like this one, I thought as I held it up. I pictured her in the whole outfit, walking side by side with Molly up the steps of Chelsea College. And then I shuddered at the thought of my daughter being friends with Bronwyn for another seven years.

My attention was distracted by seeing a police car pull up in the road. Had a resident of Oaken Avenue committed some crime? Had somebody been putting white flour in their bread-maker? But then my casual nosiness turned to panic as I spied a uniformed officer striding down my path. Inside my brain, some sort of instinctive rapid-response unit instantly kicked into action: heartbeat alarm on maximum, adrenalin mobilized, hand movements set to medium-level shaking. I must try to remain calm, I told myself. I must not appear to panic; no, I am going to remain in complete control. And then I dived behind the sofa. I lay there hidden, feeling my heart thumping too loudly against the carpet, staring into the darkness of the gap under the couch. The police had come for me, they had found out, it was all over. But at least I had located Sneezy from Alfie's Polly Pocket Snow White Cottage, so that was something to be positive about.

The doorbell made me jump even though I was expecting it. What was the point of having electric gates if I was going to leave them open in the daytime? The police had warned us about undesirable characters knocking on people's doors and now they'd been proved right. I stayed hidden. I would just ignore it and the policeman would go away again; yes, that was surely an excellent and foolproof way of dealing with this particular problem. The carpet down there was much less worn that in the centre of the room, I noticed. Give it another minute or so and the arresting officer would be gone. The doorbell rang again.

'I'll get it!' shouted Carmen, and I heard the front door open.

Since when did Carmen start answering the door for us? Ironing, hoovering and a little light dusting: that was the deal. I'd never mentioned anything about handing me over to an arresting officer.

'Mrs Chaplin, policeman to see you . . .' said Carmen, showing him into the lounge with more than a tinge of excitement in her voice.

'Ah, hello there . . .' I said smiling, my head popping up from behind the settee. 'Just getting the bits of fluff off the carpet. Carmen, don't forget to hoover behind the sofa when you do this room, will you?'

'OK.'

'But maybe you should do the upstairs rooms now,' I emphasized, getting to my feet and placing a rather paltry amount of fluff in the wastepaper basket.

'OK.' And she left me alone where I was trying too hard to adopt some sort of natural standing position.

'Alice Chaplin?'

'Yes,' I said, stiffening. I was sure this was it.

'Hi there, Alice, I'm Mike.'

Oh how lovely! How friendly and informal! Even though he'd come to drag me down to the cells and probably beat me into a signed confession, how charming that some expensive PR consultation had concluded that arresting officers should take the trouble to establish first-name terms beforehand. I'm sure when the hangman put the noose round Ruth Ellis, it would have really brightened up her day if he'd said, 'Hello, Ruth, I'm Albert. I'll be your hangman for this morning . . .'

'Hello, er, Mike . . .' I mumbled.

On his lapel, his walkie-talkie chattered away on a special frequency reserved for distorted static and bizarre non sequiturs.

'So, Alice, do you know why I'm here?'

'Er . . . neighbourhood watch?'

'Ruby Osafo?'

'Ruby Osafo . . .? Ruby Osafo . . .?' I repeated, in the hope that the name might ring some distant bell. 'Ah yes, I remember.'

'I've just been round to the flat of the family in question. They claim to be the victim of a crime?' and he looked at me with meaningfully raised eyebrows. I think that was the moment that I was certain I was done for.

When I had gone to court for causing a road accident with the model child, I never felt that bad about it because deep inside I felt no shame.

'Really? A "crime" – that's a very strong word, isn't it?' I gabbled, my voice cracking slightly. I was conscious that I was avoiding eye contact, and was also concerned that my impression of an innocent acquaintance with the Osafos might not be made more convincing if I suddenly threw up all over the fluffy carpet.

'Oh yes. But I'm concerned that this is far more serious than it looks. We might be talking fraud here, Alice.'

The excessive use of my first name was not an act of friend-ship at all – it was a subtle form of police brutality, designed to make the interviewee explode with indignation, in-advertently revealing all sorts of incriminating information in the outburst.

'Fraud?' I was fighting back the tears but had to stay strong. 'Aren't I allowed to phone my solicitor or something?'

'There's not much point in that, Alice.'

I slumped into a chair.

'Fraud? What's the punishment for fraud? A fine, maybe? A suspended sentence?'

'Ooh no, it's a very serious offence. Custodial sentence is quite common. So I need to ask you a few questions, if I may . . .'

I could just make a dash for it now, I thought. Go on the run, live wild in Richmond Park, dig out a secret den and live off raw rabbit meat and venison, occasionally popping to the Centre Court Shopping Centre, Wimbledon for essential toiletries and Belgian chocolates.

'Have you given any valuables of any sort to the Osafo family during the past couple of weeks?'

'Hmmm?' I lifted my face out of my hands. 'Yes, my old laptop computer. Why?'

'Oh. Really?' He sounded extremely disappointed. 'What sort of computer was it?'

'A little grey one – er, a Sony "Vaio" – I never know how you pronounce it.'

'Oh, that's what they said. And you'd be willing to say that in a signed statement, would you?'

'I don't understand – what's this got to do with anything?'

'Well, it's been stolen.'

'What?'

'Your laptop. The Osafos have reported it stolen.'

'Oh, thank God.'

'What?'

'Thank God, oh what a relief!' I was almost laughing. 'I thought you were, I mean, I thought that, um – it doesn't matter. I thought something worse must have happened. So you just came round to see if I had given them my laptop?'

'I had to check it out. See, it's the easiest thing in the world for them to fake a burglary, claim they lost an expensive laptop. And when they couldn't produce any receipt or anything, I thought they might be trying to defraud the insurance company.' He glanced meaningfully through the net curtains. 'Wasn't this the road where that nutty woman got done for sticking a model Tony Blair out in front of a car? One of them anti-capitalist types, you know, anarchist or whatever . . .'

'Really? No, I never heard about that. So you're saying the Osafos have been the victims of a crime?'

'Maybe, maybe not . . .'

'Poor Ruby. I'd only just given her that computer. Was it a serious burglary?'

'Well, robbery's no big news on that estate. Everyone just burgles each other; it probably all evens out in the end, Alice.'

'Actually, would you mind calling me "Mrs Chaplin", please? I don't mean to be snobby, but I don't really know you, and I can't be doing with all this Californian pseudo-mateyness.'

'Oh. As you wish, Mrs Chaplin.'

'Or just don't use my name at all. Just say "as you wish", without adding my name on the end? Do you think you could do that?'

'As you wish.'

'Thank you . . . Mike.'

Half an hour later I got round to the Osafos with a rather limp bunch of carnations to find Ruby's grandfather trying to patch a hole in the flimsy door with an ill-fitting bit of plywood. He said he would have cut the wood to size but they had stolen his toolbox. The door had been kicked in for the third time in two years. They had also lost the big telly from the sideboard, the defunct computer, the portable CD player and, of course, my old laptop. All the drawers were emptied out, mattresses pulled off beds, books and clothes scattered across the floor. Mrs Osafo had always seemed to have a philosophical stoicism about her but today she looked utterly defeated. She just sat slumped in an armchair surrounded by the chaos. 'Why do people have to steal from us?' she said looking at me. 'We don't have nothing and they steal from us!'

All that nervous energy I had expended worrying about being a victim of crime. But people like me – people with burglar alarms and light sensors and electric gates – we aren't the ones whose lives are ruined by endless burglaries. We've got too much money to be robbed.

'I'm fed up with it . . .' she went on. 'Fed up with it . . .'

'Maybe the police will find who did it and get the stuff back . . .' I offered weakly.

'Maybe,' she said. 'The policeman said he was going to make a few enquiries.'

'Ah right. Well, there you are . . .'

'But why did he go and see you?'

'Well, he just wanted to ask . . . to check the value of the stolen laptop.'

I was surprised to see Ruby arrive at the door with a small bag of shopping. She placed a bar of chocolate in her granny's hand and her grandmother pulled her close and held her there as tears spilled from her closed eyes. 'You are a good girl, Ruby. You're a good girl.' I was embarrassed to be intruding on this private moment.

'Did you come home from school specially, Ruby?'

'No, I had the day off,' she said standing up. 'Gran is taking me to the open day at my new school.'

'We can't go to that now, Ruby,' announced her grandmother. 'I have too much to sort out here.'

Ruby's face fell. In the hallway her grandfather threw a piece of wood to the ground and swore in what I now knew was Ashanti.

'Let me take her,' I said.

'Oh no, you've done so much for her already . . .'

'No, really, I'd be happy to. You'd still like to go, wouldn't you, Ruby?'

'Oh yes please.'

'You've been the victim of a crime. It's the least I could do.'

Ruby was proud to be sitting up in the front seat of our big car and called out unnecessary 'hellos' to friends some distance away on the estate. She was enjoying the job of being my local guide; after so many months of me being the tutor, now the roles were reversed.

'So you've been to this school before, Ruby?' I asked her.

'Yes, lots of times. 'Cause my brother went there. You have to turn left after this garage.'

'I must say I've lived in this area for years and never known exactly where Battersea Comprehensive was. It's not like Chelsea College; you have to go past that every time you drive to the King's Road.' Inside I winced slightly at the careless mention of the name of the school that Ruby would not be attending. I could feel Ruby staring at me.

'Did you think Molly would pass the exam for Chelsea College?'

'Well, I kept my fingers crossed you know!' The lights were red and I braked slightly too sharply.

'You must have wanted her to go there *very much* . . .' she continued. 'Right at these traffic lights.'

'Er, well, yes I did, Ruby. But of course there are lots of good schools . . .'

'No, right! Not left!'

'Oh yes, sorry.' I swerved the four-wheel drive in the other direction and vaguely heard a cyclist's bell and the sound of somebody swearing at me. 'What was I saying, er, so, jolly good, yes. I'm sure you and Molly will be able to carry on being friends.'

'Were you worried that Molly might fail the exam?'

'Goodness, you're being very inquisitive today, Ruby. Well, all mothers worry, it comes with the territory – oh, look at that advert, that's a funny dog, isn't it?'

'But, like, would you have, like, given anything in the whole world-wide-web to get Molly into Chelsea College?'

I looked across at her.

'Carry straight on down here for a while,' she added.

'Er, well, no – I knew there were other schools. We just were keen for her to go to the same place as all her friends, like you're going to. Are we nearly there?'

'Nearly; it's left down here. But you must have been pleased when she got the scholarship?'

'Well, she's always been a very bright girl; she just didn't always do well in exams. She struggles a bit with her mathematics, but then she gets that from me. I'm useless at maths.'

'I know,' said Ruby. And then we were there.

My first impression of the school was of the incredible

diversity. I looked at what I think is traditionally referred to as the 'rainbow mix' of children ambling round the playground: scruffy kids, smart kids, black, white, tall, short, Sikh boys chatting with Chinese boys, children who judging by the iconography on their hats and bags worshipped gods ranging all the way from Nike to Adidas. We were taken round the school in small groups by a couple of sixth-formers whose job it was to answer any questions with an embarrassed mumble.

'How long has the new art block been open?'

'hmnem nmemn . . .'

'Really? Fascinating . . .'

'It's even better than the one at Chelsea College, isn't it, Ruby?' I wasn't exaggerating either; even the students' paintings on the wall were more interesting. Here the self-portraits weren't all the same colour.

Battersea Comprehensive actually looked a lot better than I'd expected. There was a sixth-form common room where a girl was about twenty pages into *Ulysses*, which was a lot further than I'd ever managed. There were computer suites where pupils were designing their own web pages and no one was shouting, 'David! Everything's disappeared off the screen again!' From the way that other mums had gossiped at Molly's school, I'd imagined some unruly run-down New York holding pen, with subway graffiti in the corridors and hooded youths selling the first years Bostik behind the bike shed. Spencer House parents were frightened of the pupils in this school without ever having been here. All fear is based on ignorance really. Except if you shared a flat with that American serial killer who ate all his victims, I suppose – then your fear wouldn't be based on ignorance. 'No, no, I am not at all ignorant about Jeffrey. There's nothing in the fridge and he's suggesting I have an early night; this fear is based on a thorough working knowledge of my flatmate's eating habits.'

The tour of the school allowed us to step into lessons that were in full flow, and a few of us stood at the back of a room of children learning French. It was remarkable – this boy couldn't have been more than thirteen but he read absolutely perfectly in front of the whole class. I wondered if Molly would learn to speak fluent French like that at Chelsea College.

'Thank you, Jean-Pierre,' said the teacher as he sat down.

I have to confess that when I saw the other mums and dads waving hello to one another and chatting to friends, I felt a little jealous of them. Ruby said hello to lots of people as we walked round. 'Who's she?' I quizzed when she first waved at an elderly white lady on the other side of the playground with a family.

'That's Vera.'

Oh right, I thought, that explains it. 'No, I mean, where do you know her from?'

'She used to help at Brownies.'

'What about them?' I asked when a passing mother and daughter said hello. 'Are they from your school?'

'No. Church.'

'What about her?'

'Er, I dunno where I know her from. She just lives in Clapham.'

I was learning that in the place where I lived there was a complex local community like some huge Venn diagram. There was, of course, a big overlap between the parents at Battersea Comprehensive and Ruby's junior school. Ruby's school also overlapped with the church in the high street. Both of those overlapped with the local charities and youth clubs, and then there were other rings containing babysitting circles and dog walkers on Clapham Common and evening classes at Lambeth College, and pub quiz teams who knew people who were involved in local politics who had neighbours who ran kids' football teams in Battersea Park who had shared a flat with the lady who delivered the meals on wheels to the old woman who used to be the lollipop lady outside Ruby's school. All of their lives were intertwined and connected, everybody knew someone who knew someone else, they were all stopping and chatting with one another, and I realized that I wasn't in this Venn diagram at all. I didn't overlap with any of them; my family and friends were in their very own isolated high-security private circle, somewhere on the edge of the page.

And it was apparent that the school's intake wasn't all Joe Public, there was the occasional Charles Public and Phoebe Public as well. Using the sophisticated polling method of counting the boys with angelic choirboy haircuts and the youths with shaven bullet heads, I could see that the middle-class kids were in the minority here, just like in the rest of society, I suppose. But there was enough of a social mix to make you feel uplifted about how everyone seemed to be getting along together. Because although it was the noisiest, busiest, most bustling, excited place imaginable, there was something about the atmosphere of this school that was like being allowed to lie back in a warm bath after years and years and years of running on the spot. There was far less urgent anxiety about all the other parents or their children; it was as if the place was saying to me, 'It's fine, Alice, it's OK. Just relax.' I caught myself rushing to be first through a door for the head teacher's talk, but then realized that another visitor wasn't competing to be first into the hall at all. She held the door open for me and Ruby and said, 'After you.'

'Sorry, thank you, sorry.' I felt ashamed of myself. Ffion wouldn't have held the door open for me. She would have brought a shepherd's crook to yank all the other people's children back by the neck.

As we filed into the hall, the school choir was singing on the stage. It had the effect of making you tiptoe swiftly to the nearest seat in case you distracted the children from their performance. No one left a gap – the other parents came and sat right next to you, half crouching lest they block the others' view, then discreetly waving at friends in the crowd or proudly pointing out children they knew in the choir. Ruby was transfixed by these older singers swaying gently to the tune they belted out from the stage, singing in imperfect harmony, which somehow made it all the more perfect. And when the hall was completely full and the doors were closed, I thought they would stop, but now that they had everyone's attention, the music teacher nodded to the piano player and began conducting one last number.

I couldn't help but chuckle to myself as the student piano player bashed out the opening chords of 'Bridge Over Troubled Water'. A 1970s weepy, aimed straight at the heart of all the grown-ups in the hall. I'd owned this album when I was a wide-eyed student but at some point in my mid-twenties I must have decided it was a bit corny because I hadn't listened to it since. I adopted a benign smile to hide the cynicism that so many years had put between myself and this song. Then the children started singing. Softly at first, but with a gentleness that alerted you to the vocal power they were holding back. And as the song built, the command that the choir had over their increasingly spellbound audience was almost tangible. I felt a lump building in my throat as the raw emotional power of all these beautiful children connected with some lost part of my life. The head teacher hadn't even spoken yet, but already he had me. In pure marketing terms it was the most persuasive argument that could ever be advanced for sending your child to a school. OK, Battersea didn't get as many children to the top universities as Chelsea College, and maybe the kids didn't look so smart or win the National Debating Competition two years in a row, but just listen to that stirring crescendo: how could anyone sitting there experience the passion of that tragic climax and not want to sign on the line there and then? Please let us send our children here, we haven't even looked at the league tables, we don't need to read the Ofsted report, the siren voices have persuaded us. There is no more direct route to a parent's heart than the sound of children singing, and as for a whole stage full of kids singing a song from our own childhood, well, that was it – total and unconditional surrender.

'Why are you laughing?' said Ruby.

'I'm not laughing, dear. I'm crying.'

Once they had finished there was an explosion of applause which had most of the room standing up and cheering, so that when the head teacher walked out to talk about his school he could have said whatever he wanted – he could have announced he planned to sell all the children for medical experiments on the first day of term, everyone would have agreed that this was a wonderful idea. Instead he thanked the choir and politely asked them to step down from the stage, which they did in perfect order, one row at a time, filing out of the hall, smiling with a quiet pride for what they had just achieved together, which broke into laughter when we applauded all over again. And then he gave a talk that was unlike any head teacher's talk I had heard since I had started worrying about secondary transfer about three weeks after Molly had started primary school.

He didn't list exam grades or awards or victories in sporting competitions but he did use the word 'happy' more than once. He talked about 'well-balanced children', 'considerate children', 'compassionate children', 'kids discovering what they loved to do, children learning respect for one another', and it was like somebody talking a new language that I'd never realized I was already completely fluent in. It wasn't all upbeat and positive; he got very serious and quite scary about bullying, which he called the single greatest enemy to the happiness of a child in a school, and his determination not to tolerate bullying of any sort made me want to stand up and shout, 'Yes, yes, yes!' He was inspiring, resolute, funny, moving and sincere. When the time came for us to ask about anything he might not have covered, the only question I could think of was, 'Could you please become the leader of a political party so that I can vote for you to be prime minister?'

Battersea Comprehensive had got a bad reputation back in the 1980s when it was chronically underfunded, but it turned out that a desperate shortage of money was, in fact, a problem that could be solved by throwing money at it. The head of English with whom I chatted about all this was clearly very proud of their new 'intranet' system and the new computer clusters and the interactive whiteboards, and I tried to pretend to know what he was talking about. I explained that Ruby was a friend of my daughter's; my child wasn't actually coming here. 'Well, she managed to get into Chelsea College. She's very bright, you see, so we felt we had to go private . . .' I gabbled apologetically.

'Mmm,' he concurred. 'Whereas my children on the other hand are very stupid. That's why my wife and I felt they should go through the state system . . .'

'Oh no, I didn't mean, well, I'm sure you have bright children here too . . .' I could feel my face going red.

'It's all right.' He smiled. 'We do have lots of bright children here, and before you ask, no, they are not held back, there are extension classes in most subjects. But a good education is about more that just how many grade As a child gets in their exams. You can't judge a school by its place on a league table.'

'No,' I said absently. 'Or a child . . .'

'Sorry?'

'Nothing.'

I was so happy that Ruby would be going to such a splendid comprehensive with all her classmates, just as Molly was going to a top school with all her friends. For a brief few days it seemed that all was well with the world. Surely now I could stop worrying so much that my hair was turning grey faster than I could have it recoloured?

But the golden age of peace and reassurance is always just over the next hill. Two days later Sarah was sacked from her job at Chelsea College. It was a terrible thing to happen to your best friend; a distressing personal humiliation that left one unable to do anything other than listen and nod in agreement.

'I was good at that job . . .'

'You were good at that job . . .'

'She had no right to sack me . . .'

'She had no right to sack you . . .'

'It's a rubbish school anyway . . .'

'Erm, yes, I expect it must feel like that to you right now . . .'

It had happened very suddenly. Sarah had not realized that all her questions about the school must have been irritating for the headmistress, but every anxious query about what subjects Kirsty would be doing, which class her daughter would be in, whether the children were allowed to have water in lessons ('still *and* sparkling?') – each one was an accumulating black mark against this busybody mother.

Because I had been so impressed with the headmistress, I found a small part of myself secretly blaming Sarah for what had happened. Apparently the dismissal when it came had been executed with ruthless charm and good manners; the headmistress just didn't think Sarah was 'a Chelsea College sort of admin assistant . . .' William said that this was the preferred upper-class phraseology for all forms of exclusion or dismissal. 'Anne Boleyn learnt she was going to have her head chopped off when her husband said with a charming smile, "I just don't think you're a Henry VIII sort of wife."' The head teacher hadn't said anything about withdrawing her daughter's place from the school, but Sarah was no longer so sure she wanted Kirsty to go there anyway.

'You can't pull Kirsty out now. It wouldn't be fair to take her away from all her friends . . .' I reasoned calmly, quietly panicking inside.

'Well, we've got nowhere else to go anyway. But Chelsea College is not so great, you know, Alice, not now I've seen it close up . . .'

'Well, no school is perfect, especially if they've just sacked you. But we have to hold our nerve now . . .'

'I mean, if a child doesn't fit their narrow mould of what an Oxbridge-bound pupil should be like, then they're just not interested in them . . .'

'Wow, imagine Molly going to Oxford or Cambridge . . .' whispered the devil on my shoulder.

'If a child presents them with a problem, they just expel them.'

'No problem children to distract your child . . .' the devil continued.

'They care more about academic averages than they do about the individual children.'

'A school with high averages! How perfect for your kids!' countered the wicked voice in my ear.

'And some of the children . . . well, they're just rude. Arrogant and rude. All their lives they have been told they are innately superior and perfect and they really believe it.'

Ah, but my children would never be like that . . . I thought. Because only my children are completely perfect . . .

But what had been a mildly humiliating rebuff for Sarah turned into a disaster a couple of days later when they received a letter informing them that since Sarah was no longer an employee of the school they could no longer justify giving a place to a pupil whose entrance exam result was below the expected standard. Although the note was dictated by the head teacher, it was signed in her absence – presumably by Sarah's replacement as admin assistant. I couldn't believe it. That charming liberal headmistress I had met – this must have been forced upon her by the governors or something. Sarah and William were utterly shell-shocked. Less than two and a half months until the start of the autumn term and suddenly Kirsty had no secondary school to go to. Sarah said they were appealing, and had even written to their local MP, but suddenly everything seemed uncertain once again. She wept and wept down the phone to me and at some deep level I felt this must somehow be connected with my initial misdemeanour.

I decided I would try to cheer them up by taking them on a surprise evening out to the theatre. 'Is it the National?' quizzed Sarah as she climbed into the car, looking, I realized, a little overdressed for the occasion.

'Not exactly . . .'

'The Royal Shakespeare Company?' asked William.

'Not Shakespeare, no – maybe England's second greatest writer . . .'

'Fantastic!' said William. 'It's that Jeffrey Archer play . . .'

At first I was pleased when I heard that Battersea Comprehensive would be doing the classic musical *Oliver!* A good Dickensian story, some great songs and a couple of weepies to boot; how would Sarah and William be able to resist that? But it was only when the performance began that I realized they were doing a reinterpreted version set in the present day. The songs had all been rewritten to say things like, 'Who Will Buy This Week's *Big Issue*?' and 'You Gotta Nick a Mobile or Two!' Fagin's gang consisted of a lot of dodgy-looking fifteen-year-olds with their hoods up. 'The muggers looked worryingly convincing,' said William in the interval. 'I wonder how much research they did?'

'Interesting idea to make Oliver Twist an asylum seeker . . .' Sarah chirped bravely. 'I suppose that has the stigma that an orphan would have had in Victorian times.'

'Either that or they needed an excuse for why he could barely speak English.'

'No, he just has rather a strong accent, that's all. Nice pictures . . .' I added as I finished my lukewarm cup of tea with biscuit. William was staring at the programme: a single sheet of folded yellow A4 listing the cast, with some fairly amateurish scratchy drawings round the edges.

'Hmm . . . I think the Royal Academy is safe for another year.'

I had only meant to plant the possibility of this school in the minds of Sarah and William, but I found myself willing them to like it as much as I had, and I watched their every reaction to the teachers and the other parents. Please make the play better, I wished; make it so good they will think about sending Kirsty here with Ruby . . .

By the time Nancy successfully fought off Bill Sikes using Thai-Bo, I had developed a headache from facing the stage while trying to gauge Sarah and William's reactions alongside me. At the end William applauded politely, even though his mind was clearly somewhere else. We peeked in a couple of classrooms on the way out, and they nodded inscrutably as I pointed out the computers and the new sixth form and the art block. But they were very quiet. I feared that they were silently appalled by it all.

It was very subdued in the curry house afterwards. I realized it was impossible not to make a comparison with the operetta we had seen a couple of weeks earlier, and clearly the production at Chelsea College had been much, much better. None of us spoke as we pretended to stare at the menus that we knew off by heart. The only noise came from David breaking little bits off his poppadom as if he was working on some two-dimensional sculpture.

'What are you doing?'

'Trying to make Cyprus,' he replied, proudly holding up a shape I think we were supposed to recognize.

'Very good,' I said. It looked like a bit of poppadom to me. He attempted one more tiny adjustment, but swore as the whole of the northern peninsula snapped off. 'Shit! Cyprus has split in two,' he announced. 'Appropriate enough, I suppose . . .' he added before dipping the

Turkish half of the island in the mango chutney and popping it in his mouth. 'You have a go, William . . .' he said.

'What?'

'Making a country . . .'

William clearly wasn't really in the mood and lifted up the spiciest tub of pickle. 'Chile,' he said.

'Very good. Actually Chile is about the hardest country of all. It always snaps somewhere north of Santiago . . .'

'David, I think they've got more important things on their mind . . .' and that was the cue for Sarah to break down in tears.

'It's just not fair, everyone's got a school except Kirsty . . . Five different tests she had to take. Two and a half years' extra tutoring and for what? To have no school to go to, no place anywhere, totally rejected at the age of eleven.'

William put his arm round his wife and David looked a little sheepish as he popped Greek Cyprus into his mouth. I told her she might yet win her appeal to the governors at Chelsea and she wiped the tears from her eyes. The waiter looked a little concerned. 'Is everything all right, madam?'

'Yes, yes, it's just this hot Indian food . . .' she said sniffing, pointing to the little tub of cucumber raitha.

'Well, I just wanted you to see Battersea . . .' I mumbled. 'Just in case it might be an option. But I know the play was a bit . . . well, I've never seen a version of *Oliver!* in which Fagin was served with an antisocial behaviour order.'

'No, splendid idea . . .' announced my husband, clearly gearing up to launch into a sarcastic overdrive. 'In order to plant the idea of sending their privately educated middle-class child to the local comprehensive, you took them to a play about an upper-class orphan abandoned into a den of kids from the criminal underclass. Perfect! Spot on!' And at least this prompted Sarah to laugh a little.

'Look, I know the Chelsea College play was much more impressive—'

'Yes,' said William, cutting in. 'That's exactly what Chelsea's play was. More impressive.'

'But you can't judge schools by which one put on the best play.'

'No one said Chelsea did the best school play,' he asserted. 'I said theirs was more impressive. Different thing entirely.'

Sarah looked up from where she had been dejectedly pushing some pickle around her plate. 'What do you mean?'

'Chelsea's play was more impressive because that was the object of the exercise. To impress. Don't you see? Chelsea's play was put on for the parents. Battersea's was for the children.'

The waiter carried a loud sizzling curry dish behind me and for the first time ever I didn't turn round to see what it was. It sounded like my insides felt.

'In *The Pirates of Penzance*, the child who was the very best singer sang the solo . . .' he continued. 'So what? They know he can sing; what does anybody gain from that? But did you see the expression of the child who sang the solo in *Oliver!* She wasn't a trained vocalist, but she tried her very hardest and then gave that little smile when everyone clapped and cheered; you knew that this was the biggest thing that she'd ever had to do in her whole life. After she came off the stage did you see the way her teacher crouched down and told her how fantastically she had done?'

'Er, no, I was watching you two most of the time . . .' I stammered.

The waiter wheeled a trolley of curry dishes beside the table and ostentatiously wiped the plates as he placed them in front of us.

'Battersea's play wasn't staged to impress us, the parents,

the consumers,' continued William, 'it was put on to help the children develop, to build their confidence, to teach them about creating something together, attempting things they had never thought themselves capable of. The Chelsea play kept the shy children off the stage, banned the mediocre singers from singing; Sarah told me that the other lead performers in *Pirates* were not even from Chelsea College. They borrowed the best singers from another school!'

'No?'

'That is true, actually,' confirmed Sarah.

'What sort of message does that send to the other kids? And it turns out that brilliant soloist sang the solo last year and the year before, so tough luck all the other kids. That wasn't a school play. It was an exercise in PR, to make the parents feel better about paying out so much in school fees.'

'Hang on, it wasn't that bad,' I heard myself saying in defence of Molly's next school. 'I mean, the kids were still quite cute . . .'

'It was awful,' he went on. 'A complete sham. All the values are all upside down. It's not "Can you get better?", it's "If you're not already the very best, don't even bother turning up" . . . At Battersea I nearly cried when Nancy sang "As Long As He Needs Me" even if I didn't recognize that line about "having a career to fall back on if the marriage doesn't work out".'

There was a stunned silence around the table.

'Well, it's certainly a very cosmopolitan school . . .' said Sarah, terrified of mentioning the word 'race'.

'One chicken tikka masala,' said the waiter.

'Thank you.'

'Isn't that part of what their education should be about?' said her husband.

'One king prawn korma?'

'Over here.'

'Don't we want them to mix with Muslims and Hindus and Afro-Caribbeans?'

'And one steak and chips . . .'

'Er – that's mine, thank you,' said William. 'Sorry, I don't really like curry . . .'

'Well, anyway . . .' said Sarah. 'We'll see if the governors at Chelsea College let Kirsty back in and then we'll take it from there . . .'

'Excuse me,' I said, calling back the waiter. 'What is the Bengali for "thank you"?'

'*Dhonnobaad.*'

'I've been coming to this curry house for ten years and I don't even know how to say thank you. So, er – *dhonnobaad.*'

'You're welcome, luv, innit.'

The subject was dropped and we found something more agreeable and reassuring to talk about: things that really annoy us about Ffion. Apparently their au pair had quit because she wanted a job with less stress. William said she'd applied for a job with Air Iraq. David ordered himself a lager, which inadvertently informed me that I was driving home. Since the equality of the sexes had not yet extended to a man ever being the slightest bit concerned about what time we got home for the babysitter, Sarah and I eventually left them in the restaurant while they ordered brandies and pondered such profound emotional issues as: 'If the Nazis had won the Second World War, would The Beatles still have recorded *Sergeant Pepper's?*'

I had offered Sarah a lift home and we headed down the high street together towards my car. 'That's one of those completely ridiculous arguments, isn't it?'

'Totally. I mean, Hitler would never have allowed all those psychedelic army uniforms for a start.'

I had parked down a side road. A couple of street lights were out, and away from the main drag the shadows suddenly felt colder and more isolated as the moon disappeared behind the clouds.

'Hang on, now where are we, ah yes, I came down this alley . . .'

In the middle of some low-rise council houses was a narrow paved path, and I felt a shudder of nerves from Sarah as she followed me into the brick-built warren, but it was only eleven o'clock, the pubs hadn't even emptied out yet. I'm sure it's safe, I told myself.

Three youths appeared on the pathway ahead of us. They had been around the corner, just waiting there, three teenage black boys with their hoods up loitering by the bend in the path. One of them was sitting astride a pushbike, the other two were leaning against the wall. If we wanted to get past we would have to walk through the middle of them. Sarah grasped my arm as our pace involuntarily slowed. 'Oh my God . . .' she stammered. 'This is it.' Her arm was shaking. 'Let's turn round,' she whispered. I could feel her body tensing up; she was squeezing my arm so hard that it hurt. Finally we were face to face with them.

'Oh hello Kofi, hello Carl, hello Aubrey-from-Norbury,' I announced brightly.

'Hello, Mrs Chaplin . . .' they mumbled.

'Kofi, I meant to ask you, did you get on to that fashion design course at the college?'

'Nah, I've got to have an interview. I'm going next week . . .'

'Oh well, good luck. And Aubrey, how are you?'

'I've finished college now. I'm working at Blockbuster for a bit.'

'Oh well, I'll see you in there. Give my regards to your family, Kofi.'

'Yeah, all right.'

And we walked on. I said nothing to Sarah, even though I could feel her incredulous eyes boring into the side of my face. It was as if some aliens had stepped out of a flying saucer and I had effortlessly conversed with them in fluent Venutian.

'How on earth do you know them?' she said when we were safely seated in my car and she had pressed down the door lock.

'They live round here. Except Aubrey-from-Norbury, he lives in, er, Norbury. But the other two live very close to you, as a matter of fact.'

'I've never seen them before.'

'You've probably seen them hundreds of times. But just never looked at them, that's all.'

'Fancy that enormous boy wanting to be a clothes designer. Is he gay?'

'I don't think so.'

'It's such a tragedy when young people aren't given the guidance towards the right careers. Do you know what occurs to me: he might well have a great future ahead of him as a professional basketball player, but I bet no one has ever suggested it.'

The next day David was in the garden playing table tennis with Jamie. I watched them rally back and forth for a while. David even contrived to use ping-pong scores to give Jamie extra lessons on important dates from history.

'Seventeen fifteen. First Jacobite rebellion!' chimed David as he hit the ball into the net. David served again and then deliberately missed Jamie's return.

'Eighteen fifteen. Battle of Waterloo.'

'David . . .' I interjected. 'Would you be interested in maybe having a proper look round Battersea Comprehensive?'

'What on earth for?' he said, trying not to look away from where he was patiently returning every eager shot from our bouncing, effervescent son.

'Er, well, it's just that we never really considered it, and maybe Molly should have a chance to look at it before we finally definitely commit to Chelsea.'

'We have definitely committed to Chelsea: we've bought the uniform, sent back the form and told Molly that's where she's going. Eighteen sixteen. Argentina declares independence. Anyway, shouldn't you be taking Molly to ballet by now?'

'Oh, she said she doesn't want to go, so I told her that's fine . . .' I shrugged as if this was how our family normally operated.

'What has got into you lately? Why don't we take both kids out of school as well – they can just watch Cartoon Network all day and we'll keep our fingers crossed that *The Powerpuff Girls* is one of their set texts at A level.'

'Are we going to get Cartoon Network?' batted Jamie optimistically from the other side of the ping-pong table.

'No!' returned his father with an unequivocal forehand lob.

'No, school *is* important,' I continued calmly. 'But why can't we just lighten up a bit? What does it matter if she has nothing to do sometimes? Maybe it would be good for her to be bored sometimes, and have free time that she has to learn to fill on her own?'

'Come on, Dad!'

David absently served again, too hard for Jamie to return the shot.

'Damn, now you made me win my point. It should have been nineteen sixteen, Battle of the Somme. I don't know anything that happened in 1817. It matters because we agreed we wanted her to grow into a fully rounded adult who isn't going to turn around to us and say, "You never gave me the chance to learn ballet or play the violin or understand mathematics" – because childhood is the best time to learn all these things. And if we let her just give everything up when she can't be bothered, then she'll never do anything with her life, will she? Nineteen seventeen – Russian Revolution!'

'What about having fun? What about just mucking about? When did we last timetable that in?'

'Jamie and I are having fun right now. We're just playing table tennis, which also improves his hand–eye coordination. You make it sound like we never let up, like it's all learning and constant cramming, but it isn't. Nineteen eighteen. End of World War One.'

'Good, well Molly doesn't think ballet would be much fun this evening and if she wants to relax instead of climbing back in the car for the next appointment in her packed schedule, then that's fine by me.'

And with his father irritated and distracted, Jamie sent a low shot spinning over the net, which sent his father completely the wrong way and had him clumsily banging into the corner of the table and clutching his side in pain.

'Twenty eighteen . . .' said Jamie triumphantly, 'Dad gets a new hip.'

The following morning the debate continued. I had just returned from dropping Molly and Jamie off at Spencer House and was clearing up the chaos of the breakfast table when I saw David studying the slight changes I'd made to the children's timetable, which was pinned up by the fridge.

'What's this that Jamie has to do between five and six on Monday evenings?'

'*Whatever.*'

'What do you mean, *Whatever*?'

'Er, that's his new subject. I'm cancelling French, because I'm worried that he's falling behind in *Whatever*.'

'I don't understand.'

'Oh yes, and on Tuesdays, if you look, from now on Molly's got *Double Whatever*. I want her to be top of the class in *Whatever*. To take her GCSE *Whatever* a year early.'

'What if she doesn't want to do *Whatever*?'

'Well, you know. *Whatever*.'

'I know why you're being like this. It's because of William, isn't it?'

'What on earth are you talking about?'

'Look, we are not suddenly changing the whole ethos of our children's upbringing just because William has been forced to see Battersea Comprehensive in a wonderful idealistic new light.'

'This has nothing to do with what William thinks . . .'

'Of course it does. He wouldn't be talking like that if they still had their place at Chelsea College. You watch, the moment they win their appeal they'll be straight back in the fold.'

'And if they don't win, Kirsty will go to school with Ruby and her friends, and think how much better the world would be if we all went to school together . . .'

'Sure. I agree. In a perfect world that would happen. But we don't live in happy-bunny fairytale land – we live in inner London, and *you* try and change the world if you want to, but don't use our daughter as the first wave of infantry.'

'Oh, will you just shut up about *war* for five minutes. You've completely missed the point. Maybe this way would be better for society *and our daughter* – that's what I'm saying. I am a selfish mother, I only want what's best for Molly. That's why I want to be completely sure that she's going to the school where I think she will be *happiest*. And I'm just not sure that's the school where she'll have two hours' homework every night and feel a failure if she doesn't get five A levels at grade A and an unconditional offer from Oxford.'

'Cambridge,' corrected my husband.

'What – you've already decided which top university she is going to, have you? I bet you've already chosen a particular college!' His embarrassed silence revealed that my sarcasm was spot on. 'You *have* decided which college you think she should go to, haven't you?'

'No, I was, er, just scrolling through a website and it happened to mention Trinity College, Cambridge, and I thought that would be a good college for Molly . . .'

'What was the website?'

'Oh, I can't remember . . .'

'What was the website?'

'All right, it was Choose Your Child's University dot com. Look, I know she's still at junior school, but we have to start thinking about these things now . . .'

'No, we have to *avoid* thinking about it now, because the kids pick up on it, they feel the pressure. It wasn't until I put myself in the place of one of my children that I realized we were forcing them to be adults. That's why I want us to be really sure we know what we are doing before we send her to Chelsea. Because once Molly finds herself on that academic hamster wheel, she won't be able to stop running until her childhood is over.'

He didn't have time to answer. At that moment the front doorbell rang and I strode down the hall muttering to myself.

Why did I still feel so much anxiety, even though my long-standing wish for Molly had been granted? Maybe the abrupt change in pressure had been too much for me; maybe I'd got the bends. Was that what all this worry was about, was it purely a physical need to keep fretting about something? Far-off school playing fields seem greener – or, rather, they would do if they hadn't all been flogged off to developers years ago.

I opened the front door, wiping my hands on my apron, and a striking black lady stood towering above me.

'I'm Ruby's mother,' she said.

'At last! I've been wanting to meet you for so long!'

'Who is it?' shouted David down the corridor.

'It's Ruby's mother! Come and say hello.'

She must have been well over a foot taller than me and wore a bright red leather jacket. There was definitely a family re-semblance, but where Ruby's face was open and optimistic, her mother's face was somehow severe and intense. 'We've been so hoping we would get to meet you,' I continued, 'Ruby's such a lovely girl.'

David joined me in the doorway but our welcoming smiles were not returned.

'You stole my child's place,' she spat.

'I beg your pardon?'

'You stole it. Ruby told me she sat next to you in the Chelsea College entrance exam and you pretended to be your daughter.' I noticed that she was shaking.

'Now hang on a minute,' interjected David.

'No wonder your daughter got the scholarship! Because you stole it from mine by copying her answers.'

It was then I spotted a scared-looking Ruby waiting back on the pavement, failing to make herself invisible behind a lamppost.

'That is a ludicrous allegation,' said David. 'No one would ever believe you.'

'Is that a challenge?' she said. 'Right. Well, I'm going straight to Chelsea College to tell them.'

The Secret of Good Parenting
***How to ensure your child has the best possible start
in life***
By Alice Chaplin – Prisoner number FG 489775

Sunrise Books £6.99

*Children learn by example and the best start you
can give your child is being sent to prison for
fraud. Nothing will beat the quality time you'd
be able to spend reading to your children during
their monthly visits to Holloway Gaol. Watching
Mum being found guilty of attempting to swindle a
charitable trust fund will teach them all the values
and morals that you always hoped they would take
out into the world. A high-profile trial in which
the child's name is constantly repeated in the
press and on the television will do wonders for
your child's self-esteem, especially if, for example,
the world was to learn that you thought disguising
yourself as a hideous and spotty weirdo was the best
way to impersonate your sensitive eleven-year-old
daughter.*

*And how much better if their father could be an
accessory to the crime! If he too was to receive a*

custodial sentence, your children might be lucky enough to be taken into care by social services, which is widely recognized as exactly the sort of stable, loving environment in which high-achieving children can really thrive!

— II —

'Come on, come on!' shouted David throughout the interminable seconds that we waited for our electric gates to heave themselves open. David was poised in the driving seat like a greyhound in a trap. He revved the engine and then screeched off the moment that the gap between them was wide enough, our spinning wheels sending gravel from the drive flying up against our front door.

'We have to get there before she does.'

'What are we going to say?' Inside I was still hoping that there might be another way out of this that did not involve me entering that darkest of dragon's lairs, the headmistress's office. I had this nightmarish vision of me standing in front of the principal's desk staring at the floor in frozen silence as she repeatedly asked me to explain myself.

'We'll say she's making it up, of course. I mean, that's just how desperate these parents are to get their kids into the right school; these are the sort of lengths that they will go to, inventing a story as ludicrous as this.' The 4x4 changed gear with a guttural roar as David drove it at full speed down the long straight racetrack of Oaken Avenue. A mother with a pushchair had been about to cross the road but was forced to pull back from between the cars and shouted angrily at us as we zoomed past.

David was right. If we got to Chelsea College first, we could warn the headmistress that there was a desperate mother going around making wild allegations; we could say how distressing it was for us and that we just wanted to warn her so that she could protect the good name of the school. Then by the time Ruby's mother actually burst in, the head would treat her with scepticism and maybe outright hostility. I just thought it might be better if David did this on his own while I waited in the car.

'And what was that nonsense about you copying your answers from Ruby? I mean, the woman's clearly unhinged!' he said, speeding down a side road.

'Er, no, I um . . . I did copy some answers from Ruby actually . . .'

'WHAT?' He turned his head to face me. A car tooted and David swerved to avoid it. 'You copied your answers off Ruby?'

'Only a few. Some of the trickier maths questions . . .'

'But that's cheating . . .' he said as if some moral line had been crossed by this adult pretending to be a child.

We swung out into the main road. 'Thank God!' he declared, seeing that the traffic was flowing freely. 'We'll be there in five minutes.'

'I still say we should have telephoned first . . .'

'No, the head might have been in a meeting or something and we would've been given an appointment in a week's time while Ruby's mum was in there ranting and raving about us. About *you* copying off her daughter!'

'Oh my God, there she is!' I shouted. Ahead of us the striking figure of Ruby's mother was standing on the pavement, looking out for a bus with Ruby standing beside her. Suddenly it felt as if it was going to be a lot more difficult to lie.

We drove straight past them. I realized I'd put my hand up to obscure my face as we'd got near, but Ruby's mother wasn't interested in passing cars. She still looked angry but I couldn't help but feel a tinge of pity mixed with guilt as I saw them standing there so helpless. I thought it probably not worth suggesting to David that we stop and offer a lift for a second time. We were two mothers engaged in a desperate race, but it was a race that she was forced to undertake using public transport. Her powerlessness could not have been more obvious if she'd been chained to the bus stop. This is how the battle lines were drawn: four-wheel drive versus double-decker bus. Public versus private, the past versus the future. Surely it would be no contest?

Objectively speaking, I knew that she was right and I was wrong. But I believed I possessed the card that counted for more than any collective social morality: I was a mother doing what I believed was best for my own children, and that is the ace of trumps that tops everything else in the pack. Yet after we passed her I could feel myself shaking. My insides felt like they were at the centre of some terrible earthquake: two tectonic plates impacting. In one world I had merely assisted my daughter through her entrance exam and then been kind enough to help another child. But in this other world that was now crashing into my consciousness I had robbed a disadvantaged child of her one chance to get a privileged education, cheated and lied and deceived my own daughter, and it was all about to erupt and I would be publicly disgraced.

'Faster, come on!' I urged David as we hovered behind a lorry. 'Overtake him on the inside . . .'

'Shit!' said David, looking in his mirror. 'Her bus is here . . .' I looked round to see a 137, the one route that went all the way there. We were still over a hundred yards ahead when Ruby and her mother climbed on board.

'But the bus is going to have to keep stopping. Surely we must get there ages before they do,' I said. 'I can't believe she was so stupid as to speak to us before she went to the school . . .' I added.

'Well, she was acting emotionally, not rationally, wasn't she? Typical woman. WHAT IS THIS BLOODY IDIOT DOING?' ranted my husband as we ground to a halt and a stream of traffic flowed by on our nearside. 'Oh, now he indicates right . . . Stupid bastard!' he screamed. Luckily David seemed to know some secret driver's code for this situation and he gave the special signal that meant: 'The vehicle behind requests you move out of the way as quickly as possible.' It involved pressing his horn and holding it down for ages.

'Can't you cut in?'

'There's no gap . . .'

Cars continued to whizz by us as the bus got closer. It was then that we saw that the lorry driver had climbed out of his cab and was coming across to remonstrate with us.

'What is your problem, pal?' he said aggressively. 'Do you want some or what?'

On reflection David decided that he didn't 'want some', although it was a very kind offer. He had a strict rule never to get into an argument with any man with cobweb tattoos on his neck. He quickly reversed back up the road and now at last he managed to cut into the traffic, but only after the bus had gone steaming straight past us.

Ahead of us I saw a little boy was walking beside his mother and my heart sank as I saw that they were passing a pelican crossing. No small child can pass a button without pressing it, and sure enough, as they ambled straight past, his little index finger casually activated the pedestrian light control. He didn't even look round to where a couple in a Land Rover Discovery were shouting obscenities as they screeched to a halt. David's fingers drummed impatiently on the steering wheel: ten seconds, twenty seconds – still the pointlessly red traffic light refused to change. And then he quickly looked all around to check there were no police cars within sight before he just took off, driving straight through the red light and prompting the elderly driver behind to begin to follow before anxiously stopping once again and looking confused.

Ms Osafo's bus was now a hundred yards ahead of us. It taunted us by stopping to pick up a few more passengers and then politely indicated while some idiot lorry driver actually stopped to let the bus pull out. It was so selfish. There was a big sticker on the back of the lorry that said, 'How's my driving?' followed by the freephone number of some road safety agency that you were supposed to ring on your mobile while you were speeding along. I wanted to call the number to let them know. 'This lorry's driving is completely in-considerate. He just stopped to let a bus pull out.'

Ahead the road widened into two lanes. The right-hand lane was jammed solid with queuing private cars. The left-hand side was a completely empty bus lane, with only Ms Osafo's bus zooming up towards Chelsea. They never had this problem in the Monaco Grand Prix. 'And there goes Schumacher in the Ferrari, but oh no, he's hit the rush-hour traffic and he's not allowed in the bus lane between 7am and

9pm, and suddenly he's overtaken by some elderly shoppers on board a big red double-decker . . .'

Public Transport was increasing its lead, Private Transport was not moving at all. 'Go in the bus lane, go in the bus lane . . .' David shouted to the car that blocked the way in front of us. Public Transport sailed through a green light; Private Transport revved its engine hoping this might edge the rest of the traffic forwards. The empty road stretched out like some exclusive business-class avenue, but instead of crossing the white-painted Rubicon that separated the unused half of the road, the lemming in front patiently inched his way forward to take his place in the choking traffic jam that stretched out into the hazy distance.

Finally David was able to mount the pavement to squeeze past the car in front, manoeuvring the 4x4 into the bus lane where he could race past the line of patiently queuing traffic on our right. With half a dozen bus stops between here and Sloane Street, soon we would be back in front and first to Chelsea College; nothing was going to stop us now. It was then a policeman in a Day-Glo jacket stepped out into the bus lane and very unequivocally directed that we pull over. David may have momentarily considered running over and killing him, but though we'd already stretched the boundaries of acceptable morality, he must have concluded that this might have been overstepping the line.

We arrived at Chelsea College around twenty minutes later.

'Remember we should remain calm and reasonable . . .' gabbled David as we scurried into the reception. 'If she's been all angry and mad, that'll help when it comes down to our word against hers . . .'

'You sound like you've got it all worked out – are you sure

you wouldn't rather speak to her on your own while I wait in the car?'

It turned out that Ms Osafo and her daughter had only been admitted to speak to the headmistress a few minutes earlier. The school secretary was adamant that we could not go in, but David insisted that we had come to help clear up a misunderstanding that was being discussed in the head's office at that very moment. A brief hushed conversation took place on the other side of the closed door and suddenly Miss Reynolds appeared with a smile and an outstretched hand. If it hadn't been the middle of summer the whole school could have been heated by the glow from my reddening face.

'Mr and Mrs Chaplin, how nice to see you again . . .' she beamed, even though she'd never met David before. 'It appears that we have another parent making a rather serious allegation about your daughter's entrance exam. If you bear with me I will try and finish with the lady in question and then perhaps we could have a little chat?'

This sounded ominous. David glanced at me and then blurted: 'Well, if false allegations are being made against us then I think we have the right to hear them.'

'Er, well, Ms Osafo has her daughter with her. I don't think we want her witnessing any sort of ugly scene.'

I saw a possible way through this.

'Would it help if David came in on his own and I just waited in the car . . .'

'Although,' Miss Reynolds continued, 'Mrs Osafo seems quite calm and I usually find that animosity evaporates when people actually get together and talk these little problems through . . .'

And so the door was swung open. The headmistress's office beckoned, and I took a deep breath as I stepped over the threshold. The witnesses for the prosecution were already seated on the other side. Ms Osafo was impassive; Ruby was even worse at hiding her embarrassment than I was.

'Hello, Ruby,' I said as neutrally as possible.

'Hello,' she said without her usual smile. Beside Miss Reynolds sat the clerk of the court, Mr Worrall, the nervous deputy head whom I recognized from our first visit to the school. He gestured for us to take a seat after his boss suggested we take a seat. Finally Lady Justice Reynolds took her place and inhaled deeply in preparation for a very difficult hearing. What would happen if I was found guilty here in this very courtroom? Would Miss Reynolds place a black cap upon her head before she passed sentence on me? Would the tabloids call me the most evil woman in Britain? Would a mob of fat people be waiting outside to spit at me as I was bundled into the police van with a coat over my head?

'Right . . . now I understand that Ms Osafo has already communicated the nature of her allegation to you . . .'

'Yes,' said David.

'Yes,' I confirmed.

There was an awkward silence. A police siren wailed in the distance. David cleared his throat. Nobody quite knew where to begin.

'Why don't I make everyone a cup of tea?' suddenly chirped an upbeat Mr Worrall, getting to his feet. 'Cup of tea, Mrs Chaplin?'

'Er, not for me, thank you.'

'Tea or coffee, Mr Chaplin?'

'Nothing, thank you.'

'Ms Osafo – how do you take your tea?'

'Milk and two sugars . . .'

'Milk and two sugars coming right up.'

'But I don't want one right now, thank you.'

'Oh . . .' he said as he sat down again. 'Ruby, I don't suppose you drink tea yet, do you?'

'Yes please,' she said, and I couldn't help feeling vaguely proud of her as the deputy headmaster found himself forced to get up again and go and switch on the kettle for this eleven-year-old girl. I noticed that Miss Reynolds now had her fingers pressed to her temples as she attempted to refocus above the noise of the clattering around by the sink in the corner.

'So you are aware of the allegation made by Ms Osafo and her daughter here, and I presume from what you just said outside the office that you completely deny this.'

David was magnificent and appalling all at the same time. Instead of being cross and indignant, he played it like the understanding social worker: not angry so much as concerned. 'Look, we are as aware as any family of the terrible stress that all these examinations and tests place on young children. We've got to know Ruby here over the past few months and it must have been very hard for her to see Molly, who already has so much, also get one of the coveted scholarships to Chelsea College. Now I don't think Ruby is deliberately lying. Rather that in her disappointment she has convinced herself that she was robbed of her place as her way of coping. It's a surprisingly common syndrome . . .'

Miss Reynolds seemed very reassured by this; she had given little positive nods of her head as he talked but her face perceptibly fell as Ruby's mother cut in.

'I know my daughter and she doesn't tell lies.'

'I think what Mr Chaplin is saying, Ms Osafo, is that *to Ruby* this isn't telling lies; that in her mind this really happened because it is less painful for her than to deal with what really did happen, that is to say—'

'Sorry . . .' interrupted Mr Worrall from the other side of the room. 'Ruby, there only seems to be Earl Grey tea, is that all right?'

Miss Reynolds pinched the top of her nose and gave the impression she had suddenly developed an overpowering migraine.

'What's Earl Grey?' asked Ruby.

'It's like ordinary tea except it's flavoured with bergamot.'

'What's bergamot?'

'It's like a flavouring that they use in, well, Earl Grey tea; it's quite nice . . .'

'OK.'

'THAT IS TO SAY . . .' continued Miss Reynolds emphatically, 'that is to say, um, I'm sorry, I've completely lost my train of thought now . . .'

'I know my daughter and she wouldn't make this up. Ruby, tell the lady what you told me . . .'

Ruby glanced nervously at me and then stared at the floor before speaking slowly and quietly.

'In the exam I sat next to Mrs Chaplin, only she didn't look like that. She was wearing children's clothes and wore glasses and had spots on her face.'

'But you said it was definitely her?' prompted her mother.

'Hang on, you're putting words into her mouth there . . .' objected David.

'It was definitely her,' confirmed Ruby without looking at me.

Ruby's certainty coupled with this extra detail seemed to add a worrying credibility to her story. David felt forced to take a dangerous line of attack that would never stand up if pursued any further.

'Well, all I can say is that our own daughter has a very clear memory of sitting the exam, and that I remember bringing her here and collecting her afterwards, and so it is a case of Ruby's word against everyone else's . . . I mean, I could go and get Molly out of school and you can ask her about the exam if you want . . .'

Miss Reynolds considered this for a terrifying second.

'No, I don't think we need to go that far . . .'

'Digestive biscuit, Ruby?'

'No thank you.'

'Ruby, do you know any other children who got scholarships?' quizzed David.

'What do you mean?'

'Apart from Molly – do you know any other children who have got into Chelsea College – kids from your school, for example, any neighbours or friends?'

'Er, no?'

'Isn't it something of a coincidence that the one person you made this claim about happens to be the only person you know who's got into the school?'

There was a moment's silence. Miss Reynolds looked suitably impressed with this point.

'What difference does that make?' interjected Ms Osafo. 'She'd have to know you to recognize you, innit? You stole her place by cheating and we just want it back.'

The head interjected quickly to prevent the temperature rising. 'Now, Ms Osafo, I have to remind you that this is a very serious allegation and many schools wouldn't have invited you here to hear your side of the story at all . . .'

'You didn't invite me, I just come.'

'Er, no, but my point is that we have to proceed with—'

'Sorry, Ruby, do you take milk and sugar?' shouted Mr Worrall from the other side of the office.

'Yes please.'

'That's milk *and* sugar?'

'Yes please . . .'

'We have to proceed with—'

'How many sugars?'

'Two please.'

'What was I saying?' frowned Miss Reynolds.

'You don't even need a scholarship. You've already got a big house and flash car – like what's the point of giving a scholarship to rich people?'

'Oh dear, this is degenerating into exactly the sort of horribleness that I was hoping we might be able to avoid. That is an entirely separate issue, Ms Osafo; suffice to say it is not the school's business to go prying into parents' financial status.' The brusqueness of Miss Reynolds's tone made it clear that she felt inclined to take our side in this dispute. We were almost there.

Mr Worrall placed the tea down in front of Ruby, who thanked him quietly. It looked like this would be all she would be getting from Chelsea College.

'Is there any sort of *partial* scholarship that might be open to Ruby, since she came so close?' asked David constructively, knowing full well that there wasn't.

'She don't want a partial scholarship, she wants a full scholarship,' barked Ruby's mum.

'I'm sure everyone would like to have their school fees paid in full, Ms Osafo . . . but the bottom line is that Ruby got 91 per cent whereas Molly got an unprecedented 100 per cent.'

'100 per cent! No kid gets 100 per cent – didn't that make you suspicious?'

This was a direct hit for the prosecution. David seemed momentarily flummoxed, so I jumped in.

'Well, Molly is very clever actually . . .' I proudly pointed out. 'I mean, her whole class had to write a poem called "My Mother" and Molly got an A plus! I keep the poem in my handbag. I can prove it to you if you want.' I took the tatty scrap of paper out of my bag and pointed to the big red letter at the bottom of the page. ' "A plus" you see, so I mean it's no surprise she did so well in the exam, is it?'

'Well, that's all the evidence we need, isn't it?' said Miss Reynolds. I'd won it. We were home and dry.

'Quite. I mean, A plus. That's the best you can get . . . It was read out in assembly.'

'No, I meant Molly's handwriting,' said the headmistress calmly. She buzzed through to her secretary. 'Meg, can you dig out an entrance exam paper from the files for me. Molly Chaplin: one of next term's scholarship girls, thank you.'

'Molly Chaplin, OK, I'll bring it in,' buzzed the robot voice from the speakerphone.

I was momentarily confused by this development, but sensing that it may not be to our advantage, I glanced nervously at David. All the blood had drained from his face. I hadn't seen him look that appalled since I put all his LPs up in the loft.

'All we have to do is compare the handwriting on the examination paper with the writing on the poem . . .' said the headmistress brightly, '. . . and that will put an end to this unfortunate episode once and for all, won't it?'

I think I may have tried to say something but my throat had seized up. A strangulated noise came out that was an attempt at an upbeat, affirmative 'Mmm!', but sounded more like an old dog whining before it was put to sleep.

'May I see the poem?' said the headmistress.

David kept trying to think of something to say but no words

would come. His mouth opened and closed silently like a fish gasping for oxygen on the deck of a boat. I stammered and prevaricated, with Molly's girlish loopy handwriting clutched tightly in my hand. 'Well, I . . . but . . . I mean, she wrote this some time ago, and their handwriting changes so much, doesn't it?'

'Not that much actually, you'd be surprised . . .' The head-mistress's hand was outstretched but I was clutching the poem so tightly that I was in danger of tearing it in two.

'The thing is . . .' said David, 'that it's actually quite a personal poem about a daughter's love for her mother and I think we should respect Molly's privacy.'

'Yes!' I concurred, looking gratefully at David.

'I thought you said it was read out in assembly?' she said, her hand reaching out to take the scrap of paper once again. There was a second's pause while the head teacher continued to smile at me and the paper remained locked in my fist. At that moment the door opened and the school secretary scurried in. 'I've got the files with all the entrance exams, but I can't find Molly Chaplin's paper.'

Oh *thank you* God! I thought. Just when we needed an unlikely piece of luck, here it was delivered straight from the heavens. I promised myself never to question the existence of our Lord God ever again.

'Oh sorry, Meg . . .' said the head teacher. 'Of course. I've got all the scholarship papers in my desk here' – and she opened a drawer and pulled out a file. There on the top of the pile was the paper with Molly's name on the top. Yeah, right, thanks a lot, God, I thought, as if you even existed, which you so obviously don't . . .

She placed the sheet of my handwriting directly in front of her.

'I'm sorry we have to do this, but it's important that these sorts of complaints are seen to be dealt with properly when they come in. We aren't just talking about a place at the school, after all – there are thousands of pounds of scholarship money involved here . . .'

I looked hopelessly at David, and with neither of us able to think of a way out of this suicidal situation, with a forced smile I slowly handed the piece of paper across.

Miss Reynolds placed the poem down on her desk beside the examination sheet. I knew that no two samples of handwriting could have been more different. Well, perhaps if Molly had written in Egyptian hieroglyphics, although with a big smiley face in the middle of the letter 'o' in the title she was already well on the way. But there could be no similarity at all. My sloping tiny spindly writing beside Molly's curly round letters. My thin stooping consonants beside the youthful puppy fat of my daughter's boisterous vowels. They were also in different coloured inks, but I thought it might be a little too obviously desperate to point this out.

'Well . . .' said Miss Reynolds, studying the two exhibits before her as Ms Osafo craned her neck, straining but failing to see for herself. I braced myself for Miss Reynolds's reaction, hoping in that split second that she would at least opt for disappointment rather than anger.

'Yes, well, I think there's not too much difference between these . . .' She was blinking rather rapidly. 'Yes, given the different pens and the time difference and everything . . .' She twitched manically. 'Er, excellent match, yes.'

'Let me see . . .' said Ms Osafo.

'No, I don't want to get into a protracted debate about this and, as Mr Chaplin said, it is a private poem by a child about her mother and I think we should respect that . . . so that's that cleared up, yes, jolly good, I have to say that I am satisfied with this evidence. I'm so sorry that we've had to have all this horribleness and nastiness . . .'

'So that's it then?' said Ms Osafo. 'You're just going to believe her? That poem doesn't prove a thing – she could have written it out herself.'

'That's not the point, Ms Osafo. I pride myself on being a very good judge of character. That is one of the things that helps Chelsea College set the excellent standards of which we are all so proud.'

At this moment Ruby suddenly and noisily spat her first gulp of Earl Grey tea back into the delicate little teacup.

'Urgh. It's still got washing-up liquid in it!' she announced.

'No, it's supposed to taste like that,' said Mr Worrall helpfully.

'I don't like it.'

'Oh well, not to worry, just leave it on the desk.'

Miss Reynolds looked skywards in exasperated disbelief at this complete waste of time. She was irritated now. Mr Worrall thought this might be the moment for him to offer the Osafos some sort of way out.

'Ruby, I put it to you that perhaps you were so disappointed not to get the scholarship that it might have affected your memory of the examination? That you might have imagined you saw Mrs Chaplin sitting in that exam?'

Ruby said nothing. The deputy leaned across his desk and folded his fingers together slightly too meaningfully. 'Ruby, your mark of 91 per cent puts you next on the waiting list for a scholarship to this school. But unless you now withdraw this very serious accusation, Miss Reynolds will never be able to offer you a place were one to come up. Do you understand?'

'Yes.'

Miss Reynolds raised her eyebrows at her deputy with a look that suggested he might be speaking out of turn here.

'So let me put it to you again. Do you think it is possible that you were mistaken? That what you saw was Mrs Chaplin's daughter, who would obviously have a strong family resemblance to her mother? That's who you saw, wasn't it, Ruby?'

Ruby looked at me and her mother and shook her head. 'No. It was Mrs Chaplin . . .' she said quietly. Ruby had thrown away her last chance. All she had to do was go along with a gift-wrapped lie that was being presented to her, that would allow everyone to get out of this with a little dignity intact, but instead she rose above all that and took the far more difficult option: she did the right thing. I cannot pretend that it did not move me nearly to tears to see it. Especially as Ruby herself began to well up, her frustration at this incomprehensible injustice finally spilling over.

'No one believes me but it's true . . .' she whispered as the tears ran down her cheek and were wiped away by her mother, who only had one card left to play.

'If we were white and she was black, you would believe me and not her,' said Ms Osafo, standing up to leave.

'I beg your pardon?' blinked Miss Reynolds over her glasses.

'If we were white and we told you that a black family had cheated, you'd believe the white people not the black.'

Miss Reynolds shook her head sadly. 'I'm disappointed that you have accused us of racialism, Ms Osafo, though not surprised. As a matter of fact we have several coloured children at the school, including the son of the Nigerian ambassador, and we've even gone to all the effort of putting up basketball nets for him, so I think that proves we are not racialist, don't you agree, Mrs Chaplin?'

Ruby was just staring at me. I had made a liar out of her. There was a little less optimism in her watery eyes, as if all the knock-backs that she would experience for the rest of her life had suddenly loomed into view. She blew her nose on a tatty piece of tissue and gave me a look that said: I know that you know that I know.

'Actually I don't feel very well,' I said into the silence.

'There's a cup of Earl Grey tea going if that might help?' offered the deputy.

'Mum, I don't want to come here now anyway . . .' Ruby whispered. 'I want to go to Battersea.'

'That's fine, darling, come on, let's go. We're not going to get nothing from here.' Ruby followed her mother out of the door and it slammed behind them. Miss Reynolds looked more disappointed than ever. 'Double negative . . .' she sighed. 'Not really a Chelsea College sort of family . . .'

'Not really a Chelsea College sort of family . . .' repeated Mr Worrall.

'See you in September, Mr and Mrs Chaplin . . . I hope you'll be coming to our newcomers' assembly. One last thing, here at Chelsea College we do pride ourselves on our discretion and I'm sure you'll be able to support us in that. Oh, and here's your daughter's poem back. It is amazing how much a child's handwriting can change!' – and she gave a conspiratorial laugh. But I couldn't return her little chuckle. I finally had the prize but it had turned to dust in my hands. I felt nervous and sick and disorientated all at once. And then the school bell went and I wanted to get out of there as soon as possible.

Kids Say The Funniest Things!
A hilarious collection of delightful real-life quotes
from the little children of Spencer House Preparatory
School.
Collected by Alice Chaplin

                 £6.99 (or just priceless, bless 'em!)

'What do you mean, you only have one home? Where do you stay at weekends?' Bronwyn, aged 9

'Mummy, the stupid chalet girl put my ski-pass in the wash.' Julian, aged 9

'Molly didn't even know the difference between a gelding and a colt!!' Jemima, aged 11

'I'm better than Kirsty and Molly at EVERYTHING.' Bronwyn, aged 10

'No potato for me, thank you. I'm on the Atkins diet.' Druscilla, aged 10

'Mum, why can't the nanny come in the same bit of the plane as us?' Charles, aged 7

'Mum, Alice just called me a precocious little brat.' Bronwyn, aged 11

— 12 —

Finally it was September. The first day of term. We had made our decision, we had settled on our choice of school – whatever our reservations, we had to do what was best for Molly. She had to have a secure and happy teaching environment to compensate for those anxious parents constantly fretting about her education. I had to select a school that would turn her into a highly qualified adult, so that when the time came she could afford to put me in a half-decent old people's home.

The early morning traffic on the first school run of the year seemed less aggressive than usual: tanned drivers glowed with the warm goodwill of the summer holidays, car headlamps still sporting the sticky-tape eye-shadow they'd worn for their tours across the continent. Outside a dangerous wind was whipping through the dappled plane trees, spinning polythene bags up into the air and bringing down chunky angular twigs with leaves too green to fall yet. As I got nearer to the school I could see more and more children and parents, all headed in the same direction, mothers still allowed to clutch their darlings' hands for what might be the last time. Finally I pulled my 4x4 up outside the teeming gates of Chelsea

College. Dozens of other outsize vehicles were depositing fresh-faced children, all modelling stripy new blazers that it was hard to imagine them ever growing into. One young chap arrived on his own in a London cab and nonchalantly told the driver to keep the change. I sat there watching the scene for a while and turned and looked at the empty seat in the back of the car. Molly could have been one of those children heading in there today. Molly could have attended this private club of the privileged and cosseted. But twenty minutes earlier I had dropped her off at Battersea Comprehensive. I had kissed the top of her head, and then watched that shiny sweet-smelling hair disappear into the crowd. I had cast one last anxious look over my shoulder as I drove off, my view partially obscured by the 'For Sale' sign in the back of our 4x4, but Molly was gone. And then I had driven up here to see for myself what I had surrendered. Just one last glimpse at the strange tribe I had inadvertently been part of for the past decade. Obviously there was a part of me that still wondered if I had made the right choice. That morning on the way to Battersea Comprehensive, I had reached Queen's Circus where I would have turned off for Chelsea Bridge.

'Mum,' asked Molly, 'why have we just driven round and round the roundabout four times in a row?'

David had been hard to convince that we could make such a giant leap. 'This is Molly we are talking about, our real live daughter!' he exclaimed during one late-night discussion. 'Not some model child on the end of a pole that we shove into the middle of the comprehensive to see what happens!' But I came to realize why he was so agitated about it all. It was because he just didn't know the answer. He knew more bare facts than anyone I'd ever met, but when he had to decide what was best for our children, the answer couldn't be found on the cards of his *Trivial Pursuit Third Reich Special Edition*. David just had to trust me. The only fact I could offer was a gut reaction, an intuitive understanding. 'I may not know the capital of bloody Mongolia,' I told him, 'but I know what's best for our children.' He was quiet for a moment, but was unable to resist mumbling 'Ulan Bator'.

I'd simply felt so uplifted when I went round Battersea, like an adopted child finally meeting her real parents. I was appalled by the hypocrisy of Miss Reynolds at Chelsea College. It reminded me of the darker side of me. And so I became resolute that Battersea was the only choice. In any case, the little fisherman's cottage on www.lundy-properties.com was snapped up by someone else.

Of course, I was still concerned about that old problem of class sizes in state schools. The working class is just too big. Maybe the comprehensives could adjust their curriculum to attract more middle-class parents like us, I wondered. Woodwork lessons could involve teaching children how to hover nervously behind a carpenter saying, 'We tried to assemble it ourselves, but found the instructions a bit con-fusing . . .' The cycling proficiency test would simply require fifteen minutes sitting on a bike machine watching daytime television. School dinners would feature tiny portions of monkfish tail on asparagus soufflé, while table monitors led conversations about house prices and whether one should take the au pair skiing. But Molly would now be part of a society made up of children of all sorts of colours, different religions and varying social classes. She'd have friends who didn't think it was completely normal to put the au pair staring out of the back of the 4x4 alongside the golden retriever. She would meet Muslims and would learn that Islam wasn't all jihads and fatwas but was a peace-loving religion based on the belief that

– well, whatever it's based on. I can't say, I don't really know any Muslims. She'd grow up in a school in which all sections of society were represented – like the queue in the post office but with no one slapping the children.

Whether we could have ever crossed that social chasm without having our best friends make the leap with us, I don't know. William's born-again certainty undoubtedly helped persuade my husband. For a man who normally sat in the background making the occasional sarcastic comment, William was suddenly very loquacious on the subject. 'Thinking you can get a complete education at private school is like going to Claridge's in Delhi and thinking you've travelled,' said William audaciously. 'The whole journey of childhood is about learning that you are not the only person in the universe, that you are just one person in a society. First you have to learn to share with siblings, then you have to learn to consider friends and classmates; the biggest lesson of the first ten years of your life is fighting the infant instinct to push in and say "Me first!" and "Biggest piece for me!" But then all those overanxious parents like we were pay good money to send their kids to schools where they are actually taught "me first" and "biggest piece for me", and it's no wonder they revert to grabby, greedy toddlers all over again. I want my kids to learn that they are *special*, but not that they are *better*.'

'Sure, William,' I said standing on the doorstep, 'but would Kirsty like to come to the park with us or not?'

Having spent so long indoctrinating our daughter on why she would be happiest at Chelsea College, we did not have very long to perform a complete back flip and now convince her of the exact opposite. What would be the best way to do this, we wondered. Leave a small typed erratum slip in her homework diary? *Please note: administrative error by parents.*

'Darling, you'll be really happy at Chelsea College' should have read, *'Darling, you'll be much happier at Battersea than that silly old Chelsea College, don't you agree?'* Or maybe we could hire a hypnotist. 'You will forget everything your parents have told you about your new school . . . Yes, yes, you much prefer the other one . . . and while we've got you, you're going to remember to clean out the goldfish bowl . . .' In the end we just told her the truth. That the reason we didn't want her going to an aggressively academic school was the same reason that she didn't have to learn bridge with Ffion any more or go along to children's book club or do all those extra lessons that used to eat up every evening.

David and I didn't see F-f-f-fion and Ph-ph-philip socially any more, though Sarah and William kept us up to date with all the gossip. Apparently Ffion's life coach had recommended she commit suicide. Once when I had to be out early I did see her setting off for school at about seven thirty with her children's pasty faces pressed against the car window. If Ffion saw me, she didn't acknowledge it. The only annoying thing about all that was that Ffion and Philip's software idea ended up being a huge commercial hit, the computer craze of the year with parents and single people alike. Suddenly everyone was buying into this new obsession of designing personal league tables in which they or their children always seemed to end up in top place. I didn't sink to such tragic self-delusion. Ffion and Philip had struck gold and probably thought it finally proved their total superiority over everyone they knew, but of course I secretly knew it was me who had said to Ffion that you couldn't measure a child by just one exam result – the whole thing had been my idea all along, so in my personal league table I would have been way above the two of them.

As part of the formal closure of that hypercompetitive

phase of Molly's life, I helped her clear out her bedroom, fill-ing a black dustbin bag with old exercise books, project folders, homework sheets and revision timetables. I read about one teenager in Hackney who had left his school and the following night burnt it to the ground, which is another means of achieving closure I suppose. After Molly and I had sorted her desk, we attacked the box files in the kitchen, emptying them of completed test papers and extra homework set by expensive private tutors. Hours and hours of her life were now being thrown away, or rather, had been thrown away long ago. We laughed at all these extra test papers now, like prison guard and inmate meeting as equals after sentence had been served. 'If Simon has fourteen apples and eats twelve, what has he got?' I asked her. 'Indigestion,' she replied, remember-ing the joke I'd always recited in the forlorn hope of extracting a smile during extra maths lessons.

'What's this?' said Molly, suddenly pulling some test sheets out of an envelope.

'Just some test papers, darling . . . Do you want to keep any of these booklets or shall I put them in the recycling bin?'

'No, these aren't like the others . . . "Entrance examination, Chelsea College" . . .' she read, seeming perplexed.

Somehow, incredibly, David and I had never disposed of the test papers we had got Molly to sit when we told her that she'd be doing her Chelsea entrance at home.

'I remember doing these. How come we've got these here?' she asked.

'Um, maybe they sent them back, I can't remember, dar-ling. Let's stick them in the recycling bag, shall we?' – but my slightly less than gentle attempt to extract the sheets from her hands met with equal resistance and she began to flick through the paper.

'They've never been marked! It doesn't make sense, no ticks or crosses or anything . . .'

'Oh, er . . . that's strange, let me see . . .' – and this was my excuse to take the documents from her hands. I glanced down at the questions I had last seen under exam conditions months earlier and it sent my mind spiralling back. I could smell the floor polish of the examination hall, feel the sweat soaking into the brim of the baseball cap. It seemed perverse that David and I had never been curious enough to see what she would have got, that the papers that had caused us so many sleepless nights had just been tucked away unmarked and forgotten in a pile of old schoolwork.

'Oh, I remember . . .' I suddenly announced. 'We had to send them a photocopy. And keep the originals in case the copy got lost in the post or something . . .' And I popped the papers in the pile of rubbish, a few layers under the surface.

Just out of idle curiosity I gave the papers to David to mark that evening. And twenty minutes later he came into the kitchen with a look of apologetic astonishment on his face. 'You're never going to believe this . . .' he said. 'She would have got a scholarship anyway.'

'Really?'

'Yeah.'

'*Really?*'

'No.'

'Oh. So how did she do?'

'Not very well. She got all the dividing fractions wrong . . .'

After dinner I looked at the maths paper staring up at me from the sideboard and a curious thought crossed my mind.

'David, could you rub out all of Molly's answers? I want to see if I can do this now . . .'

'What's the point? Molly's got the school we want now.'

'It's not for Molly. It's not for anyone else. Just for myself.'

And so in the twilight peace of my own kitchen, with the audio water-feature of our dishwasher churning away in the background, I worked my way through the Chelsea College entrance exam maths paper. And where once I would have seen a fog of random numbers, now there was a logical staircase, a sequence that I could tackle one step at a time. '0.7 x 0.9 = 0.63.' Yes, even though you are multiplying, the number actually gets smaller; it's perfectly rational once you get your head round it. In fact, there is a little internal buzz of satisfaction to be had at the symmetrical logic of it all. That was the strangest thing. I was enjoying it. It was gratifying to be in total command, to be capable of producing the appropriate response to every challenge that was hurled at me. From all angles the questions attacked, like the drug-pushing pimps in PlayStation Scum-Slayer 7, or Urban Vigilante, but I was ready for every one of them: I had an Uzi pistol in both hands, I'd acquired the kung-fu skills and tucked a flick-knife in my boot, and could shoot and stab and stun them however the sums came at me. Why could I never make the children see that doing arithmetic was just as thrilling as patrolling the streets of the Bronx exterminating heavily armed social deviants? Take that, 270 − 280! In your face, 12 x 12,000! Hurr! Splat! You're history, 7 x (7 + 13)! I realized I'd begun to add explosive sound effects as I worked. But I was unstoppable now. I had vanquished all adversaries on the first level. 'Congratulations Player One − you have successfully completed the initial phase. Now you must do battle with more formidable opponents: converting fractions into percentages!'

It had taken me several lessons but I had finally overcome the mental block I had about these. David had attempted to explain the basic principle but the tutorial had broken down when I'd accused him of coughing in an impatient and patronizing manner. Only Ruby had managed to illuminate me – when I'd been supposed to be the one tutoring her. We had laughed about this when she'd come to play during the summer holidays. We had bumped into Ruby and her grandmother in the high street one Saturday morning and her granny was as warm and friendly as ever, chatting and laughing as if nothing had ever happened between our two families. She was delighted that Molly would be joining Ruby at Battersea, and welcomed my suggestion that her granddaughter came round to play. Ruby was as polite and well behaved as ever. Except that towards the end of the afternoon, Molly and Ruby were playing a board game and some sort of argument developed over whose go it was. A few months earlier Ruby would have let Molly have her way, but a little bit of my daughter had rubbed off on her since then.

'Shut up, Molly, you cheater. It's my go!'

'Ruby is your guest, Molly. Let her have her go if you can't agree,' I interjected.

'That's not fair,' protested my daughter. 'Why do you always believe Ruby?'

'Because I have never heard Ruby say anything that wasn't true . . .' and I smiled at her and then as she understood the full meaning of what I was saying, her eyes opened wide before she looked away a little embarrassed. 'And you can tell your mother that from me, Ruby . . .'

Now, only months after I had copied my maths answers off an eleven-year-old stranger, I was able to do it properly. I turned to the final sheet and allowed myself a satisfied nostalgic smile. Multiplying and dividing fractions. What is a half divided by a half? That's *one*. One whole unit. That's what I am, whole again; complete. 'David's wife' is only half a person. 'Molly's mum' is only half a person. Alice Chaplin, that is me, that is the entire thing. 'You must know Alice Chaplin: rather small, brown eyes, good at maths.' What is 4 in binary? Why, that would be 100; I can think about that without checking out the availability of the nearest toilet. And now I was proud of myself instead of my children. This wasn't 'well done, Molly' or 'isn't Jamie clever', this wasn't the vicarious pride of the soccer mom hovering on the touchline. This was me, centre stage: in the movie poster of my life I had finally reclaimed top billing. 'Those with small children be sure to attach your own oxygen mask before helping others . . .' Was that what this was all about? Had my brain craved the oxygen of independent learning to give me the sanity to cope with three children? Had I done this to be a happier person or a better mother, or are they inevitably the same thing? All these impossible questions – now I understood the attraction of mathematics. You work out that x equals 7 and that's the end of it. Unless you're Ffion, of course, in which case x equals 7 but has a reading age of 9.

Molly was brimming with excitement and enthusiasm when I picked her up at the end of her first day at Battersea. She and Kirsty came dashing out into the playground, where William was also just arriving. For some reason I felt enormously grateful to William, as if he had sent his daughter here just for Molly's sake, and when he reached us I gave him a long and meaningful hug. I was so happy that my daughter was so happy, and felt so indebted to him for helping it happen, I wanted to kiss him full on the lips. In fact, what I wanted to do was have sexual intercourse with him right there in the school playground, but children that age are quite self-conscious, and seeing her mum having it off with her best friend's dad is one of those silly little things that might have embarrassed my eleven-year-old daughter.

Molly gabbled at me about how each of them had been given their own computer password and how they had different teachers for different subjects and she was learning German and Maths and Drama and Information Technology and English and Netball and Humanities and Science and Maths, and I couldn't believe she had said Maths twice and I breathed a secret sigh of relief that she hadn't spent the whole day painting yoghurt pots. In addition, there seemed to be a whole parallel curriculum taught by the older children: how to wear your huge tie knots at half-mast and how to blot out certain letters on your blazer badges to turn the motto into a swear word. The two girls from the private prep school were in the same class together and I knew that they would have to learn to play down their privileged backgrounds, but adolescents invent an image for themselves wherever they are. Molly became a bit self-conscious about the little treats I put in her packed lunch, which is a shame because she used to love quail's eggs. But she was happy. My daughter was happy at her new school and exuded such pride in herself and goodwill towards the whole world that even though her friends were around I noticed her quietly take the hands of her two younger brothers as we all walked back towards the car.

The following day, I walked with Alfie to take him for his first day at his new school, Ruby's old primary just down the road. And after that David and I found ourselves in an empty house, all the kids at school for the first time ever, just the two of us, alone. I made a pot of coffee and we sat opposite each other across the kitchen table. 'What's this?' said David, picking up a newspaper in which I had circled an advertisement.

'Oh, I don't know, I just thought I might send off for the details . . .'

'A job? Excellent idea. If there's an exam, let me know and I'll put on a wig and a dress and take the test for you . . .'

Seven hours later Molly walked home from school on her own and it was still a beautiful summer's afternoon, and the kids wanted to get the hosepipe out in the garden and of course we said yes. 'Shouldn't they put their swimming costumes on?' suggested David and I said, 'What does it matter?' and in their crisp clean cotton underwear the kids took turns to run through the spray from the lawn sprinkler, giggling with delight each time they leapt through the glistening curtain of cold water. They looked so healthy and happy, Jamie with his little tongue sticking out of the side of his mouth, his resolute brow furrowed in determination as he prepared to make the courageous dash once again, and then whoosh, and hysterical laughter as he slipped right over on the wet grass and landed on his bottom.

'Quick, quick, the water is coming back!' screamed his overexcited sister, running into the oncoming wall of spray to help him up, getting soaked herself but pulling her little brother to safety. 'Alfie's turn!' shouted the older two, and Alfie just ran and stood still in the middle of the downpour, getting himself deliberately soaked, laughing because his big brother and sister were thrilled with his courage, and their skin was so smooth and perfect, glowing pink under a shiny film of cold clean wetness, and then suddenly I ran down the garden and I jumped through the spray as well, and all the kids clapped and cheered and I ran back again and Molly picked up the hose and threatened to completely soak me with it, and David came and stood beside me and said, 'If you soak

her, you're going to have to soak me too . . .' and then with all
three of them holding the hose, they turned the jet onto us
and shrieked in delight as we were completely soaked, both
parents falling to the floor, 'Please, we beg you on our knees,
don't wet us any more . . .' which was their cue to hold the
spray directly over our heads, relishing the brief reversal of
power, almost sadistically drenching us from head to foot as
we pretended to beg them to stop. Actually we weren't pretending any more, we were now genuinely begging them to
stop – they'd switched to the most powerful jet and it hurt –
but Alfie was clapping his hands in delighted hysterics and
then all of us took turns to deliberately soak one another, until
I grabbed all three of them and held their precious slippery
bodies close to mine: 'Please don't grow up any more, my
lovely beautiful precious children, please stay like this for just
a little bit longer . . .'

The period in which your children are totally dependent
upon you is such a short phase of your life. You think it's for
ever, then suddenly it's over; before you've even looked up
from checking their coats were buttoned up properly, it's over.
One day you are in your kitchen when the doorbell rings and
it is your own child arriving home from school, staggering
over the threshold with a four-ton rucksack of books on her
back and her mind weighed down by a million thoughts that
you will never know. And you glance up at those framed
photos on the stairs of when they were so little, wearing
clothes you chose, sitting in swings you had to lift them into,
laughing uncontrollably as you pushed them back and forth.
And it's gone. That's it, she's grown up – that expression of
total trust in her face, it's gone for ever; just a memory. There
was always so much to think about, so many potential pitfalls
that sometimes it was easy to forget to enjoy it. In the

playground of parenthood there's always going to be a big seesaw between fun and fear, but if you keep plonking your big fat worries down on one end, it's never going to be any fun, not for kids or parents. You have to let them fall and fail and then try again. Nobody ever learnt anything except by doing it (said a book I'd read to make me a better parent).

On Molly's third day at Battersea there was an incident during the lunch hour. Three girls from the year above grabbed Ruby in the playground and told her she was going to be 'happy slapped'. Ruby knew what this meant: that she would be struck in the face and her subsequent tears would be recorded on a videophone for posting on the internet or broadcasting on Al-Jazeera or whatever. It was a particularly unpleasant craze that was currently sweeping through secondary schools – though all credit to those emotionally disturbed bullies for learning how to put video files onto a website.

It happened very quickly. One second Ruby was on her way to the dining rooms, the next she was jumped on from behind and found her arms were pinned behind her back.

'Look into the camera, new girl . . .' said the fat one of the three, holding up a mobile to her face. Ruby's eyes were screwed up as she did her best to recoil in anticipation.

'Get off her!' shouted an approaching voice that Ruby recognized. 'Get off her!'

Without pausing to think, Molly dashed into the melee and simply placed the palm of her hand directly in front of the camera lens.

'Get out the way, you stupid-ass bitch . . .' said the lead bully, whose summer at that Swiss finishing school seemed to have been a complete waste of money.

'Let go of her!'

'Do you want a slap an' all?'

'No,' said Molly, which was an honest if not particularly inspired answer, but she continued to move her trembling hand to block the view of the lens. But the moment had passed and Ruby had struggled free and then both new girls made a dash for it.

'Right, I'm filming you so I'll know you next time,' shouted the bully, pointing her video mobile at the fleeing girls. Perhaps it would have been wiser to have kept running, but something in Molly made her stop and turn to shout at the lens. 'Why don't you find something more worthwhile to do?' she said. 'Like shaving off that hideous moustache, you big fat walrus.'

And the two sidekicks couldn't help but burst out laughing at the expense of their ringleader, who nervously fingered her upper lip before ordering one of her mates to 'shut it'.

'Are you all right, Ruby?' said Molly, once they were safely in the clear.

'Yeah, I'm fine. Thanks.'

'Yes!' proclaimed a triumphant voice from nearby. Under the tree, the shy spotty girl with the baseball cap punched the air as discreetly as she could. I'd just wanted to be sure, but now I'd seen it for myself. Molly was going to be OK. My daughter was courageous and she was kind and it moved me nearly to tears to see her deal with this all on her own. She had stood by her friends and she could stick up for herself. She was safe and she was happy. There was nothing more I could ask. Though it also turned out that my daughter was in fact quite bright after all. Because after the bullies had wandered away, after Ruby had dashed off to tell the others what she'd said, Molly looked left and right, and then walked slowly over to the spotty girl with the baseball cap, put her arm round me and whispered, 'Mum. Go home. I can manage.'

THE END

AUTHOR'S NOTE

This is of course a work of fiction; the schools are all invented and none of the characters portrayed are intended to represent anyone dead or alive, particularly if they have access to a good lawyer.

To my many friends and colleagues who have chosen to educate their children in the private sector, please do not think that I condemn you out of hand. Your decisions are none of my business and your particular choices were no doubt made with your own child's interests in mind, yer big snooty social-climbing Tory snobs. No, really, there are all sorts of schools and all sorts of children, and you have to do what you think is best for your child, and I think that monocle and top hat really suits them.

Enormous thanks are due to Georgia Garrett, Bill Scott-Kerr, Tim Goffe, Mark Burton, my wife Jackie and my children Freddie and Lily – for whose sake I hope that this book actually sells a few copies so that I can finally afford to pack them off to some posh boarding school.

JO'F – March 2005